CALL ME NOT A MAN

Mtutuzeli Matshoba

Longman

Longman Group UK Limited,
Longman House, Burnt Mill, Harlow,
Essex CM20 2JE, England
and Associated Companies throughout the world

First published 1979 by Ravan Press (Pty) Ltd., Johannesburg,
in association with Rex Collings Ltd., London
First published in Longman Drumbeat 1981
First published as Longman African Classic 1987

Produced by Longman Group (FE) Ltd
Printed in Hong Kong

ISBN 0-582-00242-7

Contents

An Autobiographical Note

I was born in 1950 in the early Soweto of Orlando (East and West), Shantytown, White City Jabavu, Pimville and Moroka. Today's Soweto, the sprawling dirt- and vice-polluted giant matchbox city, was more or less my age when my environment began to register in my consciousness.

It was in Orlando East, in the three-roomed house of an aunt with a family of six, that I spent the first four years of my life. I can faintly remember my father and mother paying me visits at weekends and my being unsure that they were really my parents, only believing what I was told. They had not yet found a house of their own, were still on the everlasting waiting list, maybe. My mother stayed at the Nurses' Home in Baragwanath where she was a 'lady of the lantern', as she is today. This much I know of the early days. Of my late father who died in 'seventy-four, I knew next to nothing then.

Half-way through these first four years the loneliness of being the only child, and away from my parents for most of the time, was suddenly soothed by the arrival of a younger brother, Diliza, who would one day find himself in chains, en route to Robben Island — thus inspiring 'A Pilgrimage to the Isle of Makana' for our magazine, *Staffrider*.

In 1954 my parents got their own matchbox at Mzimhlope, a part of Orlando West II, and the four of us — mother, father, myself and Diliza — moved there. 'Cousin sisters' or aunts came to join the family from time to time, baby-sitting us — no, it was only Diliza they had to keep an eye on, because I was already running around, safe in the company of other toddlers. In the ghetto one learns to take care of oneself early in life.

At seven I entered 'Sub-A' in a Salvation Army school in Orlando East. We had fish and apples at break — but that soon stopped when the government took over the school completely. After 'Sub-B' I was shuttled to Mzimhlope Primary School for Standard I.

I remember the menacing saracens two years later (1960). We were not allowed to leave the house and at night we slept on the cold floor. It was then that I first heard the sound of real gunfire. It was then that I first saw the black man standing his ground with a clenched fist in front of the barrel of a gun (fortunately, no one was shot that I knew of at Mzimhlope). It was then that I had my first faint acquaintance with the name of South Africa's recently resigned President. It was then that I saw pictures of dead or dying black men, women and children after they had been mowed down with bullets at Sharpeville. It was also in that period that I saw pictures of a row of coffins containing the remains of Coalbrook victims, lined up next to the gaping earth. Then that a slogan, "Release Mandela", was imprinted in my mind.

Later, with growth, I would ask and try to answer the *why* of it. Why did all these things happen? Why did a man called Patrice Lumumba sit in the back of a truck, hands bound behind his back, his hair being pulled from his scalp by men surrounding him with jackboots?

I entered puberty and launched on an adventurous growth. Adventurous because it was hard, as it still is, to grow in the dog-kennel city. On Saturday and Sunday mornings there was always a corpse covered by wind-blown papers in Mohale Street, which passes my home on its way from the station to the hostel for migrant workers. From time to time someone that I knew would stab someone else that I knew, fatally. Occasionally someone would hang himself. My friends started going to the Van Ryn place of detention for juvenile delinquents or to 'Number Four', and returned to relate their episodes. I knew prison long before my turn came to pay a visit there.

To save me from all this my standard 5 and 6 teacher, Samuel 'Maviyo' Ngcobo who had trained a keen eye on me, advised my parents to send me to boarding school after standard 6.

Wilberforce, near Evaton, thirty or forty kilometres from Soweto, was the first choice. It was discovered that I was in Soweto more often than I was in class at Wilberforce.

Lovedale, 18 April, 'sixty-four, four hundred kilometres from it all. A boys' school, then. I felt lost but soon adapted. I was 'proud' of my white lady teachers and when on holiday at home I boasted about them to my friends, who said: 'So what?' Now I think I should not have been so proud, for I remember they used to send us to 'Corona', the principal's office for a tanning at the average rate of twice per week, particularly a Mrs. Uys who taught us *Rekenkunde* (Afrikaans for Arithmetic) and a farmer's wife, Mrs. Kirsteen, who taught us Afrikaans and 'Sosiale Studie' and said our intelligence was as short as our hair.

In standard eight a composition titled 'Fire! Fire! Fire!' won me the acclaim of my class teacher and English master, Mr. Maneli, who passed it on to Victorian Mrs. White, who taught English at Matric level. She marked me at forty-five plus out of sixty and from then on wanted to mark my English scripts and read them to her classes. I made sure that I did not disappoint Mr. Maneli and Mrs. White. I read any paperback that came my way. I spent hours studying encyclopaedias in what was supposed to be the school library. I loved English poetry and I interpreted Shakespeare for my classmates. I hated enforced church attendance and played hookey, thus avoiding the endless ranting of the preachers who came our way.

There was a strike the following year. It was raining when we were sent home. My friend, Thandi Jaantjies (a Xhosa) did not return, and I heard later that year that he had been buried alive in some mine. At the end of the year I passed Junior Certificate with a first class, and regretted that I had not put more effort into it. The new principal, Engelbrecht, had caused the strike.

I was excited about Matric. The new principal, Van der Merwe, and his vice, Van Wyk, sneaked up on us and gave us tannings for the slightest transgression. They enjoyed it and my friends and I began to enjoy it, too — more than our studies. Many of us failed at the end of Matric year. I was a teenager, and unimpressed by the 'fall'. I knew I could do it. I told myself I was marking time.

In 1969 the police seemed to take a special interest in me. Maybe because I had spent five years away in the Cape and they wanted to teach me the discipline of Soweto that I had been missing. I re-adapted, and that was the year of my first and last visit up to now to Number Four, although police stations were like toilets, as they are to all blacks here, to me. Their pull is like that of the call of nature. Twice that year I engaged in fisticuffs with reservists (the same people who inspired 'Call Me Not a Man') because they were showy and pushy when they gave you the shakedown and wanted your pass.

The St. Martin's (Catholic) parish priest called me to his church office at the end of the year and told me that I had been admitted to Inkamana High School in Vryheid, Natal. I went, because I thought God would strike me down if I refused his servant's advice. I did well there, always among the first two in tests and exams. This time I passed Matric with a good second class. It might have been a first, but for the nun who repeated Mrs. Kirsteen's words about our hair and our intelligence.

I still 'liked' to pay the people at John Vorster an occasional visit.

Fort Hare, across the Tyume River from Lovedale, old adventurous friends, listening to Strini Moodley, Harry Nengwekhulu and Steve Biko talking, liquor parties, soccer, a strike and no return in the following year, '73. No regrets. After all, science was too abstract for me. I wanted to know more about human beings.

I worked as an 'assistant' draughtsman at a die-cutting factory. I always could draw and I felt a strong desire for artistic self-expression, but had no money for art equipment. Technical drawing held little artistic appeal, and I was paid slave wages while doing all the work, not simply assisting. My boss began unearthing new clients. One day he asked me: 'Matshoba, how would you like to be a millionaire?' out of the blue. I did not give any notice when I left. The firm went bankrupt a year or two later.

Back to Fort Hare. Our alma mater was sick with apathy but I told myself that I had to persevere for the sake of a B. Com. (Law) certificate. Two years. Past graduates came back after not finding work. Third year: June 16, 1976 exploded in my face. Memories of old were revived, my life was so full that I knew that if I did not spill some of its contents out I would go beserk. I started scribbling and burning the scraps of paper on which I wrote, torn between writing or heading for the beckoning horizons, my country become my enemy. The moment I had been waiting for since the standard eight composition had not yet arrived.

It came when *The Voice* newspaper asked for literary contributions in 1978. I met Mothobi Mutloatse there and handed him my first story: 'My Friend, the Outcast'. Mothobi's remark after reading it was: 'Keep on writing, Mtutu. Don't stop until you get what you want to say off your conscience.' Through Mothobi I met Mike Kirkwood of Ravan Press, the publishers of *Staffrider*, and he said much the same thing. I have kept the words of these two men in mind, and I am still writing.

I want to reflect through my works life on my side of the fence, the black side: so that whatever may happen in the future, I may not be set down as 'a bloodthirsty terrorist'. So that I may say: 'These were the events which shaped the Steve Bikos and the Solomon Mahlangus, and the many others who came before and after them.'

Mtutuzeli Matshoba

My Friend, the Outcast

Woe to them who devise wrong,
And work out wickedness upon their beds.
In the morning light they do it,
Because it is in their power.
They covet fields and seize them,
And houses, and carry them off.

His name is Vusi. For his whole life he has lived with us at our location. I have known him ever since I started to notice that there were other people in the world besides those whom I saw at home. We made trains with mealie cobs together when we were small; we hunted the delicious wild rats and little birds of the highveld on the mining land where we were not allowed, together; we learnt to swim in the Klip rivulet together when it had rained and the water was deep enough; we went to old, and now gone, Harlem cinema next to Faraday station together; we learnt to smoke and to lie in wait for the little girls at the shops together; we played 'chailence' soccer with a tennis ball against the boys from the other streets, together. He quit school first and sold apples and sweets on the trains while I went to school, but we were together at all other times. Ah, there are countless other things that we did together, and if I counted them I would never get to telling you about what happened the other day.

Roughly, here is the story of my friend. Mind you, I was not there when it all started to happen, but I can just imagine what took place; what with such things being part of life for us darkies. We read about them in the papers, we hear about them every other day, we come across the people who bring them about, who cause our friends pain and sorrow, many times in our lives. But when you read about it or hear about it, it is never as real as when it happens to someone who is close to you.

Last month on a Wednesday morning, when the eastern horizon was beginning to be etched out against the grey light cast by the first rays of a young day, there was a loud knock, that rattled the dishes in the cupboard and vibrated the window panes in their frames, at the front door of Vusi's home. Vusi's mind was wrenched painfully from the depths of slumber. At first he thought that he had just woken from a terrible nightmare in which ghouls had converged upon the house screaming for his blood. When he recovered from the shock, he realized that it was the unmistakable knock of the police that had jolted him from sleep. While he reached for his trousers on the small bench near the bed, he tried to remember what he had done wrong. 'A guy's mere existence is a crime in this cursed world. You break the law without being aware of it, no matter how you try not to,' he thought.

'*Vula*, open up, or we break in!' a furiously impatient voice with a Xhosa accent shouted from outside, followed by another nerve-wrecking knock.

From the other bedroom Vusi's mother's tremulous voice sailed. 'Who is it, Vusi?'

'It's the blackjacks, ma. I wonder what they want,' answered Vusi, having peeped through a slit in the curtains to see. He felt a slight relief: Usually the WRAB police did not mean serious trouble.

'Let them in quickly, my child,' Vusi's mother said, and to herself she muttered, '*Thixo wami.* At this time of the night! It must be something bad. But we've been paying the rent. Let me rise and see what they want.'

'Okay, I'm coming. Stop knocking like we were deaf,' Vusi said exasperatedly as he went to open. Dikeledi's eyes shone in the semi-darkness. She smothered the cries of their baby, who had been woken by the rude knocking, with her breast. The other baby, two-year-old Nontsizi, was whimpering with fright on the floor beside the bed. Temba, the little boy who had come with Dikeledi from the dusty streets and was now calling Vusi *baba,* slept soundly next to his sister. In the other room on the sagging sofa, Muntu was sleeping off the last dregs of the *skokiaan* he drank every day, snoring like a lawnmower. Vusi felt an urge to kick him in the ribs. He knew, however, that he could never bring himself to do it, in spite of the revulsion he felt towards anyone who drank excessively; Muntu was his brother, moreover his elder brother.

He switched the light on and the big bulb flooded the room with a glare that sent the cockroaches scampering for cover. They made the grimy walls look more grimy and Vusi felt ashamed that he was about to let strangers into such a house. It was slightly better when Dikeledi had spruced it up. The insects were a nuisance as well as part of the family, having always been there, surviving all the insecticides on the market.

He unlocked the door and heaved. There was a screech that set everybody's teeth on edge as it swung open, and in strutted three 'blackies'. Recently their uniform had been changed from a depressing pitch black over a khaki shirt and tie into another dull colour that only a painter can name for you.

'Where's the owner of the house?' asked the first one in a gruff voice. He had a bushy moustache, puffed cheeks, and an air of importance.

The others did not want to be left out of the fun. 'Are you the *mnumzane*, you? Ha, ha, haw,' the fat one with an oily face and a neck like an accordion said. They had not even removed their caps.

'No. This is not my house. There's the old lady. She's in bed,' Vusi answered, ignoring the goading.

'We want the father of the house, maan. And we haven't got forever, too,' the third one butted in, not to be left out either.

'There's no father. Only the old lady. The old man is late.' Vusi felt a tightening in his chest as he remembered how many years ago they had been told without really grasping what was meant, that their father had committed suicide by hanging himself from the rafters of his bedroom with a thin wire, leaving them to face a merciless life which had defeated him, a man, alone with their mother. He had always asked himself what had made his old man, whom he could only remember very faintly, decide that the only way out of hardship was death.

'Wake your mother, boy. There's nothing we can talk to a *tsotsi*,' the one who had come in first said, with the smirk of a coward who had got a chance to push someone else around.

Vusi's mother appeared from behind a tattered curtain which was meant to give a little privacy to her bedroom. All seventy-five years of her, woken up unceremoniously at ungodly hours.

'Hawu, my children, what has made you pay us a visit at this early hour?' she asked slowly, in the manner of the ancient.

The dignity of old age overcame some of the visitors' braggadocio. 'It is *abakhulu* who have sent us, *magogo*. Are you the registered tenant of this house?' Bushy Moustache asked. He had pulled out a battered chair and seated himself while the others remained standing. Muntu continued to snore.

'Yes child, but he pays the rent,' she replied, pointing at Vusi.

'He pays it under your name. Don't he?'

The old woman nodded.

'It's you that's wanted then. Come with us to the office.'

'Is it trouble, my children?'

'We don't know. Our duty was just to bring the owner of the house in. *Asazi*, you'll hear from the big ones,' the fat one said and moved towards the door. His behind reminded Vusi of an ox.

That morning they took the old woman away for an interview with the superintendent at Uncle Tom's Hall. Vusi wanted to go along but the 'blackies' would not allow him in the van. Dikeledi persuaded him to go to work: everything would be alright, they had never failed to pay the rent on time. He had a bad day at work.

It was not until about four hours later, at nine, that the white staff started showing up. There were three of them, the superintendent and his two assistants. As soon as their cars came into sight, the blackjacks who had seen them first rushed forward and waited to open the doors for their gods. One even went so far as to carry a briefcase inside the building for the white man who arrived last, trotting behind the latter like a schoolchild who had beaten others in the race to aid the principal with his case. Those who had been caught unawares appeared to be-grudge the others their alertness. Two of the new arrivals wore shorts which seemed too big for their thin dry legs.

It took the superintendents another hour of browsing through their morning papers to assure themselves that they were the masters of the fates of hundreds of thousands, before they could really get started with their work. With single strokes of their pens they decided the com-fort and discomfort of the people who came before them.

The old man who had been called in ahead of Vusi's mother came with his passbook, the old folding *dompas* type, held in front of his eyes, squinting and tilting his head to read whatever he was trying to make out in it. He stood there shaking his head dejectedly, his shoul-ders drooped, unlike when he had been called in. There was no doubt that he had received a stroke of grief.

The interpreter-clerk-aide stood at the door and shouted at the top of his voice, 'Mrs. Nyembezi!' The frail old woman tottered painfully from where she had been sitting. It took her some time to reach the door and in the meantime the clerk coaxed her dryly: 'C'mon, c'mon, *magogo, phangisa. Umlungu* will not wait for you. We are working here!'

'*Awu*, my child, the years have passed. The bones have gone weak, child of my child,' apologised Mrs. Nyembezi with a wrinkled smile. She tried to quicken her step but all she did was give herself fiery pangs in her joints.

At last she was sitting on the bench before one of the superintendents, a middle-aged man with a beaky nose, thin down-turned lips, a pale pinkish, leathery, veined complexion and impersonal grey eyes. He kept toying with his pen on the blotter while his underscrapper buzzed around arranging the house files and the rubber stamps on the desk so that his lordship could reach them without straining himself.

'*Ja, ouma. Wat kan ek doen vir jou?*' The thin lips barely vibrated. He asked this absent-mindedly, opening the file.

Mrs. Nyembezi tried her best to comprehend what was said, although she knew that she understood scarcely one word of Afrikaans or any other white man's language. She looked from the man to the clerk. 'My child, please come and help me here. I can't understand a single word of what he says,' she pleaded.

'*Jong!* You can't even speak Afrikaans?' the white man went on in the same language. He sounded as if he regarded it as a grave sin for the poor granny not to be able to speak his tongue.

He looked up from the papers into the old eyes. His face was expressionless. Again he studied the file. 'Tsk, tsk, tsk . . . ' He shook his head.

'Why don't you pay rent, *jong*?' And the clerk translated.

'But . . . but, my child, I pay. I've never missed paying. We'd rather go with empty stomachs at home than fail to pay. And I keep all the receipts. I could bring them to prove that there is not one month in all the years that we lived in the house that we did not pay,' Mrs. Nyembezi explained, wringing her shrivelled hands weakly. 'There must be a mistake somewhere, *bantu bami.*'

The clerk interpreted.

'You want to say I'm lying *ouma*? It says here you are in arrears to the amount of one hundred rand with your rent, *maan*!'

The sudden outburst made Mrs. Nyembezi cower, frightened even more. '*Nkulunkulu*, the white man is so angry. What shall I say to him?'

And aloud, 'Please child of my child, ask *nkosi* not to send me to jail.'

The clerk looked exasperated. 'No one is sending you to jail, *mago-go. Umlungu* says you owe rent. You know you owe, so I don't see why you're making such a fuss about it.'

'But I don't owe anything. Honestly, I paid. Where could I get the receipts if I did not pay? Ask him my child, ask him.'

'So you think you're smart about the receipts, huh? Didn't your children steal them when they burnt down the offices? And if you bring them, against what do you think we are going to check the black power period and that which comes before it? We don't have the re-cords. Your own children destroyed them with fire. Moreover who do you think has the time to check your stupid record of payment? Get this straight, *ouma*. First you should teach your children not to burn down things that have been built for you people out of our taxes and, secondly, I want that money paid — are you working?' A ridiculous question.

'No *nkosi*. My son works. I receive old age pension.' The old wo-man's distress was audible in her undulating voice, which trailed off hopelessly.

'How much does that son of yours earn, and how much is your pen-sion?' the superintendent demanded.

'I don't know how much he earns but I receive thirty rands every al-ternate month.'

'I don't see what beats you in paying your rent when you've got in-come. Or perhaps you drink it in shebeens? Tell your son to stop drink-ing and help you with your rent — understand?'

She nodded because there was nothing else to say. The white man was really angry.

'I want that money paid as quickly as possible. Otherwise you go back to the bantustan you came from and your son gets a room in a hostel; and somebody who is prepared to pay his rent gets the house. There are thousands on the waiting list. Now go. I don't want to see you here again. You're lucky I don't throw you out immediately. Say thanks I don't,' the superintendent said and clamped his thin lips.

'Thank you very much, *nkosi*. We'll raise the money and pay.'

It was like saying she would get a duck and make it lay eggs of gold for her.

During the first month after the interview, the going was tougher at Vusi's home. They had to sacrifice some of their basic needs which in the circumstances acquired luxury status. Protein was one thing they could not afford at all, the little ones having to make do only with sour porridge, and when the smallest baby got sick Dikeledi had to stay a-way from work to take her on day-long visits to the babies' clinic at Or-lando, seeing that she could not spare five rand for a quick visit to the private doctor. No one whined. Dikeledi did not ride Vusi about money, careful not to drive him to desperate measures.

When one day Vusi had come home talking about how people be-came rich only by stealing from others, she had discouraged him from nursing such thoughts by saying what he was thinking was the same as a woman resorting to prostitution to ease the pressure on their children. They agreed that such practices were the surest sign of weakness in the face of desolation.

At the end of the month they paid forty rand of the money they had come to accept that they owed, plus that month's amount; and braced themselves for the next one. At least that month it would be slightly better because the old lady's pension was also due.

Someone had told Dikeledi that what was happening to them was what had happened to her before she was thrown out into the streets after her own husband had been stabbed to death in a Soweto-bound train. A person with money goes to the superintendents and tells them that he needs a house badly. They tell him that in view of the fact that nowadays there's so little money and so many people going around without any, those in possession of the little carry more weight than those who have none at all — so what about a coupla hundred rand and a solid, electrified, four-roomed matchbox at, say Mzimhlope? 'You see,' they go on, 'you Bantus think that all Europeans are rich and well-paid in their jobs. But I and my colleagues here can assure you that we don't get enough; so we have to make a little for ourselves on the side too. How much can you afford?' they ask.

'Three hundred,' answers the prospective buyer, the thought of what would happen to those who lived in the house never having entered the minds of both men.

'You have a house,' and the green tigers exchange hands.

'Righto! Come and see us at the end of the month.'

At the time Dikeledi's friend was relating this, little did they realize that a similar deal was the subject of difference between a superinten-dent and a man who had paid money to get a house. The person who had paid was getting impatient. He was demanding service or his money back, and the money was no longer available.

'You said to come and see you at the end of last month. When I came you said to wait a bit. Now you tell me that the house is not yet ready and meanwhile you've taken and spent my money. I doubt if there was ever any house or if I'll ever get one. It's either I have the house now or you give back what you took from me. Otherwise I'm going to expose the whole thing through the papers,' the young man said heatedly. He had decided that the only way in which he could compel the superintendent to perform his obligation or return his money was to show him that he was capable of embarrassing him.

While the superintendent listened to these taunts, the whole of his body turned hot with rage at being addressed that way by an 'inferior', but especially the bit about the newspapers unsettled him. 'Nowadays the WRAB is getting a lot of bad publicity as an organization to disorganize the lives of Bantus. These English papers!' he thought. 'Now the bloody unmannered kaffir is threatening to bring them into our money-making scheme, our secret. That's what comes of an opposition that plays *verligte* and screams at you to give the Bantus a decent education and a better deal. Build them a machine to run their affairs and the first thing is for you to fashion houses with a magic wand to keep up with their galloping birthrate. *Here,* how I wish for the good old days when Bantus were Bantus and knew their place. Bring them out of the bush and teach them to read and write and they think they're smart enough to swear at the *baas.* Good old Bantus . . . that rings a bell! That old woman. The one who owed a hundred rand. Let's see how much she managed to pay. If she hasn't paid all, it's the bantustan for her and the stupid in front of me gets off my neck. Then I can breathe freely again, without thinking of the damn English papers that are busy agitating the kaffirs to demand rights; ha, ha, rights in a whiteman's land? They should have been banned too. I don't know why they were left out because they endanger our security and therefore that of the state too.'

He brightened up at stumbling upon a solution for his problem. He remembered that the *ouma* had shown little resistance when confronted with the amount she supposedly owed. If she had not paid all, which he was positive was as beyond her reach as the faintest star that she could see on the brightest night, he would bring down the wrath of god upon her. This trick always worked. She would relinquish the house to him, no, to the board, and go live with her relatives. The good thing with them is the way they can live in crowded conditions. He put that down to their strong family ties, and 'the way they breed'; baby girls with child before they know where they themselves came from. 'That is what they know best, sex and liquor.'

8

To the fuming man in front of him he said, 'Now, now, quiet down. Don't flip your top, man. How can we solve your matter if we make threats at each other?'

'You better be quick. I'm not prepared to listen to your cheating anymore.'

Barely restraining himself from striking out at the 'cheeky Bantu', the superintendent ordered the clerk, and not in the kindest terms either, to produce old Mrs. Nyembezi's file.

'*Hawu*, my friend, you haven't gone to work today?' I asked when I met Vusi at the station at about seven in the morning the other day, a time when he should have been at work. He had to be on the five o'clock train to be on time.

His hands were sunk deep in his pockets and his shoulders hunched. His head was not held as high as I had known him to hold it. He dragged his feet when he walked and he took a long time to return my greeting. I knew immediately that my friend's spirits were down. Something was wrong and I knew from his dejected semblance that I would not like it when he told me. Yet I wanted to know. That was what friendship was made for.

'I didn't go my friend, *is sleg*,' he replied slowly in a downcast voice.

'Why, what's it, Vus'? Why do you look like your homestead has been burnt down? Is it because your *baas* is going to halve your wages and make you work overtime for nothing to cover lost production when you return to work? Don't fret about money, that is the root of evil. Your teacher taught you as much, didn't he?' I went on in an attempt to cheer him out of the doldrums.

'I'm going to the office. The "blackies" took my mother there for the second time this morning. The first time was last month,' and he proceeded to tell me about what had happened since that first visit from the WRAB. He blurted out his story with unbridled bitterness, emphasizing that the debt was a fabrication aimed at squeezing them out of the house. His bitterness spilled over to me and by the time he got to the end I was helping him to curse those who were bringing his already destitute world crumbling down around him. He finished off by saying, 'South Africa! A cruel, cruel world with nothing but a slow death for us. I hate it, *mfo*, I hate it!'

I accompanied him to the office. That was all I could do to help my friend to try and save his home, the four-roomed centre of his life. He kept asking me what he could do and I hated myself for being so im-

potent in the face of a friend's distress. He told me that he did not
know where he would go if all this was building up to an eviction. Let
alone Dikeledi and the three children, because the other one, his late
sister's retarded daughter, would be returned to a home at Krugersdorp
where she had spent the previous year. I tried to strengthen him by
telling him that everything would turn out alright in the end; he was
only being pessimistic, the WRAB officials were also human and would
not be so callous as to throw them out into the dusty streets.

We did not stay long at the office either, for as soon as he and his
-mother came before the superintendent concerned, the one with the
beaky nose, all hell broke loose. They were told in the crudest terms
that, seeing they had been given two months to pay and they had
managed only forty percent, the board had no choice but to repossess
its house and give it to another person who would pay the rent without
trouble. When Vusi tried to point out that the time had not been stipu-
lated and neither had the two months mentioned expired, he was cut
off by the inevitable question, 'Do you mean to say I'm telling lies,
boy? Your mother lied to you, huh? Your mother's fault. She should
have told you that the money was wanted immediately.'

And turning to Mrs. Nyembezi, he asked, 'You are not ashamed to
lie at your age, *ouma*?' But she did not understand.

'Would you please give us another week, *meneer*? We've got another
thirty-five rand with us; we'll do all we can to raise the balance this
week. Please help us, sir, we haven't anywhere to go if you chase us out.
Here's the thirty-five rand. Show him, ma, show him,' Vusi said in his
best pleading voice. The old woman produced the folded notes which
were tied in a knot of her handkerchief and gave them to Vusi who
tried to hand them to the superintendent. The latter threw Vusi's hand
so violently aside that the money flew out of his hand. 'Can't you hear,
I say your time to pay is long overdue!' he screamed. 'Now get out. By
sunset I want you out of that house or I'm having you arrested — hear?
I'll be there to make sure.'

The clerks who were working at their desks and the two other white
men continued unperturbed by the scene. Only one or two black clerks,
one of them a woman, threw half-interested glances. The people who
were there for their own problems ogled and hissed softly, the way
black people do to express sympathy without words.

One ten rand note had landed on the desk of one of the other superintendents. As Vusi took it, their eyes met. There was a smirk of sadistic satisfaction in the man's eyes, like one who was deriving pleasure

out of a tragic scene in a drama. To show his approval to the villain, he winked at the latter and smiled. His thick eyebrows, large facial bones and the bristles growing out of his nostrils made him look like a lion.

I saw it on their faces the moment my friend and his aged mother stepped out of the hall. I did not ask them anything because I wanted to save them the agony of going over the details of their disastrous meeting with the superintendent. I wished that I had not been there to share those first moments of their tragedy because it was now my responsibility to console them and I did not know what to say I was dumbfounded and so were they. It was hard for all of us to accept that they were now homeless. We said very few words all the way from Phefeni to Mzimhlope, and Vusi's mother moaned from time to time. I hated to think that I was going to be there when they were removing their belongings from the house, actively assisting them to carry out the heartless bidding of the superintendent.

When we came to the house Vusi's mother asked him to make tea before everything. 'At least I'm entitled to a last cup of tea in what has been my home for the great part of my life,' she mumbled. Old as she was, her composure was remarkable. That desperate look had gone from her creased face. She gave me the impression that she looked forward to the bleak future as if it were one more challenge in addition to the many which had comprised her life.

Before the tea was ready, Beak Nose and Lion Face, true to the former's word, arrived in the van. There were three black men in overalls with them. The two officials alighted from the vehicle with a marked urgency and the three other men followed them and stood waiting for orders on the stoep. Beak Nose and Lion Face barged into the house without knocking. There was no need to knock.

Seeing an official van and whites coming out of it into the house brought the neighbourhood out to watch. Children who had been playing in the street abandoned their games and ran home shouting, '*Abelungu, abelungu!* At Temba's home!' Their mothers left their chores unfinished to stand in their small yards with folded arms and curious expressions on their plump faces. Seeing a white man in Soweto was like seeing an eskimo in the middle of the Sahara desert. And when he went into a house, it could only mean one thing, namely trouble for the people living there.

'*Jislâaik* Gert! The blerry fools are still sitting!' Beak Nose exclaimed. 'Didn't I tell you to get out of this fucken house immediately? I told you that I shouldn't find you here!'

11

Gert played up to the tune. 'And you're still sitting! Can't you hear what says the *baas*? All you want now is the fucken police to come and show you the gate. C'mon, get moving, I say!' and I ducked as he made as if to strike me with his open hand.

I joined Vusi in the kitchen and we stood there, reluctant to start moving the things. It was all so untrue and yet so true that they were being thrown out by the scruff of the neck, like a drama enacted in a cruel nightmare. Mrs. Nyembezi did not move from where she was sitting, holding her hands together and looking her persecutors in the face, no longer afraid of them but hating them — no their deed — with all her being. I say their deed because I never knew that old woman to bear hatred for another human.

Gert saw that we were not getting started and called in the three waiting outside to cast out everything into the street, as well as the three of us if need be. They got to work like mules and soon everything down to the last rag was in the street. When they finished, Beak Nose demanded the keys and the house was locked. The officials got into the front of the van and the three black men behind. With screeching tyres they were gone from sight.

The people, who had all along watched from a distance, converged upon Vusi's mother to ask what was wrong although they had already guessed. They came with shawls draped over their shoulders as if someone had died and they were joining the bereaved in mourning. They did the only thing they could to show that they were grieved at losing a long-time neighbour that way. They collected fifteen rand, saying that perhaps it would help them to persuade the office people to take the payment if only ten rand was short. Some advised that it would be better to take the money to the WRAB offices at New Canada where there were white social workers.

Mrs. Nyembezi now had fifty rand in the knot of her handkerchief. Vusi began to cheer up a little at this. 'This is the best thing for us to do, my friend,' he said. 'I'll take the money to the social workers at New Canada. They'll understand the whole bleeding thing better than those sadists at Phefeni. What I'll do tomorrow is to go and borrow the ten rand from the *mashonisa* where I work and by the time they open the offices at New Canada I'll be waiting for them.'

'Ya. I agree that's the best thing to do. How the hell did we overlook that angle when those Phefeni people would not understand? If we had gone straight to New Canada from Uncle Tom's perhaps all this would have been prevented.'

As the following day's events at New Canada proved, we were presuming too far as regards both the readiness and the ability of the social workers to help our cause.

Dikeledi's arrival from work coincided with that of the new tenant's to see what sort of place he would be moving into. The stranger arrived in a Chevair, which placed him among the fortunate of the sprawling locations.

It had been decided that there would be no harm in returning the furniture into the backyard while it was being decided where it would be taken. So, of the two, only Dikeledi saw that something was terribly wrong, from the way in which those who knew her looked at her as she walked from the station. The first thing that entered her mind was her three children. When she approached the house the missing curtains told her the whole story.

She was opening the battered gate when the stranger stopped the car behind her and called out, 'Sorry, girl.' He was not being disrespectful. Dikeledi was no more than a girl. 'May I ask?'

She turned and went back to the car.

'Do you stay here?' he asked, noting the way she swallowed nervously.

'Yes *buti*. I stay here.'

'I . . . er. Okay, let me come out.'

He came around the car and stood with his hands on his hips. He wore a navy blue suit, a snow white shirt and a blue tie with small white dots. There was the air of confidence about him which is characteristic of those who have just found a way to keep their heads above the water. Most probably very recently married and badly in need of his own four-room. Dikeledi felt uneasy standing before him, the way she felt when she faced a white man.

'*Awu,*' and he paused, perplexed. 'I thought this was a vacant house, *mos.* Is anybody else around? I see there are no curtains.' Dikeledi thought he had a friendly, though puzzled voice.

'I don't know, *buti*. I'm just arriving from work and I'm just as baffled. I'll see if they're there.' She turned and headed for the gate.

'Let's go in together,' he said and followed her.

She knocked on the front door but there was no response. They went round to the back of the house along the small passage, jumping to avoid the puddles made by the water from the leaking drain-pipe which Vusi had recently repaired as best as he could, after it was reported twice and in vain at the office. The drain-water turned the dust into a rank paste that brought the flies in swarms.

Vusi and I had gone out to buy fatcakes. We could have sent little Temba but we had to have an excuse to get away from the continuous sympathisers and location gossip mongers.

Dikeledi and the stranger came upon the backyard scene unexpectedly. It struck them with an impact which broke down the girl's composure and she wept uncontrollably. She had gone to work knowing that her mother-in-law (by her common law marriage) had been hauled out of bed to face the authorities at the office. Until she saw the curtainless windows and, finally, their rags strewn around in the backyard, she had not thought the visits in the small hours of the morning to be anything more than little inconveniences that were an integral part of a black person's life.

The stranger stood at the corner of the house, taking in everything slowly. The dilapidated state of the furniture and the piles of rags, the extreme poverty that he was witnessing did not shock him, because it was part of his life too. He had come upon such desolation a million times in his life and perhaps he might have come through it too. What made his heart bleed more than anything was the realization that he had contributed to everything that he saw before him. Where would these people go if he took their home from them? It had been stupid of him to think that he would be given a vacant house. There simply was not a single vacant house in the whole of Soweto. That was why people stayed on the waiting list for houses for decades. He had thought that he could avoid waiting for eternity, when more houses would be built, by paying to be considered whenever a house became vacant. Those who had tricked him into causing anguish to this poor family had assured him that houses did become vacant. He had not delved deeply into what they said and had been only too pleased when they took his money. His idea of an empty house was, say, that people there were leaving of their own accord. The shock wave of 'seventy-six, the year of the tumults, had sent many a timid soul packing for the sleeping countryside. He also knew that there were many lonely old people with no one to look after them, who kept their houses on doles so that they might at least die under a roof and not like dogs, in the wilderness. These derelict humans were only too prepared to accept young couples who would take over their houses and give them shelter and food until death arrived to deliver them from unrewarded lifetimes.

The thought that a whole family would be thrown out to make way for him had never entered his mind. It was immoral and he would not be a willing party to it. He wanted his money back and he would add to it to build himself two small rooms in the backyard of his home and wait there for eternity. They were still childless and by the time they were really forced by circumstances to leave home something might have cropped up for him or he might have saved enough to have a room built for him on the new thirty-year lease system.

We came as he was telling Mrs. Nyembezi what to do. 'Please ma, do exactly as I'm telling you. You said your son would try and get the rand, neh? It's a pity I have nothing on me, otherwise I would help. Tell him . . . '

'Here he is, my son. I was hoping he would turn up so that you could tell him what is to be done.' She called Vusi. 'Come and meet your brother here. He has been very good to us. God works in wonders.' The goodheartedness of the young man of slightly more than our age was reflected in her eyes.

She introduced them and left them to discuss the matter by themselves, 'because you are young and understand the ways of the white man better than we old people, who allowed ourselves to become their sacrificial lambs.'

I went to join them.

We listened carefully to each word that the man told us. In short he advised us not to waste precious time by trying to take the money to the superintendent who had ordered the eviction, because he would still refuse it and sell the house to someone else so as to raise the money he had received from the young man. 'The best thing to do is, take the money to New Canada, as the old lady has told me you've already planned to do. The social workers there might be of some help in persuading the officials to take the money. But this man is a *skelm* as you have seen for yourselves. He might have tipped off the others at New Canada and you might never even get to explain your problem to a social worker. Don't make a mistake about it, my friends, these whites benefit together from our sufferings. So I doubt if, when you come there looking for a social worker to help you with such a problem, you will be taken to the right people. If they don't attend to your matter satisfactorily, go either to the *Daily Mail* or *Star* offices and tell them the whole thing. Don't leave out a single scrap of information. The *Star* or *Mail* people will do their best to help.'

We thanked him heartily for his noble deed in refusing the house because of Mrs. Nyembezi and her family, and giving advice about what was to be done. The old ladies accompanied him to his car.

Everybody was blessing the stranger for his kindness. I was inclined right then to become a little superstitious by thinking that if the affairs of man *are* run by a just omnipotent, then that was the subtle way in which he made his presence known to us.

'Do you think it would be wise to put the things back inside?' Vusi asked me.

'It's locked up, *mos*. How are we going to open?'

'I should have asked for the key from that guy. He couldn't have come here without one. They must have given him one at the office,' Vusi said.

'What do we do then? Commit HB? It would be too risky. Remember that the bloody house is under the control of those sadists and boy, should they find you here!' I opined.

'You're speaking the gospel truth, my friend. They might return in the middle of the night. It means our troubles are not yet over, then. Let me sound the old lady.'

'*Awu*, women!' she said to the five or so matrons who were crowded around her. 'The little ones are not lying when they sing that the burden of our lives is heavy. A glimmer of hope in the dark and you follow it. Before you're anywhere up crops another problem. Vusi here asks whether it's safe to go back inside the house since that boy, who is now the rightful tenant, wouldn't mind us keeping the house.'

'Hey, my mother's child, that good child is not the superintendent. You may make matters worse for yourselves if you do that. Wait until you get permission to go back into the house,' one woman gave as her sound opinion.

The neighbours offered to divide the furniture and other things and to keep them until everything was back to normal. Some wanted to give them a place to sleep in their own crowded homes, but Mrs. Nyembezi declined politely, saying that they had already done enough for them by donating the fifteen rand and taking their belongings for safekeeping. She would take one of the children to her sister at Orlando East and the two little ones who still needed their mother's care would go with the latter to Mofolo, to her sister. The retarded one would be returned to the 'welfare' at Krugersdorp. She turned to Vusi. 'Where will you go Vus'?'

'I haven't decided yet, ma. But I'll see. Maybe I'll go to uncle at Klipspruit. But today I'm sleeping here at Mzimhlope. I'll find a place somewhere with my friends.'

But we slept in that controversial matchbox that night with the two blankets that Vusi had taken saying that he wanted to contribute those at least wherever he was going to sleep — which would have been at my place, only then he insisted on sleeping 'home'. He told me that the whole police force, let alone the 'blackies', would never stop him from sleeping there that night. I couldn't help but sleep there, also. You might not care to know that we remained on edge the whole night. The hard floor and thin blankets did not worry us very much; we were used to that in jail. It was the possibility of being found there by the WRAB people that robbed us of sleep.

The morning brought us great relief. We washed at my place and set out to where Vusi worked to see his *mashonisa* about the ten rand. Moneylenders are only too obliged to extend credit.

Vusi explained to a pleasant young white man why he had not turned up the previous day and that he wanted that day off, too. Without demanding the usual 'proof' he gave Vusi permission to attend to his affairs until they were settled and he assured him that that would not affect his paypacket. How contrasting people can be!

Our next destination was New Canada. The white so-called lady social worker sat with her stony face balanced in the palm of her left hand. By the time Vusi came to the end of his story I wasn't sure that he was not reciting his tale of woe to a wax mannequin — but for the incessant yawning of his listener. The problem was not communication, because Afrikaans is one of the seven languages that Vusi can speak with reasonable fluency, the others being: Zulu, English, Sotho, Pedi, Xhosa, Shangani.

'I'm sorry I can't help you boys. Go back to your superintendent and seek his forgiveness. You must have been disrespectful for him not to take your money. That's all I can suggest.' And she erased us from her attention as if we had suddenly vanished.

The next train took us to Westgate station. At the *Star* offices we were received cordially. A statement of my friend's plight was taken down and he was assured that it would be thoroughly dealt with. He was told to return in a fortnight to hear the result.

Meanwhile we stay with crossed fingers and prayers that things may take a better turn. Vusi is at Klipspruit with an uncle. It is two days since I last saw him. He passes my place on his way back from work. I wonder what is keeping him from coming.

Call Me Not a Man

For neither am I a man in the eyes of the law,
Nor am I a man in the eyes of my fellow man.

By dodging, lying, resisting where it is possible, bolting when I'm already cornered, parting with invaluable money, sometimes calling my sisters into the game to get amorous with my captors, allowing myself to be slapped on the mouth in front of my womenfolk and getting sworn at with my mother's private parts, that component of me which is man has died countless times in one lifetime. Only a shell of me remains to tell you of the other man's plight, which is in fact my own. For what is suffered by another man in view of my eyes is suffered also by me. The grief he knows is a grief that I know. Out of the same bitter cup do we drink. To the same chain-gang do we belong.

Friday has always been their chosen day to go plundering, although nowadays they come only occasionally, maybe once in a month. Perhaps they have found better pastures elsewhere, where their prey is more predictable than at Mzimhlope, the place which has seen the tragic demise of three of their accomplices who had taken the game a bit too far by entering the hostel on the northern side of our location and fleecing the people right in the midst of their disgusting labour camps. Immediately after this there was a notable abatement in the frequency of their visits to both the location and the adjacent hostel. However the lull was short-lived, lasting only until the storm had died down, because the memory tarnishes quickly in the locations, especially the memory of death. We were beginning to emit sighs of relief and to mutter 'good riddance' when they suddenly reappeared and made their presence in our lives felt once again. June, 'seventy-six had put them out of the picture for the next year, during which they were scarcely seen. Like a recurring pestilence they refuse to vanish absolutely from the scene.

A person who has spent some time in Soweto will doubtless have guessed by now that the characters I am referring to are none other than some of the so-called police reservists who roam our dirty streets at weekends, robbing every timid, unsuspecting person, while masquerading as peace officers to maintain law and order in the community. There are no greater thieves than these men of the law, men of justice, peace officers and volunteer public protectors in the whole of the slum complex because, unlike others in the same trade of living off the sweat of their victims, they steal out in the open, in front of everybody's eyes. Of course nothing can be done about it because they go out on their pillaging exploits under the banners of the law, and to rise in protest against them is analogous to defiance of the powers that be.

So, on this Friday too we were standing on top of the station bridge at Mzimhlope. It was about five in the afternoon and the sun hung over the western horizon of spectacularly identical coalsmoke-puffing rooftops like a gigantic, glowing red ball which dyed the foamy clouds with the crimson sheen of its rays. The commuter trains coming in from the city paused below us every two or three minutes to regurgitate their infinite human cargo, the greater part of whom were hostel-dwellers who hurried up Mohale Street to cook their meagre suppers on primus stoves. The last train we had seen would now be leaving Phefeni, the third station from Mzimhlope. The next train had just emerged from the bridge this side of New Canada, junction to East and West Soweto. The last group of the hostel people from the train now leaving Phefeni had just turned the bend at Mohale Street where it intersects with Elliot. The two hundred metre stretch to Elliot was therefore relatively empty, and people coming towards the station could be clearly made out.

As the wheels of the train from New Canada squealed on the iron tracks and it came to a jerking stop, four men, two in overalls and the others in dustcoats, materialised around the Mohale Street bend. There was no doubt who they were, from the way they filled the whole width of the street and walked as if they owned everything and everybody in their sight. When they came to the grannies selling vegetables, fruit and fried mealies along the ragged, unpaved sides of the street, they grabbed what they fancied and munched gluttonously the rest of the way towards us. Again nothing could be done about it, because the poverty-stricken vendors were not licensed to scrape together some crumbs to ease the gnawing stomachs of their fatherless grandchildren at home, which left them wide open for plunder by the indifferent 'reserves'.

'*Awu*! The Hellions,' remarked Mandla next to me. 'Let's get away from here, my friend.'

He was right. They reminded one of the old western film; but I was not moving from where I was simply because the reservists were coming down the street like a bunch of villains. One other thing I knew was that the railway constable who was on guard duty that Friday at the station did not allow the persecution of the people on his premises. I wanted to have my laugh when they were chased off the station.

'Don't worry about them. Just wait and see how they're going to be chased away by this copper. He won't allow them on the station,' I answered.

They split into twos when they arrived below us. Two of them, a tall chap with a face corroded by skin-lightening cream and wearing a yellow golf cap on his shaven head, and another stubby, shabbily dressed, middle-aged man with a bald frontal lobe and a drunk face, chewing at a cooked sheep's foot that he had taken from one of the grannies, climbed the stairs on our right hand side. The younger man took the flight in fours. The other two chose to waylay their unsuspecting victims on the street corner at the base of the left hand staircase. The first wave of the people who had alighted from the train was in the middle of the bridge when the second man reached the top of the stairs.

Maybe they knew the two reservists by sight, maybe they just smelt cop in the smoggy air, or it being a Friday, they were alert for such possibilities. Three to four of the approaching human wall turned suddenly in their tracks and ran for their dear freedom into the mass behind them. The others were caught unawares by this unexpected movement and they staggered in all directions trying to regain balance. In a split second there was commotion on the station, as if a wild cat had found its way into a fowlrun. Two of those who had not been quick enough were grabbed by their sleeves, and their passes demanded. While they were producing their books the wolves went over their pockets, supposedly feeling for dangerous weapons, dagga and other illegal possessions that might be concealed in the clothes, but really to ascertain whether they had caught the right people for their iniquitous purposes. They were paging through the booklets when the Railway policeman appeared.

'Wha . .? Don't you fools know that you're not supposed to do that shit here? Get off! Get off and do that away from Railway property. Fuck off!' He screamed at the two reservists so furiously that the veins threatened to burst in his neck.

'Arrest the dogs, *baba*! Give them a chance also to taste jail!' Mandla shouted.

'Ja,' I said to Mandla, 'you bet, they've never been where they are so prepared to send others.'

The other people joined in and we jeered the cowards off the station. They descended the stairs with their tails tucked between their legs and joined their companions below the station. Some of the commuters who had been alerted by the uproar returned to the platform to wait there until the reservists had gone before they would dare venture out of the station.

We remained where we had been and watched the persecution from above. I doubted if they even read the passes (if they could), or whether the victims knew if their books were right or out of order. Most likely the poor hunted men believed what they were told by the licensed thieves. The latter demanded the books, after first judging their prey to be weak propositions, flicked through the pages, put the passes into their own pockets, without which the owners could not continue on their way, and told the dumbfounded hostel men to stand aside while they accosted other victims. Within a very short while there was a group of confused men to one side of the street, screaming at their hostel mates to go to room so and so and tell so and so that they had been arrested at the station, and to bring money quickly to release them. Few of those who were being sent heard the messages since they were only too eager to leave the danger zone. Those who had money shook hands with their captors, received their books back and ran up Mohale Street. If they were unlucky they came upon another 'roadblock' three hundred metres up the street where the process was repeated. Woe unto them who had paid their last money to the first extortionists, for this did not matter. The police station was their next stopover before the Bantu Commissioners, and thence their final destination, Modderbee Prison, where they provided the farmers with ready cheap labour until they had served their terms for breaking the law. The terms vary from a few days to two years for *loaferskap*, which is in fact mere unemployment, for which the unfortunate men are not to blame. The whole arrangement stinks of forced labour.

The large *kwela-kwela* swayed down Mohale Street at breakneck speed. The multitudes scattered out of its way and hung onto the sagging fences until it had passed. To be out of sight of the people on the station bridge, it skidded and swerved into the second side street from the station. More reservists poured out of it and went immediately to their dirty job with great zeal. The chain-gang which had been lined up along the fence of the house nearest the station was kicked and shoved to the *kwela-kwela* into which the victims were bundled under a rain of fists and boots, all of them scrambling to go in at the same time through the small door. The driver of the *kwela-kwela*, the only uniformed constable among the group, clanged the door shut and secured it with the locking lever. He went to stand authoritatively near one of the vendors, took a small avocado pear, peeled it and put it whole into a gargantuan mouth, spitting out the large stone later. He did not have to take the trouble of accosting anyone himself. His gangsters would all give him a lion's share of whatever they made, and moreover buy him some beers and brandy. He kept adjusting his polished belt over his potbelly as the ,38 police special in its leather holster kept tugging it down. He probably preferred to wear his gun unconventionally, cowboy style.

A boy of about seventeen was caught with a knife in his pocket, a dangerous weapon. They slapped him a few times and let him stand handcuffed against the concrete wall of the station. Ten minutes later his well-rounded sister alighted from the train to find her younger brother among the prisoners. As she was inquiring from him why he had been arrested, and reprimanding him for carrying a knife, one of the younger reservists came to stand next to her and started pawing her. She let him carry on, and three minutes later her brother was free. The reservist was beaming all over his face, glad to have won himself a beautiful woman in the course of his duties and little knowing that he had been given the wrong address. Some of our black sisters are at times compelled to go all the way to save their menfolk, and as always, nothing can be done about it.

There was a man coming down Mohale Street, conspicuous amidst the crowd because of the bag and baggage that was loaded on his overall-clad frame. On his right shoulder was a large suitcase with a grey blanket strapped to it with flaxen strings. From his left hand hung a bulging cardboard box, only a few inches from the ground, and tilting him to that side. He walked with the bounce of someone used to walking in gumboots or on uneven ground. There was the urgency of someone who had a long way to travel in his gait. It was doubtless a *goduka* on his way home to his family after many months of work in the city. It might even have been years since he had visited the countryside.

He did not see the hidden *kwela-kwela*, which might have fore-warned him of the danger that was lurking at the station. Only when he had stumbled into two reservists, who stepped into his way and ordered him to put down his baggage, did he perhaps remember that it was Fri-day and raid-day. A baffled expression sprang into his face as he rea-lised what he had walked into. He frantically went through the pockets of his overalls. The worried countenance deepened on his dark face. He tried again to make sure, but he did not find what he was looking for. The men who had stopped him pulled him to one side, each holding him tightly by the sleeve of his overall. He obeyed meekly like a tame animal. They let him lift his arms while they searched him all over the body. Finding nothing hidden on him, they demanded the inevitable book, although they had seen that he did not have it. He gesticulated with his hands as he explained what had caused him not to be carrying his pass with him. A few feet above them, I could hear what was said.

'Strue, *madoda*,' he said imploringly, 'I made a mistake. I luggaged the pass with my trunk. It was in a jacket that I forgot to search before I packed it into the trunk.'

'How do we know that you're not lying?' asked one of the reservists in a querulous voice.

'I'm not lying, *mfowethu*. I swear by my mother, that's what hap-pened,' explained the frightened man.

The second reservist had a more evil and uncompromising attitude. 'That was your own stupidity, mister. Because of it you're going to jail now; no more to your wife.'

'Oh, my brother. Put yourself in my shoes. I've not been home to my people for two years now. It's the first chance I have to go and see my twin daughters who were born while I've been here. Feel for an-other poor black man, please, my good brother. Forgive me only for this once.'

'What? Forgive you? And don't give us that slush about your child-ren. We've also got our own families, for whom we are at work right now, at this very moment,' the obstinate one replied roughly.

'But, *mfo*. Wouldn't you make a mistake too?'

That was a question the cornered man should not have asked. The reply this time was a resounding slap on the face. 'You think I'm stupid like you, huh? Bind this man, Mazibuko, put the bloody irons on the dog.'

'No, man. Let me talk to the poor bloke. Perhaps he can do something for us in exchange for the favour of letting him proceed on his way home,' the less volatile man suggested, and pulled the hostel man away from the rest of the arrested people.

'*Ja*. Speak to him yourself, Mazibuko. I can't bear talking to rural fools like him. I'll kill him with my bare hands if he thinks that I've come to play here in Johannesburg!' The anger in the man's voice was faked, the fury of a coward trying to instil fear in a person who happened to be at his mercy. I doubted if he could face up to a mouse. He accosted two boys and ran his hands over their sides, but he did not ask for their passes.

'You see, my friend, you're really in trouble. I'm the only one who can help you. This man who arrested you is not in his best mood today. How much have you got on you? Maybe if you give something he'll let you go. You know what wonders money can do for you. I'll plead for you; but only if I show him something can he understand.' The reservist explained the only way out of the predicament for the trapped man, in a smooth voice that sounded rotten through and through with corruption, the sole purpose for which he had joined the 'force'.

'I haven't got a cent in my pocket. I bought provisions, presents for the people at home and the ticket with all the money they gave me at work. Look, *nkosi*, I have only the ticket and the papers with which I'm going to draw my money when I arrive at home.' He took out his papers, pulled the overall off his shoulders and lowered it to his thighs so that the brown trousers he wore underneath were out in the open. He turned the dirty pockets inside out. 'There's nothing else in my pockets except these, mister, honestly.'

'Man!'

'Yessir?'

'You want to go home to your wife and children?'

'Yes, *please*, good man of my people. Give me a break.'

'Then why do you show me these damn papers? They will feed your own children, but not mine. When you get to your home you're going to draw money and your kids will be scratching their tummies and dozing after a hectic meal, while I lose my job for letting you go and my own children join the dogs to scavenge the trashbins. You're mad, *mos*.' He turned to his mate. 'Hey, Baloyi. Your man says he hasn't got anything, but he's going to his family which he hasn't seen for two years.'

'I told you to put the irons on him. He's probably carrying a little fortune in his underpants. Maybe he's shy to take it out in front of the people. It'll come out at the police station, either at the charge office or in the cells when the small boys shake him down.'

'Come on, you. Your hands, maan!'

The other man pulled his arms away from the manacles. His voice rose desperately, '*Awu* my people. You mean you're really arresting me? Forgive me! I pray do.'

A struggle ensued between the two men.

'You're resisting arrest? You — ' and a stream of foul vitriolic words concerning the anatomy of the hostel man's mother gushed out of the reservist's mouth.

'I'm not, I'm not! But please listen!' The hostel man heaved and broke loose from the reservist's grip. The latter was only a lump of fat with nothing underneath. He staggered three steps back and flopped on his rump. When he bounced back to his feet, unexpectedly fast for his bulk, his eyes were blazing murder. His companions came running from their own posts and swarmed upon the defenceless man like a pack of hyenas upon a carcase. The other people who had been marooned on the bridge saw a chance to go past while the wolves were still preoccupied. They ran down the stairs and up Mohale like racehorses. Two other young men who were handcuffed together took advantage of the diversion and bolted down the first street in tandem, taking their bracelets with them. They ran awkwardly with their arms bound together, but both were young and fit and they did their best in the circumstances.

We could not stand the sickening beating that the other man was receiving anymore.

'Hey! Hey. *Sies*, maan. Stop beating the man like that. Arrest him if you want to arrest him. You're killing him, dogs!' we protested loudly from the station. An angry crowd was gathering.

'Stop it or we'll stop you from doing anything else forever!' someone shouted.

The psychopaths broke their rugger scrum and allowed us to see their gruesome handiwork. The man was groaning at the base of the fence, across the street where the dirt had gathered. He twisted painfully to a sitting position. His face was covered with dirt and blood from where the manacles that were slipped over the knuckles had found their marks, and his features were grotesquely distorted. In spite of that, the fat man was not satisfied. He bent and gathered the whimpering man's wrists with the intention of fastening them to the fence with the handcuffs.

'Hey, hey, hey, Satan! Let him go. Can't you see that you've hurt that man enough?'

The tension was building up to explosion point and the uniformed policeman sensed it.

'Let him go, boys. Forgive him. Let him go,' he said, shooting nervous glances in all directions.

Then the beaten-up man did the most unexpected and heartrending thing. He knelt before the one ordering his release and held his dust-covered hands with the palms together in the prayer position, and still kneeling he said,'Thank you very much, my lord. God bless you. Now I can go and see my twins and my people at home.'

He would have done it. Only it never occurred in his mind at that moment of thanksgiving to kiss the red gleaming boots of the policeman.

The miserable man beat the dust off his clothes as best he could, gathered his two parcels and clambered up the stairs, trying to grin his thanks to the crowd that had raised its voice of protest on his behalf. The policemen decided to call it a day. The other unfortunates were shepherded to the waiting *kwela-kwela*.

I tried to imagine how the man would explain his lumps to his wife. In the eye of my mind I saw him throwing his twins into the air and gathering them again and again as he played with them.

'There's still a long way to cover, my friend,' I heard Mandla saying into my ear.

'Before?' I asked.

'Before we reach hell. Ha, ha, ha! Maybe there we'll be men.'

'Ha, we've long been there. We've long been in hell.'

'Before we get out, then.'

A Glimpse of Slavery

. . . For the suffering of injustice is not the part of a man,
but of a slave, who indeed had better die than live;
since when he is wronged and trampled upon,
he is unable to help himself, or any other about whom he cares.
                    — Callicles' words from Plato's Gorgias.

Magistrate: Have you anything to say for yourself before sentence is passed?

Myself: I've nothing to say, your honour. All I wanted to say has been said. The evidence I gave before the court was the pure truth. I'm only surprised now when you promise to sentence me. It is clear to everybody in this court that I was merely defending myself. The only thing I want to add is that your honour must pass sentence knowing that you, a man well versed in the principles of justice, are about to violate the same principles that you swore never to undermine.

Magistrate: Is that all?

Myself: Yes, your honour.

Magistrate: I am not moved by your last words from my findings, which I have already explained to you. The court sentences you to twelve months' imprisonment of which nine months is conditionally suspended for three years . . .

The condition was that I should not be found guilty of assault during those three years. I turned and grinned at my people in the gallery. They smiled back at me triumphantly. Although I had deserved a discharge, we all welcomed the three months. Assaulting a white man is sacrilege in South Africa. Even the courtroom constable

27

was pleased that I had got away with a vacation on some farm. The complainant derived a different satisfaction. He had been the villain all the way, and a 'smiling, damned, villain' in the courtroom. In the first place he had tried to steal from the firm where we worked, sending us to deliver an order that was less than what was listed on the invoice. Secondly, he had insulted us first. And thirdly, he had struck me first, about three blows before I retaliated. Because of all this I was going to jail for three months and, sure as I was being fingerprinted at that very moment, I had lost my job too.

'Hey boys, come here, come here. The goods you have just delivered do not correspond with the invoice. They are short by seven; two lampshades, two electric irons and three kettles. What's wrong?' Our firm dealt in home electric appliances and there were four van 'boys' to every medium-sized van. Our group consisted of two other youths of about my age then, twenty, and the fifty-five-year-old 'boy', Alfred (otherwise Ntate Ali to us), our driver and group leader — he signed everything and we just loaded and off-loaded the van. Ntate Ali was a goodhearted old man, his only shortcoming being that he did not allow any 'bread' to come out in his van with his knowledge, perhaps afraid to be made an accomplice, although he did not go out of his way to ensure that there was nothing extra in his van.

Ntate Ali turned to hear what the white man was talking about. He wanted us out of earshot because we always teased him about his religious fear of whites. We followed him close.

'Where are the other things?' asked the baldheaded manager type. 'Look . . . Can you read and count?'

'Yes, *baa-*, sorry, sir', Ntate Ali answered nervously, correcting himself when he saw us out of the corner of his eye nudging each other.

'Here, add these articles and come inside with me to check them.'

Ntate Ali went with the white man into the building. Presently he reappeared muttering to himself and folding a debit note, which he put between the pages of the signature book that he carried with him on our rounds.

'What is it Ali?' Sello asked. That one was on first name terms with everybody at the firm, including some of the easy-going whites.

'That man gave us the wrong order,' replied the old man.

'No, Ali, always trying to shield your *baas*. That guy stole the other stuff. He was taking a chance on the stuff not being checked before we left the place. If the mistake had been spotted later the firm would have been notified and the order rectified just like any other mistake. That's how Jan operates — if you don't know, Ali, said Sello. 'The man uses you to steal and you pretend you don't see. One day you'll go to jail for him.'

'Awu, shaddup Sello. You think everybody's a thief like you. Either this is a wrong order or he made a mistake counting,' insisted Ntate Ali.

'Oho. Go ahead and remain sleeping. You'll see. He's going to tear up that debit note and tell you to deliver the things.'

We pushed the matter to the back of our minds and continued our round. If I had known where it would lead me, perhaps I would have given it a little more thought.

Manyathela — he was flat-footed and knock-kneed and waddled like a duck when he walked, so we called him that — stormed at us as we went in through the wide, sliding glass door. At first we hardly took notice of him waddling towards us. He was an aggressive type and you never knew whether he was really angry or not until he was upon you. Most 'boys' at our firm had tasted his wrath, which he was inclined to unleash physically. Until that day he had stepped clear of me, maybe sensing that I was not the kind that is easy to push around. However sometimes his guard slipped, and in such moments I had caught him looking at me with a doubtful eye, as if he wanted to try me and see if I could stand up against him. I tried my utmost not to give him a chance to carry out his experiment, in spite of his relentless goading, which even extended to pulling me up for minor mistakes in my work.

'Hey you stupids! Why did you tell those people to phone the firm for the undelivered things? Since when have you done that?' he screamed at us.

'Er . . . Mr Du Toit. It was a, a mistake . . .' Ntate Ali stammered.

'What? A mistake? Whose mistake? Your bloody mistake of course!' He advanced threateningly on the old man.

The next thing I found myself between him and Ntate Ali. He raised his balled fists but hesitated to strike.

'Either your own mistake or nobody's mistake. You know that this old man has nothing to do with stealing. He just drives his van where you send him, that's all,' I heard myself saying in a nice even voice. I had the disturbing feeling of welcoming the confrontation. Maybe it was because I had long been coiled up inside and the person who had done the coiling up was standing in front of me, giving me a chance to unwind.

The white man was beyond himself with anger. He sucked in a deep breath through his slitlike nostrils and clenched his teeth, grimacing as if he was in pain.

'Who told that manager to phone here? Why didn't you tell him to phone dispatch?'

'There's only one phone number here,' I said. 'Or do you have your own?'

'Then why didn't you tell him you didn't know why you were short?'

'Why?' Aggression contaminates. The anger was welling up inside me.

'Because kaffers don't know anything! And what's more, don't you stand here asking me questions — hear?'

I did not reply to this. We were going on like a pair of schoolgirls. If he was not going to do to me what he had started out to do to the old man, then I might as well proceed to the changing room. The knock-off buzzer had gone and the rest of the firm was packing up for the day. Those who had finished came to form a sort of ring around us, a sprinkling of whites and Indians included. They stood there silently and expectantly, with their arms folded, some of them holding their chins, the whites more towards Manyathela's side, forming part of the arc behind him, the Indian guys on the sides, except for good old Moosa, whom I could not locate and guessed was behind me.

I started turning. By so doing I gave Jan the chance he was waiting for. His vicious right caught me above the temple. I staggered a good two metres and just managed to stay on my feet. He had snatched the advantage, the cowardly bully, and he hung on to it, but only for the two more blows he landed on my jaw and chest, both not hard enough to stun me or knock the breath out of me, because I was moving away from him as he waded in on flat, awkward feet. I hadn't grown up in the rough streets of Soweto without learning to defend myself. Everything I did next was purely instinctive. You live in a brutal environment, you develop an instinct for violence. As simple as that. I went for Manyathela like a rabid dog. I came to when I had him on all fours before me and was working my legs on him like pistons. It was not a white man I was belting, don't mistake me. It was a bully who needed some straightening out. I was doing to him what he would have done to me if he had had the makings of a good fighter. In our own dialect he had 'come to the stop station'.

Someone was pulling me off him. My half circle was cheering madly, and it was this noise that brought the manager from the first floor. When he appeared on the staircase, all went suddenly mum. I think nobody wanted to be caught cheering.

'What's going on here?' the manager demanded to know.

The first to answer was Manyathela's friend, who called himself *'Vrystaat'* when he was in a happy mood. Miss Malan, the receptionist and the only woman on the ground floor, was quick to pick up the phone. Maybe if there had been only men on the ground floor the matter would have been settled in a manly way. Everybody had been treated to a good, though unbalanced duel. All men enjoy watching a man-to-man tussle, that is why boxing is such a prosperous sport. The worst I might have come by was to lose my job.

The lady and *'Vrystaat'* were the star witnesses at the trial. Ntate Ali was bound by the fact that the fracas had started over him to stand by me. The others I left out of the matter so as not to jeopardise their positions at the firm. Ntate Ali was terror-stricken through the whole circus in which the main bone of contention was why I had taken the law into my hands, not who had been the aggressor and why.

Koos de Wet, the man I was later to learn had once been heavyweight wrestling champion of the Transvaal, had a torso that was not much smaller than that of the oxen his servants, or rather slaves told me he had trained with. He was barrel-shaped and suntanned to a brick red. This hulk was covered with a short thick khaki suit, cut Safari style, and on his head, the facial portion of which reminded me of the nose of an archaic aeroplane with its propeller represented by his grey brush of moustache, was perched a scout's hat with a leopard-skin band. The wide brim of the hat was pinned to the dome on one side.

Farmers had come to choose their labour since morning, when we were herded into the square yard. They stood on the other side of the wire fence and pointed. Others had only stated the number they needed and taken their men away. The other three sides of the square were bounded by walls. I assessed each bidder and pushed the other prisoners ahead or hid behind them. But now it was about twelve and there were few of us, about twenty, left in the yard, which had grown in size as the occupants diminished, and there was no way you could hide. Up to now no bidder had taken my fancy and I had stuck around hoping that a more Christian-looking person would turn up. I did not like Koos de Wet at all. He was taking in my physique with the practised eye of a livestock buyer.

'*Ek soek vyf gesond jonges. Daardie, daardie, daardie, daai en daai.*' Koos picked his men, starting with me. I regretted waiting all morning only to be picked out by the most unsettling human being I had seen for a long time. I had heard tell of fearsomeness in people, but Koos took the cup by a wide margin.

He was filling his pipe as we filed out of the small gate. When I passed him I felt my scalp shrinking. My whole body knew the sensation of expecting a blow. The others detoured, to leave a safe distance when they passed him. I guessed that we were all feeling the same. Our behaviour tickled the ogre for, as he signed the papers at reception, he kept eyeing us with dead grey marbles and what I thought must have been a smile twitched at the corners of his mouth. He had bought us (we did not know how the actual transaction, payments and all took place) and we belonged to him. He could do whatever he liked with us, faraway in the wilderness where nobody would know. He could kill us, bury us on his farm, and report that we had escaped. We would have to do all we could to slip out of that slave-master's hands alive.

A battered misshapen pile of green metal sheets that might have been a van once waited for us outside the Modderbee prison grounds. We were still in our own clothes and I thought how easy it would be to run. But where would one run in that open sea of brown waving highveld grass? These thoughts were wiped from my mind when we came to the van. The slave-driver opened the cab of the vehicle and leant inside. When he came erect there was a rifle in his right paw. I don't know anything about arms, so I don't know what model it was. It was a rifle right enough.

He raised the gun and shook it at us. 'Climb in,' he growled in Afrikaans. 'I'd like to see if this old *roer* can still spit fire. I ask you to give me a chance to try it, kaffers.'

We sprang to obey the order. I was afraid that the contraption we vaulted ourselves onto would fall apart under the strain of our weight. To my surprise it remained intact. It protested loudly when Koos de Wet got into the cabin. Then it quaked, whined, purred, and at the third try roared to life. With a screech of gears that set my teeth on edge we were moving. The petrol fumes smothered us but soon cleared when we picked up speed on the infinite tarred road to the shimmering distances of the Transvaal. By way of speed that battered tin could do wonders. The world came at us from where we were going and swept past us in one great blur. The few vehicles we passed on the road appeared to have been hurled from somewhere ahead of us by some monstrous force.

After what appeared to be an eternity — there was no way we could estimate the distance we had travelled on the never turning road — we felt a reduction of speed.

We turned into a dirt road that branched off at a right angle to the north (all along we had been driving eastward). By the look of it, it was not very frequently used. Grass grew in the middle, making the dirt road look like two parallel footpaths. The dust mushroomed behind us like a nuclear explosion cloud. None of us spoke. Trying to do so would have been futile with the racket that our conveyance to the unknown raised. On that meandering dirt road our main concern became trying to hold on to the sides of the carrier as best we could in order not to be thrown off. The violent bumping and twisting prevented us from placing landmarks which might have helped us know our bearings. However I did my best to note the general direction of the main road and changing landscape. We were ascending some hilly and craggy land; the roar of the engine and the fact that I could see the road way down below us where the dust had thinned, told me that.

The farm lay in the second, shallow valley, a rich saucer-like country bounded by three low hills. Did you ever travel on land that has been left undisturbed since it was made by the Creator, and when you were beginning to think you would never arrive anywhere, suddenly come upon a place to which people once somehow found their way? The symmetrical human touch seemed to be a wry joke in the face of nature. What Koos de Wet had done was to choose a fertile dale for himself, place a city homestead on one hillside and below this, plan his farm, totally neglecting artistic considerations. He had arrested what must have been a beautiful twinkling stream in the middle of the valley, flattened acres of the downstream land, divided this with criss-crossing fences, planted maize, potatoes, onions and green pumpkins on four fields, and let perforated asbestos pipes distribute the water from the dam formed by a wall running across the valley. The pipes, some of which were not perforated, opened into a kind of trough from which the stream continued on its way. The usual farm buildings dominated by a large hay-shed, were scattered over the farm. The hay was the feed for his innumerable livestock grazing upstream on the other side of the dam. That was the place where I would learn the extent to which cruelty and hatred can turn man into something less than a wild beast.

We passed the servants' shacks. They were low, crooked mud walls on which were placed rusted corrugated iron sheets, kept there with boulders the size of a man's head. From one end to the other the shanty was a hundred yards. Dark holes which served as doors gaped in the walls. The foreground was nauseatingly filthy. Either it had rained or they threw their waste water there, and the sour smell of rotting trash was similar to that of a pigsty, which I would have mistaken the clumsy construction to be, but for the two ragged women, one heavily pregnant and the other lean and old, who came out of two of the gloomy holes followed by a swarm of dirty children with soiled noses and tear-marked faces, all of them not much more than babies. Some of the children were stark naked and those who had something on looked no better. The ones who might be girls wore straight dresses made of cotton flour bags and the boys wore old shirts that came to their ankles. The biggest boy was sucking his thumb. They greeted our advent passively.

Turning left, Koos drove down between two lucerne fields. Figures were crouched in rows two hundred metres away, cutting the lucerne with sickles. With ear-splitting squeaks and squeals, and one final loud roar, the van came to a stop beside a big, square brick building. Koos got out from the front and grunted, '*Klim af.*'

We jumped down and stretched ourselves.

'At least it's better than being locked up in jail — neh?' said Thabo, with whom I had paired three days previously, on a Friday when we reached Modderbee.

'Still too early to decide. If the people who live on his farm are like those we passed, what do you think we'll be like by the time we leave here? I don't trust that gorilla at all, my friend,' I answered, more convinced that Koos was a psychopath the more I saw of him.

The baas-boy appeared around the corner of the building. I concluded that he was one from the way he was dressed in heavy khakis and boots that were still in reasonably good condition. Sick people tend to be drawn together by their common plight. 'Bobbejaan' suffered from the same mental sickness as Koos and for that reason was exempt from his master's sadism. In fact he was Koos's main hand on the farm. It was obvious how he had earned the position of farm overseer. A few days after our arrival one of the farm labourers told me that Bobby, as he preferred to be called rather than his baas's full 'Bobbejaan', was born on the farm, had never been further than Benoni, the nearest town, where he accompanied Koos to the market to sell the produce, and never left the farm because he knew no relatives other than those few who lived there. He was, perhaps, also afraid that he might come across some of the people who had been through his hands on the farm. Another reason might be that Bobby knew no other way of life than farm life, and was by nature neither adventurous nor imaginative. He had been brought up with hard farm labour and as such expected everybody to be able to work like an ox. It might have been for these reasons, and the sadism in common, that he was favoured by Koos de Wet.

Bobby was about thirty-five years of age, of medium height, stone-hard muscle and extreme cruelty. His leathery face told you that as soon as you saw him. He examined us with the contempt rural people have for city people (an attitude city people hold, in reverse, for rural people). He apparently considered us in terms of work, as labour units instead of other human beings he was meeting for the first time. After sizing us up he turned his attention to Koos.

'*Basie. Baas* Van Tonder was here. He had come to see the cattle you discussed with him. He'll come again tomorrow evening,' he said in perfect Afrikaans, like a little boy telling his father how he had spent the day while the father was away at work.

'*Ja, dankie*, Bobbejaan. How's the work proceeding?' asked Koos as if soliloquizing, and took out his pipe.

'*Baie goed, baas.*'

Koos grunted his satisfaction like a pig. 'Here's five more hands from Modderbee. See that they learn the work fast, but first I want that tree stump removed from the side of the granary. I want work to begin on the extension by the week after next. Dress them and make them start now, I'm still going to see the Missus at the house.'

Bobby stared at us with baleful eyes for some seconds before speaking. '*Madoda,*' he said in a voice that might have chilled a milksop, 'you must know that here on *baas* Koos's farm no one is begged to work, more especially prisoners. If you're afraid of work, we soon make you like it. This is not the city where you come from, but a farm. Come and change.'

We followed him to the entrance of the brick building next to which the van had stopped. He took a key out of his pocket and unlocked the heavy padlock that held a horizontal iron rail across two wooden doors that were covered with sheets of tin. The doors had three right angled iron hooks each, about halfway up. The iron rail rested in the nooks of these hooks and held the doors fast. It was only when he pushed the doors open that I noticed that the room had no windows. From the sunbeam that flooded in I saw that there were piles of sacks on the floor.

'Take the sacks in the nearest right hand corner, remove your clothes and put the sacks on. They have three holes for your head and arms at the base,' Bobby said as if he was giving a most ordinary order. When they had spoken of 'change' and 'dress' it had never occurred to me that they might mean we were going to replace our clothes with sacks.

The five of us looked at each other in shocked surprise. We stood where we were without making any move to go inside or take off our clothes.

'Can't we work in our clothes, mister? Why the sacks?' I asked.

'So that you may run away all the easier? On the other hand we are saving your city clothes for you, because when *baas* Koos returns you to the prison you must be dressed as you came here,' Bobby explained curtly.

'Well, tell your *baas* that I'm not dressing like a slave,' one of us whose name I did not know replied.

'So, you're not prepared to work? You forget quickly that you are a prisoner. I'll call *baas* Koos and we'll remind you what you are.'

Seeing that all five of us stood motionless in spite of the mention of Koos de Wet's name, Bobby made a move to attack the man who had spoken.

'You touch him and we all take you apart limb by limb before that ape arrives here,' Thabo threatened. 'You just try, and you'll see.'

Without any more words Bobby spun around and ran as fast as he could after his master.

'We're in for it now, *majita*,' I said. 'But they're mad to think that we can put on these sacks.'

I should have said we were mad to think that we could refuse to obey anything that Koos told us to do as long as we were on his farm. When the pair of sadists returned, the one time heavyweight wrestler had a long braided thong whip in his left hand, and in his eyes the glint of a tamer of wild animals. Bobby stood aside and smiled — in fact sneered — like a dirty-minded person about to watch a filthy play. Koos asked no questions but started flogging us with brutish enthusiasm. I covered my face and felt the lashes cutting my skin and setting it on fire. Two or three of us were crying out aloud. In the background I heard Bobby laughing gleefully. Whip! Whip! Whip! the burning leather swished in the air. After a storm of fire and brimstone that lasted close to forever there was a welcomed pause.

'*Trek uit!*' Koos spat out. His eyes shone like a snake's. They hypnotized us into complete submission, reduced us to whimpering bags of pain. The little nerve we had had against Bobby had been flogged out by the whip that lay coiled like a thin black snake near Koos de Wet's left boot. '*Trek uit, jong!*' he spat again, and in a flash we were out of our clothes, as naked as we were born and trying to hide behind one another, both out of shame at our nakedness and because of the whip. I felt dehumanized as I stood there hiding my loins with my hands. The two in front of me had lacerations all over their backs down to their buttocks.

'Give them the sacks, Bobbejaan.' The latter went inside the building and came out with five of the said sacks. He threw them at us. I caught one and examined it before putting it on. It had been converted into a simple dress by cutting holes at the corners and the centre of the base as Bobby had told us. I slipped it on. It hung heavy and coarse on my shoulders. Where it touched the whip cuts it felt as if pepper had been sprinkled.

I looked at my companions. Their appearance made me feel like laughing, but I could not bring myself to do so. I had all along thought that such scenes existed only in the pages of history books or in films. My standard three teacher had taught me that slavery was abolished way back in eighteen thirty-three in South Africa. He was lying, and those who had told him that had fed him a lot of bunkum too.

'Bobbejaan is going to give you five picks and you're going to dig out a tree stump. You give him any more trouble and you'll see that the dance we just had was only the first rehearsal of the real party. *Nou, spring!*' We were not going to argue after our initiation.

Bobby led us to a tool-shed. 'You see now that this is not the city where you're begged to work? You'll leave Traanfontein with some experience worth relating to your grandchildren. This is where *baas* Koos's great-grandfather was killed by Ndebele savages and lies buried. Later, when the Ndebele thieves were conquered his sons claimed this land and called it Traanfontein because their tears flowed here. They vowed never to leave the land and my people came to work for the De Wets before *baas* Koos was even born.' He gave us a brief history of the farm, very proud that he too was part of it. So Koos de Wet was visiting the 'sins' of the fathers upon the second and third generations.

The tool-shed was big and full of all types of farm implements. This gave me the impression that, although his was a prosperous farm which could afford to keep pace with modern technology, De Wet was a conservative farmer. He must have preferred manual labour for two reasons — its cheapness, and the vengeance sworn by the family against black people. Each of us took a pick. Bobby showed us the stump of gumtree, five feet in diameter, about a metre from the wall of what must have been the granary. He did not leave us but sat on a rock and rolled a zoll of Magaliesberg tobacco. We spaced ourselves around the stump and started digging. In spite of the sack I still felt naked and, in addition to the painful lacerations on my body, my skin itched intolerably.

At the first few swings the picks sank deep into the soil.

'This is *(dig)*, better *(dig)* than I thought *(dig)*. The ground *(dig)* is soft,' remarked the man who had started the whip dance.

We dug about two feet down, tearing through the topmost roots easily. Then we came to the thick roots and trouble. Our picks stuck in the roots and it became difficult to pull them out, or they just glanced off the hard wet underground wood, twisted in our grips and blistered our hands. The blisters soon burst and we were holding the shafts with raw palms.

'Damn it!' I cursed. 'We won't get anywhere digging like this. Tell that swine to give us spades.'

Thabo stood erect, held his waist behind and grimaced. 'Shoo,' he said, 'My spine feels as if it's going to break.'

'Mine too. You're right about the spades,' another man said and stopped digging.

We all stopped digging and leaned on the shafts of our picks. Bobby jumped from where he had been sitting as if he had suddenly discovered that the rock was red hot, and came running at us. His eyes were shooting fire. 'What are you resting for, you bloody prisoners? You don't rest until the fucken stump is out!' he shouted. 'Come on, get on with . . .'

'Hell, maan. Don't blow your top over nothing. Give us some spades. How do you think we can dig without shovelling out the soil?' Thabo answered.

'Then say so if you want spades. You've got mouths to speak. Don't just stop working, or I'll call *baas* Koos.'

'You sure regard that ape as a god — neh? Go on, give us the spades,' I said.

Before Bobby went to fetch the spades he defended his *baas*. 'Of course he is one. He feeds me and gives me a place to live with my family on his farm. What can you do for me?'

'I can kill you and save you from your stupidity. It's people like you who spoil these whites.' And I had meant the first part of what I said.

Bobby ignored this and continued, wagging a finger like a piece of bark at me. 'If you keep calling my *umlungu* names, I'll tell him and you'll regret being yourself.'

When we had the two spades we removed the loose soil. That was as far as they were of any use to us, for they were too light and thick-edged to cut through the thick entangled roots. What was needed was an axe to chop them with. Then we'd have to bend them out of the way, loosen the soil underneath with the picks and scrape it out with our bare hands until more roots were exposed for hacking. Bobby gave us a big sharp one. The roots were still wet and it was by no means easy to cut through them as the axe just bounced off most of the time. However we made better progress that way. We strained on until sweat was running down our bodies as if we had been in a rain shower. The sacks were very uncomfortable but we tried as hard as we could to concentrate on what we were doing. The soil stuck between our nails and fingers as we scraped. Our palms were literally peeling and the blisters were covered with soil. Once we asked for water. Bobby told us to go to hell.

Three hours later — estimating by the sun, we had started working at about two in the afternoon — Koos came to inspect our work. We heard by the crack of the whip when he was still out of sight that he was coming and we increased our diligence. By then we were past the thickest horizontal roots, standing almost waist high in the hole. Only the tap-root still held fast in the ground. That would be easy.

He came to stand a few feet from us, and said, '*Ja, jong.* You must work until you drop dead. When you finish this Bobbejaan is going to give you ropes to haul out the stump so that you can refill the hole.' He cracked the whip once more and left us, commanding his baas-boy to follow him. After half an hour we tilted the stump and started chopping the tap-root. Bobby returned with a tractor, towing a two-wheeled carriage, and told us that we were to load the stump on it. The ropes we were to use to haul it out of the hole and onto the tow-cart were fetched by Thabo from the tool-shed. While Thabo was gone we had a chance to take a short breather.

I looked up at Bobby sitting behind the steering wheel of the tractor. He glared back balefully. I was very interested in this minion who allowed himself to be called 'Bobbejaan'. 'Say, Bobbejaan, is that your real name?'

'Yes. *Baas* Koos gave it to me when I was small, but no one else calls me that on Traanfontein unless they want trouble. You want to talk to me, say "Bobby",' he said and twisted on the seat to see if Thabo was on his way back.

'You like seeing other people suffering — neh, Bobby? Why?'

'I don't care. What can a black person like me do for me? I've got a job to see to it that everybody works as hard as they can on this farm so that we may always have a good harvest and I do that job as best as I can because it is my living. I don't care about another black man who's poor like me.' Bobby seemed convinced that that was the wisest thing to do to survive.

'But you could try that elsewhere than on a farm the whole of your life. What makes you prefer to stay here helping Koos to make life unbearable for other people like you? Is it because you are afraid of life outside your small realm of Traanfontein? Are you afraid that if you leave the cruel patron who keeps your stomach full of crumbs, to try to stand on your own feet and be counted with the real men of the world who face their suffering without turning judas, you'll be a loser? You're a bigger loser now Bobby, because you've lost your confidence in yourself, if you ever had it. You're as good to Koos as any of his cattle, and . . .' There was a lot more I wanted to say to Bobby, but the nonplussed face told me that I might indeed have been talking to a cow.

'You see, I don't know what you're trying to say, prisoner. If you want to find out about Bobby, bide your time and you'll soon discover me. Or ask the others. They'll tell you. They know me.' I took the last part of his advice. They told me that Bobby was selfish, cruel and as bone-headed as they come.

Thabo was back with the two twenty-foot lengths of rope. We secured them around the stump, wound them around our hands, grouped together, dug our heels into the ground as in a tug of war and heaved. Not even a centimetre of movement from the stump. We tried again and again but we couldn't budge it. Bobby jumped down from the tractor to give us a hand. 'City weaklings,' he muttered as he joined us. His additional pull was negligible.

'Bind the ropes to the tractor and pull it out that way,' one of the two men who had not spoken since we left Modderbee suggested.

The tractor pulled the stump out easily. I forgot to tell you that the tree had been cut at chest level while it stood. The stump was still wet and heavy. As I looked at it I saw that it would be impossible to lift it onto the cart. There was nowhere to grip it and six of us were too few to lift it with the ropes. Bobby realized this and, to my surprise, he chose to drag the stump to wherever he was going to dump it, with the tractor. I had expected him to force us to lift it, if only for the sake of seeing us straining against its dead-weight.

We filled the gaping ground. Bobby returned on foot and said, 'Good, tomorrow you start demolishing the wall. Go wash your hands now.' He pointed to the tap. 'We're going to the dairy now.'

'I've never milked a cow in my life,' Thabo said to me.

Bobby overheard and answered:

'You're going to learn now, come on.'

The sun stood at an acute angle as we followed Bobby from where we had been working. What struck me as odd was the way all five of us seemed to accept our lot. The sack scratched my skin. It was no use thinking about it. None of us said anything about the situation in which we found ourselves. The rules were simple: shut your mouth and follow the baas-boy, prisoner!

No, not prisoner, slave. Because at Traanfontein we were flayed of even our prison status, which was, at least, still human. In prison we were accorded a human enough status in that we were dressed in proper clothes and corporal punishment was at any rate not prescribed, although the warders had behaved in such a way as to make one suspect that they were tacitly allowed to use their discretion in the abuse of prisoners; we were entitled to two meals — if what prisoners were fed could be called meals — if we did not fall foul of prison regulations or incur the disfavour of a warder; we were also certain of sleeping with blankets, even if these were vermin infested, under a roof and on inch-thick felt mats. Considering that there were so-called free people in the locations and elsewhere in the world who could not even afford to live like prisoners, prison was to us only a limitation of one's movement. Really desperate people would opt for prison rather than accept a 'window-shopping' role in life.

We were still going to see about the food and the *slaap-plek* which

Traanfontein would offer.

The milk cows, a herd of about one hundred Frieslands, a breath-taking spectacle of black and white fur in the crimson hue of the setting sun, moo-ed their satiation and slavered a green mucus, eager to have the pressure in their swollen mammary glands relieved by milking. They were brought in by four tattered little boys. We waited at the dairy gate while the herd was driven into a mucky enclosure with hay troughs, made out of large drums cut longitudinally in halves, along the fence and scattered here and there in the kraal. The smell of moist straw, wet ground, fresh cow-dung and the milk dripping from the teats of the cows combined to make the air rich and pleasant to inhale. When the animals were all in, one of the dirty boys pulled the wide wooden gate shut. He wore an old jacket that he must have inherited from his father, its sleeves rolled up, the hem coming to his ankles, and nothing else underneath to cover his emaciated, ebony nakedness. He carried a little whip in one hand. The boy did not show any surprise at seeing us in sacks, maybe because he had grown up with it from childhood. To me he looked quite striking with his thin, flimsy, brownish hair, parched little face and bulging almost transparent stomach: such a figure in the midst of such abundance.

Farmhands were leading some of the cows into stalls where they would be milked. Bobby ordered five men to show us how to bind the hindlegs of a cow and milk it. I remember I filled eight large buckets, and I remember it because as the warm, rich milk jetted into the buckets and foamed invitingly, there was a little hope in me that when we finished, one little mug would not be regarded as a loss. When I was busy with the eighth cow, the man who had instructed me came to stand over me.

'How's it going, *mfowethu?*' he asked in a friendly voice, but I did not pay him any attention because I thought he might be mocking.

'See? I told you it's easy. Takes no time to learn,' he continued and this time I stopped milking to tell him to leave me alone. Although the sun had already sunk beyond the hill, there was still enough daylight for me to see him clearly. He wore gumboots and an old denim overall. His face was round and his smiling brown eyes changed my mind and made me respond amicably.

'Ya, it's easy. First time I milked a cow. I'm going to write home about it soon as I get pen and paper.' I continued milking. 'You work here for money?'

'Yes. And if my wishes counted, I would have gone long ago. Only I don't know where I would go. Life on this farm is too tough for a man with a family. I can't stand watching my children starving with so much food around. Only that evil-hearted spy of the *boer,* Bobby, can say life is good here. He and his family get everything they want. Other labourers' children are not supposed to taste even a drop of milk . . .'

I felt my heart sinking.

'There's no school for our children. They are made to wake up at five every morning to work in the fields. The younger ones go out with cattle every day for the whole day, taking only cooked samp with them. The samp is part of our payment — we receive a bag as big as this one you're wearing plus ten rands every month's end and, well, we live on the farm. Formerly they used to milk the cows in the pastures and eat the samp with the stolen milk, but one day *baas* De Wet's biggest watchdog discovered this. And boy, were the little imps tanned! They have many sjambok and whip scars over their little bodies but those from that day stand out. If I did not leave that day, after killing that Bobby, I'll never leave.'

'What made you stay? In fact what makes you go on staying, if you see it's that bad?'

'*Heer!* You don't know how bad life can get for a black man in this godforsaken land, my friend. I have come a long way to find myself here. You see, I grew up on a farm in Northern Natal. All my youth I worked for our landlord, a much better white man than this one but also suffering from the same sickness of selfishness they all have of thinking that black people exist only for their benefit. For, while I worked hard on his farm to make him a comfortable income, his daughters and his sons went to the best schools and became lawyers and doctors, I think. Then he sold the farm and left for somewhere overseas. All of us who had given our youth to him were left destitute and homeless, with only the farming experience we had gained on the farm but had not the slightest hope of ever using for our own advantage. So then I spent my life travelling from farm to farm looking for work. Somewhere on the way I picked up a wife — made a dairymaid pregnant and had to marry her. She has had four children since, the first-born is the naked one you saw closing the gate. She is now pregnant again, and I have no use for her because I know that she keeps bringing forth children who are fated to work all their lives for whites. I regard myself as a father of slaves. It's better with you, because you did not come here of your own free will. You've been forced because you're a prisoner, you have no choice. I have the choice, but it happens to be no more than switching farms. I would give it all up and head for the cities. But do you think my forefathers wouldn't forsake me if I left my blood at Traanfontein?' He ended his simple biography with this question.

'They surely would, my friend.' I assured him that he was doing the most virtuous thing by not deserting his family. He had told me his life story in the simple resigned manner in which our people tell about their misfortunes. I felt a touch of compassion for the friendly farm-hand. The reasons for his staying on the farm were beyond his control.

The milk would not come out anymore. I removed the bucket, unbound the cow and let it jump out of the stall. There were no more to be milked. I wanted to know where we were going to put up. 'Say man, where do we sleep?'

'Who? You who arrived today? In the storehouse where you got the sacks. You eat first and *baas* Koos locks you in there.'

I did not have to be told that the sacks served as bedding. 'What do we eat?'

'Samp or porridge and the water that remains after the cream has been separated from the milk to make butter and cheese.'

'Does all this milk go to making butter and cheese?'

'No. Very little is processed here. The rest of the milk goes to the Co-operation.'

'What's that?'

'It's a sort of organization whereby farmers sell their produce together for the sake of price control,' he explained briefly. 'Ya, samp, porridge, and the milk water is all you get, breakfast, lunch and supper. It's better during harvest time. The vegetables that are not good for the market are sold here on the farm to the labourers at cut-price, and you prisoners are given vegetable soup, the cost of which is deducted from the twenty-five cents a day that you're working for. What is not sold is dug back into the ground as manure . . .' He paused and looked in the direction of the gate. 'Go now, friend. We'll talk some other time when we have a chance. *Baas* Koos should already be around to inspect the evening work. After that he locks you up and the day's work is over.'

When the door was closed the storeroom, which was empty except for the sacks, was as dark as Hades. I could not see my hand when I held it in front of my face. However the three others we had met when we had our supper of semi-cooked and unsalted mealie-meal mixed with the water from the milk, said they had a piece of candle which we would light when Koos had gone back to his house. He did not want any fire near the sacks.

'Where did you get the candle?' Thabo asked in the darkness.

'The man who was wearing gumboots and an overall, the one in charge of the dairy section,' (he meant the friendly farmhand who had talked to me) 'he gave us the candle.'

'He is a good guy that one — neh?'

'Ya, he's alright. When King Kong and the sell-out are away we get a chance to breathe a little. He sometimes hides vegetables — carrots, cabbage, beet, turnips and tomatoes under the sacks for us. All the stuff is uncooked of course. But it's sweet and better than nothing.'

'How long have you three been here?'

'About a month. There were eight of us from Modderbee. The others ran away, first two and then the other three last week. You've come to replace them.'

'Why did you stay behind?'

'Man, I'm tired of running away from farms, getting nabbed again for the same failing to produce my pass, which I haven't got, running away and getting caught again. I don't want to go on slaving for farmers or cleaning some police-station somewhere for ever. No, *Rawuta* (the Rand) is rejecting me. I want to wait till I'm returned to Modderbee to get the twenty-five cents a day we're slaving for and take the next third class passage to Mafeking. I hear we're getting freedom next year.' The poor man apparently placed all his hopes for a better life on the last-mentioned idea.

'And the others? Are they staying for the same reason?'

'No. They're afraid to run. When they tried three weeks back, King Kong gave them an hour's start, saddled his horse, went to the hilltop above his house and scanned the surrounding valleys with binoculars, and when he spotted them he went after them with the horse at an easy lope. The rest you can imagine for yourself. They were lucky that he did not set his dogs upon them or that it was not at night when the brutes are prowling the farm. If you want to run away, do it when Koos and his overseer are away, and run during the day. If you're lucky you'll be faraway, maybe even reach the highway and hitch a lift — before they return. But you must first try to get clothes from the labourers who don't stay on the farm. Those who live here have nothing to spare. Otherwise you get to the highway dressed in a sack. It's difficult to get a lift from either the people who know why you're like that, or those who don't.' The voice came out of the dark.

I did not ask these questions with the aim of using the information they brought. At that juncture I had no intention of leaving Traanfontein. It was still too early for me to do so. On top of that, in a queer way I was curious to go through with the experience of being on Traanfontein for some time.

We talked into the late hours of the night about many things. The candle, which had been lit as soon as Koos had gone (the excited baying of hounds told us he had arrived at his residence and let them out of their cages) flickered sadly and cast our giant, dancing shadows on the naked walls. The cracks between the doors and the frame were covered with sacks to prevent the light from seeping out. Our topics ranged mainly around a central subject, the white people of South Africa. We searched for reasons why a whole tribe should suffer from such a callousness as earned the condemnation of the whole nation of humanity on the planet Earth. I say it this way because to me the whole world is the true home of all the creatures that were placed there at the beginning of time. No tribe can claim any portion of the globe as its own to the exclusion of others, because we all have to give way to posterity. We all know that the two extremes of life are birth and death, the beginning and the end, hence the African adage: *'Into engapheli iyahlola'* (that which does not terminate is an omen). The beginning can be cheated sometimes with abortions and miscarriages, but the end can never be defrauded. Once born we all must die, so that anything intermediate between birth and death becomes only by the way, a pastime until we reach the end. In this respect no one, no matter how self-important, can rise above the rest of humanity. People may not be equal in life. Some may pass their time thinking that they are better than others, causing misery to others, imposing their so-called ideologies on others in their vain attempt to assume a god-like stature, but in death we finally achieve the desired ideal state of equality which we unsuccessfully try to pursue through the hokum we call ideology — apartheid, socialism, communism, democracy and all the things that some people say they are prepared to die for: they are right in that they must first die in order to realize their desire. It is very comforting to remember, always, that your oppressor too, will one day die and be equal to you in that state of oblivion.

So we rambled on and on about whites. It had started when I told them what had taken me to Traanfontein.

'But what are they made of that they are so indifferent to, or rather delight in, the suffering of other people?' queried the one they called Temba.

'It's greed that makes them like that. In order to satisfy their greed they have no choice but to insulate themselves against the sufferings of those they exploit by convincing themselves that the latter are not really human beings but something less than that. They liken us to beasts of labour that they can force to do anything they will upon us,' Thabo said.

'But if it had been that way, there would have been no need to keep us in subjugation with guns. We would simply serve them without argument — it being only natural to do so,' another one added.

'How much longer do they think they can maintain the status quo, without inconveniencing everybody with an unnecessary war?' asked another one.

'Who knows. I heard once that Hitler wanted to try a similar thing for a thousand years. It took twelve years, after which he learned the hard way how wrong he had been; but not without having robbed the world of thirty million lives. Perhaps that is how they blackmail the world,' came still another voice, trying to answer the puzzle.

I saw that we would never arrive anywhere trying to pinpoint or diagnose the disease that was eating away part of our mottled human society, placed by fate in a most beautiful country to learn to appreciate it in amity, but failing to do so, to the utter dismay of the rest of humanity. 'It's just no use trying to find out these things. But at least let me give my opinion too. I think it's pride, an insane pride that makes them refuse to accept in the face of humanity that they are wrong. On the other hand it's cowardice, a fear of accepting failure and losing face. But then think of how great the man would be who would stand up and declare that they were indeed wrong.'

The light was put off after we had made beds with the sacks. I slept soundly that night, perhaps because I was dead tired from the first afternoon's work.

As early as five the following morning there were several bangs on the door, like someone striking it with a stick. I fluttered my eyes, convinced for a few seconds that I was waking up at home. The smell of the sacks reminded me where I was. I felt for my clothes beside me without finding them. I had forgotten that the sacks were also our clothes. The others were standing up and stretching themselves.

I asked one of the men who had long been there, 'Do you get a chance to wash here or do we go on like we are?'

'Well, I can say ya. With a piece of blue soap at the tap where the workers were washing yesterday evening.' They had queued for a tap near the granary, where we washed our hands before going to milk the cows.

A few minutes later Bobby opened the door for us and we went out into a dewy morning. There were no morning greetings between us and the baas-boy, although among us it is customary to greet others every new day. He gave Temba a piece of soap. We followed the latter to the tap, feeling naked and a little chilled under the coarse sacks. But fortunately the season was still warm, winter still a month away.

'You're going to learn what work means today, you five. You're going to bring down the wall and *baas* Koos wants it down in five days. I can assure you that if you give him any reason to doubt that you can make it, he'll stay close to you until you finish. The other three are lucky, only cutting lucerne,' Bobby said behind us, and chuckled. 'Working for nothing. Don't you wish that you were born white? White prisoners get paid for every job that they do. Twenty-five cents? That's next to nothing, *mos.* White prisoners don't dress in sacks and sleep in empty storerooms.'

None of us felt like retorting. If every time he saw us he wanted to pick a quarrel which would eventually lead to us being scourged by his *baas* we were already getting wise to him.

We ate cooked samp that was full of little stones and sand, which would have broken our teeth were we not chewing cautiously. To wash it down we had black half-sugared coffee that might have been brewed the previous evening or with cold water. Then Bobby led us to the tool shed. There we took five sledgehammers, three of which were new, bought especially for us.

'Wait for me near where you dug out that tree. I'll bring you the poles and the planks to make the scaffold.'

'Here starts the second day of slavery,' sighed Thabo as we started off to the granary.

'Every day of your life has been a day of slavery. You were born for that,' I corrected him.

'If only I had gone to school when I was young. I would not be here now; I would be in an office working with a phone and a pen,' Thabo went on.

'Ha. You'd still be serving, and you'd still not be satisfied. That would be just another form of slavery. Leashed with a tie to a desk doing the same thing half your life to make a white millionaire even richer. When a black person goes to school he does it in order to earn a certificate to serve at a better place, not for the sake of gaining knowledge to use for the betterment of his own people or to widen his scope of thinking so as to be able to analyse the world and find himself a place in it. We who serve the harder way with physical labour need not go to school for it, that is, there are no certificates sold to dig trenches and sweep streets. We're ready made as such,' I answered.

My words sparked off some interest in Jabulani, the man who had started the whip dance the previous day. 'What about doctors and lawyers? Don't they work for themselves, those people? They don't serve anybody, *mos.*'

'You're absolutely right — they don't serve anybody but themselves. The doctors rob sick people and the lawyers make money out of the distress and ignorance of people. Both have a common aim of leading jet-set lives and looking down upon other people. I don't say all are like that, but most of them are.'

'Of course you might be right, *mfo,*' agreed one of the other two men. 'You know, people don't trust the educated because they hunt with the wolves and graze with the sheep, mostly.'

The fifth man also broke his reticence. 'Ya — who can trust them when they keep only to their "high societies" and boast to the people about the money they make? They live on whisky, champagne, women and lust; vice is the mark of many an "educated" person. It must be disappointing for some of the old men who worked their hearts almost to a standstill to buy their children what they never had themselves, an education which they hoped their sons and daughters would use to recover what was lost by our forefathers.'

'So you agree with me that education or rather knowledge is used by blacks only to serve the whites, if not to steal from their own brothers who have not had the same opportunities to go to school for many reasons that are beyond their control,' I said, trying to drive my point home but not knowing the right way to put it.

'The betterment of mankind is a dead virtue. Educated people should be an investment in the futures of those around them, but it is they who are posing the greatest threat to the dignity of man with their class consciousness. Instead of raising the man at the bottom, they tend to keep him there for fleecing, or deliver him to white wolves for fleecing,' Jabulani concluded. We would have liked to pursue the subject further but had arrived where we were going to work.

'I did not notice how big this building was yesterday. These hammers seem too small,' remarked Thabo.

'Don't look at it that way. It will discourage us when we need courage more than anything. Moreover it's no use because even if it were ten times as big as this, Koos would make us bring it down if he wanted it down,' Jabulani said.

Bobby was soon there with the tractor. Six strong long poles, six thick flat planks and many vice-grip devices for fixing the planks to the poles were in the tow-cart. Four of the poles had large cross bases for keeping them well balanced as long as the ground was reasonably flat. The remaining two were longer and used as leaning supports. We unloaded the wooden scaffold and raised it under Bobby's abusive instructions, fixing three platforms with the grips, starting with the lowest and going up. The grips had flat surfaces that were uppermost when they had been attached to the poles. The flat planks rested on these. When we shook the scaffold it felt strong.

We went up and sat equally spaced on the topmost platform, facing the wall with our legs dangling. Fortunately it was a side wall that we had to demolish and the roof rafters rested on the other two walls; so we did not have to worry about the roof falling in. The bricks were home-made and appeared reasonably soft. As long as we remembered to lean forward and not to swing our hammers too far behind, there would be no danger of us falling. I looked at my comrades and said, 'There we go, *majita*. Let the hammers pound while the sickles swish in the name of Koos de Wet.'

The five of us set upon the wall with demoniacal industry. The store-room had been emptied before we arrived on the farm. The hammer-falls made a hollow noise as they struck the wall. I selected a spot that I could strike with the greatest force from the sitting position and felt the soft brick give under the first few impacts. I put the hammer down and scraped the grit out. It was a double wall, so I decided the best thing to do was concentrate on the outer layer until I had made a large gap in it. Then with one great blow I hit the inner layer. A piece of wall two feet square vanished inside. A second later it crashed on the cement floor with a shattering noise. The others paused to see how I had done it. They had been hammering the wall with blows that were intended to go through the whole thickness of the wall, which sought more force but had less effect. I explained my trick to them. They tried it and it worked. Soon chunks of wall were falling into the granary and raising a cloud of dust. The bricks from which the wall was made might have been soft, but the wall was strong enough not to make the task as easy as it sounds now. It was a snail's-pace job that required an extra sense of balance, an iron grip on the handle of the hammer, and above all, patience. The jolts of the impacts jarred the marrow in my bones and the strain of the sledgehammer, which seemed to increase in weight as the work proceeded, wrung the sweat out of my muscles. Koos came an hour later to stand below us (telling us to *'roer julle gat, kaffers!'*) obviously delighted to see the black slaves that he had bought at Modderbee labouring precariously for him. If one of us was to fall, there was a good chance of his breaking his neck or back. I paid the slavemaster little attention, but the glimpse I had of him standing there, with his mocking attitude, while we worked on the wall with violent hammer-strokes, distantly reminded me of a scene on the railway line. With my heart I sang *'Shosholoza'* and then 'Sisi-Rosy', the songs of labour known to millions of my people. The handle of the hammer became hot in my palms, adding more blisters to yesterday's raw patches.

Koos de Wet had estimated right. At midday — after an endless lifting of the hammer, closing of the eyes to avoid the flying granules, striking, lifting of the hammer, closing of the eyes to avoid the flying granules, striking — we had done the upper quarter of the wall. That meant we had about halved his estimate with our trick of attacking the layers separately. The wall would be down in two days, or three, because we had to be very careful at the corners so as not to crack the adjacent walls. The only rest we had in five hours was in the pauses between the strokes or when we shifted on the planks. Bobby had not lied when he'd said Koos would breathe down our necks. Except for cursing, groaning and remarks about the boiling sun, hardly any words were passed between us. When we wanted to pass water we made waterfalls from where we were. I was beginning to get used to, and even enjoy the jolts when Bobby called us down to eat.

Without the hammer my arms felt paper light. My back was also hurting from sitting the whole morning. We stooped around our big basin which was filled with the same half-cooked porridge after Temba and his two companions had joined us.

'Don't stuff yourself too much with this paste. Take only enough to hold you till the evening. S'phiwe, the good guy, is going to leave us some vegetables in the store-room,' Temba told us as we ate. After we stopped he took a packet of BB tobacco out of a fold in his sack and gave it to me. 'And he gave this too. Solly, give him some brown paper and matches.'

I was moved by the way our little hardship brought us together in unity. We might be prisoners and serving our punishment under the merciless selfishness of Koos and his baas-boy, but our recognition of each other as people, human beings with feelings and desires common to all people, still held us above those who lived with hatred. Because hatred and selfishness breed indifference to, and delight in the sufferings of others, they might be likened to a cancer of the soul, which steadily eats away the nobleness of human nature and leaves only a shell, a demon in human form, through which Belial works out his diablerie upon mankind. Hatred is 'the mark of the beast'.

The zoll was passed around. There's nothing like sharing a smoke in times of hardship. I believe that among us a *skyf* (sharing of one cigarette) has a greater significance than giving a man some puffs when he craves them; it is a gesture of friendship, trust and respect; and if a person is prepared to offer you a smoke, it means he is freely disposed towards you and might help in other ways too. Non-smokers may not quite grasp what this is all about, but those who partake in the habit will understand. That is where the proverb *'asibhemisani'* (we don't share smokes), meaning that people do not see eye to eye, comes from. We shared the smoke and like the Red Indian peace pipe, it meant that we were together.

Before we had finished smoking Koos appeared unexpectedly around the corner of the building. Temba and his two mates jumped up like children who had been caught doing mischief. Reacting likewise, we snatched our hammers, pretending that we were resuming work immediately after eating.

'*Ja! Julle sit?* Getting used to Traanfontein, *nê?* After work we must have another dance to remind you who you are, where you are and what you're here for,' said the ogre, like an adult who had caught children red-handed in mischief.

What could we say for ourselves? Temba and the others took their sickles and vanished around the building. The top platform of the scaffold had to be removed so that we could stand on the second one. We put down our hammers and started with this. '*Goed.* You're coming alright with it . . . Be careful at the corners . . . You work fast, *nê kaffers?* Those three are teaching you to sleep on your work. It's them that need some shaking up; and they are going to get it from *baas* Koos, because I'm the only *baas* on this farm. This is one *boereseun* they must take a long time to forget.'

What he said did not give us any relief. It would have been better were we all going to receive punishment. To us, watching was not going to provide the entertainment it offered Bobbejaan.

No one came to inspect us the whole afternoon. Nevertheless we did not pause for any rest since we never knew when Koos or Bobby would turn up. The punctured blisters on the palms of my hands had stopped hurting although the loose skin had peeled off. I laid down my hammer beside me and looked at my hands. Corny skin was forming where there had been blisters. I continued to batter the wall in front of me and, as I did so, many thoughts filled my mind. I found myself thinking that perhaps the Traanfontein experience was a destined part of my life, which had been set aside by Providence to take me out of my aimless life in Soweto and show me a practical example of how my people were demeaned because they happened to have a dark skin, while I jived around a shebeen table covered with beer bottles. The wall became symbolic of the wall of man-made laws that demarcates the black man from the rest of mankind and makes him the doormat of the races. At that stage I felt a new strength and fury rising up inside me and I beat big chunks down to the rubble inside the granary. What man has put together, man can also put asunder. The wall was falling and the day I, together with my fellow prisoners, would be free to leave Traanfontein was nearing, no matter how far away it still seemed.

At sunset we went to the dairy to milk the cows. This time I did ten cows. S'phiwe came to talk to me.

'When are you running?' He sprang the question on me. I stopped midway squeezing a teat, surprised that he should have read my thoughts, because, in spite of my resolution to stick around for a while to learn about farm slave labour, I was beginning to have second thoughts.

'What makes you think that I want to run away?' I asked, sounding a little vexed.

'*Mos,* people are always running away from this slavery.' And he told me of others who had run away, of some who had been caught and of what they had gone through at Koos's hand. This was not at all encouraging for one who was contemplating escape, though he did not tell it with the intention to dishearten. He also enumerated for me the different ways by which I could leave fast and unnoticed. I was interested in one.

'Tell me S'phiwe — not that I want to bolt . . . This truck that collects the milk for the Co-operation, how often does it come in a week? And you say that man is your friend?' It was he who had offered the information.

'Ya. Sam is my friend and, like me, he can't stand seeing people dehumanized the way you are, even if they are prisoners. And having heard why you're here from Temba at the lucerne field I feel it was unfair that you should be punished for self-defence. He comes on Saturdays and picks me up at my shack to open the cold storage for him. I'll talk to him then. Really it was unfair. I can see you're a good guy, not a *tsotsi.*'

'How could I have stood a chance? I was alone, and there were four *abelungu* against me: the man I fought with, a woman witness, the magistrate and the prosecutor.' As I counted, the four sneering white faces came up before the eye of my mind. From time to time they would rant in Afrikaans, apparently about the immorality of my striking a white man. Perhaps I would have stood a better chance if one of the court officials, either the prosecutor or the magistrate, had been black and had an insight into the indignities that blacks have to put up with from whites.

'There's no justice in this country, *mfowethu.* Your skin determines whether you are right or wrong. South Africa has its own form of 'justice' that is moulded to suit the racial obsessions of those that hold the gun and the gaol keys,' S'phiwe said.

You might be surprised that an ordinary farm labourer and a group of jailbirds dressed in sacks could talk about things that are usually reserved for so-called sophisticated scholars' minds. But then let me ask you a simple question. What would the champagne, beautiful cars and expensive vacations at the Swazi Spas have come to if those who enjoy these things discussed miseries that do not affect them personally? It is among the simple, despised people who feel the pinch of injustice, who scrape from hand to mouth to survive, that one finds a wisdom about life that is gathered with harsh experience.

'You're absolutely right, S'phiwe. The devil dwells in the hearts of the Koos de Wets and through them turns the world into a stage on which sadistic plays of oppression and suffering are played while he sits watching with satisfaction from hell. The South African show must be one of his favourites.' I tried to illustrate my concurrence with what he was saying with symbolism for emphasis.

'Ya, let me leave you, my friend. If you want to leave this hell on Saturday morning, start figuring out how to get out of the store-room, now. It's a pity I can't open for you but the others always got out in spite of the locks on the door being strengthened with each escape.'

I thanked S'phiwe, and by the time we finished milking, I had made up my mind to leave on Saturday. I would put the suggestion to the others that evening, because I was sure Sam could take others besides myself on the dairy truck. The sunset scene was the same as the previous evening's with the ragged farm labourers queueing up at the tap to rinse their dust-covered faces, arms and legs. Some wore sacks, like us over their rags, but most preferred to work bare-breast. When we were fretting about the selfishness of most white people the previous night Temba had told me that these people, family men and young men with their futures still before them, stayed at Traanfontein only on sufferance because of their free labour. They were supposed to put aside six months of the year to render service to the slave-master, otherwise their families would be cast out of the farm. During the time they worked on the farm, their salaries could not exceed S'phiwe's ten rand and a bag of maize or samp per month, not forgetting of course that the latter was a permanent and experienced farmhand. The same money went to buying the market-rejected produce as diet supplement from the landlord. These things are never heard of outside the farms because desperation and need keep the victims in silent desolation, and for any concerned person to set foot on the farms permission would be necessary from the landowner.

Take that formidable ape to keep a promise! The eight of us were still forcing down the cold samp soured with the milk water (the latter very refreshing after the day's labour) when Koos materialized behind us with Bobby and the whip. His tobacco-stained teeth were bared in a malicious grin under the bristly moustache and his colossal bulk dwarfed the medium-sized Bobby, whose face and gait reflected an urgency to unleash his cruelty. We all stopped eating. Even if the meal had been worth eating, they would still have spoilt our appetite. They marched up to us and we backed towards the building until the wall stopped us.

'*Ja*. You thought I would forget to honour my promise to remind you what you're here for?' Koos said in his fast Afrikaans. He pointed to Temba and the other two and ordered them to move to one side. Then, cracking the whip once, he gave it to Bobby: 'Here Bobbejaan, show those three who's *baas* of Traanfontein.'

Bobby took the whip, and like all farm people he knew exactly how to use it. He did not use the tip of the whip the way an inexperienced person would, but let some length entwine itself around the body and then pulled hard. A series of claps like a small pistol being fired followed as the whip untwined. These claps were caused by the tip striking the flesh and tearing the skin at the places of contact. Trying to conceal those parts of the body which were exposed, all three men lay down and balled themselves up as best as they could. It was obvious that this did not help.

'*Nee* maan, Bobbejaan! You're playing with them because they are your brothers. Give me that whip,' Koos's voice said greedily. He continued the cruel task. I grimaced at each stroke.

After five minutes it was over. We were locked up and sat silently in the dark while our friends were still licking their wounds. When they could tolerate their burning skins no one said anything about the flogging. There was nothing to say, after all. We had all watched and were too sickened by the whole thing to repeat it in words. Temba went to search in the pile of sacks and came back with a bunch of carrots, turnips and tomatoes in a plastic bag. There was a gallon of milk too! We ate in the darkness. The sweetness of the vegetables provided us with a wonderful variation of diet, and the milk was refreshing.

I put forward my Saturday morning intentions. '*Majita,* I don't think I can stand it much longer here. Saturday . . .' and I proceeded to lay out my plan. Everyone agreed that it was an easy way to leave the farm, but only Thabo and Jabulani wanted to go.

'*Madoda,* you must know what lies in store for you when you stay behind. Of course I do not think Sam would have been able to take all of us at the same time,' I said, feeling sorry that others were going to have to explain how we got away and why they did not stop us.

Getting out, which I had thought would present a problem, was going to be very easy. I did not deny it when Thabo said, 'You guys all think as far as your own height. You forget that there's also some space occupied by many other things above you. If you're always looking down on the ground like pigs you'll miss a lot of things.'

The riddle was self-explanatory. We slept earlier than the night before because of the unbearable fatigue. My whole muscular system felt numb and dully painful, the way muscles not used to strain do. Before sleep overtook me I pictured myself at home.

Our wall was down in three days flat. The routine was exactly the same. After an endless pounding of the wall we went to milk the cows, ate our supper and were locked up. S'phiwe always came to chat with us at the dairy. He had told me that there was no way he could get me my clothes, but in the truck Sam had some old white overalls which belonged to men who worked at the Co-operation whom he had to pick up on his farm rounds. He also told me that Koos de Wet did not report people who had escaped because he wanted to avoid paying the money he owed them to the prison officials. The latter always assumed that it had been paid to the prisoners when they left the farm, as long as Koos reported that he had dismissed them according to the dates that he had been given for their release. The jail-warders at Modderbee were also his friends.

On our fourth day at Traanfontein we were given sickles to go and join the others on the lucerne field, but it was found that they had almost reached the number of bags that was wanted. So we were to start the reaping of the maize fields instead. Bobby made us take a pile of the sacks to the field and bind them in twos with strips of other sacks which were being cut by three black women who reminded me of the three witches in *Macbeth*, with their gaunt set faces. Their deep-set eyes had the wariness of the starving mongrels of Soweto. I had seen many like them at *matikitwane* (the ash and rubbish dumps of Soweto), scouring the whole day long (I never did find out what for) while their white counterparts were being driven in 'China-eyes' Mercedes Benzes to the city for eternal shopping sprees. Go to *matikitwane* any day and you'll find black women wading in the filth. Funny how poverty and filth go hand in hand.

The idea of binding the sacks, we found out later, was to make a sort of sling across the shoulders. You slung three pairs of the sacks and walked between two rows of maize, plucking the ears and dropping them into two sacks hanging down your sides. As the sacks filled up you got to know what was meant by gruelling work. When a pair of bags was full you left it where it had been filled and started a new pair.

There were many of us going down the whole width of the kilometre square field, men and women who arrived in groups of four and five, each going down his or her own row while Koos de Wet sat on his ginger horse marking down the names of his slaves. He looked like a mounted soldier of the Anglo-Boer war with his rifle slung on his back after going out in the early morning to hunt a jackal that he suspected of killing his small stock. Having failed to bag anything he thought it fit to come and drive the human wave going through the field, on horseback. He shouted, 'Kom, kom, kom, kom,' as he galloped up and down behind us. We prisoners who were not used to what we were doing found it hard to match the pace of experienced farm labourers, and this lagging behind was our undoing. Koos harried and drove us. We stumbled and fell and rose and plucked, and the hot breath of the horse blew down on our necks; we were drenched in sweat and when the sun began to gain height it baked us and parched our throats. The more bags we filled, the more Koos's chances of catching the early market increased, and the more his chances increased, the greater his impatience became. The ground was marked with an endless maze of small paths made by field rats that scampered between our feet. During 'lunch' S'phiwe told us to be careful of snakes.

The following afternoon I had an unpleasant experience with Koos de Wet. S'phiwe had told us the truth about snakes. I stumbled on a black cobra as thick as my arm. Fortunately it was replete with two rats and it lay there without attempting to bite me. I dropped the maize on it and killed it with a rock as it tried to wriggle free from the weight of the almost full sacks. At that time Koos had gone up the column and when he saw the disruption of work — Thabo and the others nearby came to help me kill the reptile, six feet long and scales as big as your fingernails on its back — he came galloping towards us.

'Who killed the snake?' he asked from the saddle.

'It was me,' I answered, thinking that there was nothing wrong with killing a poisonous snake where people were working.

He alighted slowly from the beautiful gelding, as if he wanted to take a closer look. A snake dies in a peculiar fashion. For hours after it has died its body keeps on moving slowly with ripples of muscles under its glossy skin. The sight is not at all pleasing to the eye or the nerves. Koos was unruffled. He sank to his haunches and turned the snake around studiously.

'Do you know that this snake eats these rats that destroy the maize?' he soliloquized, his eyes remaining on the dead snake. He took out a pocket knife and cut the snake where its thickness bulged out. Two wet, dead rats came out. 'You see? I told you; two dead rats that might have put away tons of grain and bred more rats. Did you think about this before you killed the snake?'

'I know that snakes eat rats. Someone might have been bitten,' I answered in unwavering Afrikaans.

'*Jy praat goeie Afrikaans — nê?*' was his answer to my explanation that I had killed the snake because the people were in danger of being bitten. No, that did not matter to Koos de Wet. What mattered more than the lives of the people who slaved for him was the grain. 'Have you been to school?'

'A little.'

'There is an English poem about a sailor who killed a bird he was not supposed to have killed and they hung the bird on his shoulders.' He meant Samuel Taylor Coleridge's *Rime of the Ancient Mariner,* and the implication of his example was clear to me.

He stood up with the snake held by the tip of its tail between his thick forefinger and thumb. 'I want you to wrap this around your neck like a scarf.'

Most people have a terrible phobia of anything that crawls, and more so of snakes because snakes can kill. I am no exception to other human beings. I might have been afraid of Koos de Wet, but I feared a dead snake more. I backed away, and this brought the smile I had seen at Modderbee to the wrestler's face. 'Here. Take it, it won't bite. It's dead.'

It was like someone coaxing a child to touch a toy made of fur that the child did not trust. I was not going to wrap a snake around my neck even if it meant that Koos de Wet was going to kill me if I did not. He threw it, but I ducked, having anticipated his move. The dead snake sailed over my head and landed behind me without touching me. For some reason missing me infuriated the ape. He rushed at me and, before I could turn, struck me down with his large hairy arm. I fell on my back. His oversized boot pinned me down on the side of my neck. The soil got into my mouth, nostrils and eyes. He unslung his rifle and I thought he was going to shoot me cold-bloodedly, a thing of which I knew him to be perfectly capable. I saw him turning his rifle in his hands and holding it by its barrel and I thought he was going to bash my skull in. He did neither, but pressed the butt into my ribs with slowly increasing pressure. I felt my ribs caving inward and prayed that I should pass out before they snapped. Crying out was impossible. The priority during those nasty moments was to get some air into my lungs without inhaling the dust as well. Just when I thought I heard the ribs cracking under my skin, he let go. I staggered and gasped and coughed to my feet.

'That'll teach you to do what I tell you, kaffer,' he said and went to his horse. 'Now, get on with the work!' he roared. Everybody scattered to their rows in a split second. The beast of prey had roared and the timid stampeded to catch up with those who had not stopped working. Within a minute we were in line with them.

At dusk when the day's drudgery was over I felt the painful lump as big as my fist under my right arm. I could not inspect it until we were in the store-room because I was naked under the sack. If I had had any doubts about leaving the following morning, the incident with the snake had evaporated them.

At the dairy I told S'phiwe to make arrangements with Sam for three people. He apologised: Sam could take only two in the cab, because the truck carried nothing but milk containers and had no canopy. The two would have to ball themselves up in the cab where nobody was likely to peer. This precaution proved wise the following morning because De Wet went to the dairy to sign the receipt book. Those were tense moments we spent crouching in the cab while De Wet moved around the truck.

The iron bar with which we would prise open the roof from inside had been hidden in the storeroom under the sacks.

I did not eat that evening. Who could eat knowing that he was leaving Traanfontein, ahead of time? It might not have been a jailbreak exactly, but we felt an excitement worth mentioning. We knew that we could beat the security of Koos de Wet's farm, which was its remoteness from anywhere, and that we could beat the hounds. Putting aside the sure flogging that those who remained would get when our absence was discovered, we knew that we were going to be free from the oppression and cruelty meted out to blacks on the hidden farms.

Jabulani had received the disappointment like the man he was. As soon as we heard the hounds barking at the start of their night prowl, we started tearing the sacks into wide strips that would hold our weight. All eight of us were tearing the strips and knotting them into a 'rope'; in no time it was ready. The roof was as high as that of the granary, but for Thabo it was easy meat to get up there and put his house-breaking skill to use with the flat iron bar.

He took one end of the rope and bound it to the flat bar. He threw the bar over one rafter and as near the wall as he could. It dangled low, swinging like a pendulum. 'Two of you hold this end tight and put your weight to it while I climb.' He went up the wall like a fly using both feet to walk on it and the rope to winch himself up. Holding onto the rafter, he hooked his leg over it, twisted himself to sit astride it, pulled the bar up, and unbound it. He felt for where the corrugated iron sheets overlapped. When he found the spot, he wedged the bar in between the sheets and told us to hold the rope tight. He slithered down.

I lay down for the last time on the sacks, which no longer felt as much like sandpaper as they had when I first came. My mind left Traanfontein and went ahead of me to where I was going. I saw myself sleeping at home under the kitchen table, the cockroaches trying to explore my nostrils and ears, not giving me a chance to sleep. The hounds that barked in the background reminded me of the location night. I thought I would soon hear the frightened scream of a woman being raped; or running footfalls of the dark night's children chasing a victim of *inkunzi* (mugging); or the victim crying, '*Anginamali, akina chelete, bafowethu*' (You can take everything but please don't kill me) — the voice of a man facing death and begging it to pass him by just that once; or the drunken voice of a daughter of darkness laughing lazily as she was tickled by her boyfriends; or the Zionists' cowhide tomtom and songs of supplication receding into the distances of sleeping Orlando East and Diepkloof, on the way to shrines that strengthen the hope but bring forth no realization; or the answering tomtom of a *sangoma* invoking the ancestors to chase away the evil spirits and strengthen a certain household. I thought about the coming months when I would have to play hide and seek with the hunters of 'illegal Bantus' until my three month term was over and I would be able to go to *Esibayeni* at 80 Albert Street to get another workseeker's permit to remain in Johannesburg. Going there sooner than that would be a risk because the harbingers of fate follow you to Traanfontein, to Bophuta-Tswana if you were the man sleeping next to me, and, eventually, to Avalon, the city of the dead, so like the neighbouring city of the still living.

I wished I had a talent. When I was small I wanted to be an artist, a painter. I made sketches that were commended by everybody who had a little appreciation of creativity. Unfortunately my parents wanted me to go to school and qualify for a white collar job, to be a *mabhalane* (clerk) they said, instead of sitting around the whole day drawing pictures. My teachers did no better either; they searched my exercise books for any missing pages or drawings that I had forgotten to rub out, and whenever they found these things they punished me for 'destructiveness' — which they never forgot to state in my reports. I wanted to go for the free lessons organized by the few established artists of Soweto at Orlando YMCA, and they refused. I ended up drawing 'dirty' pictures which were burnt when discovered and earned me a peach-tree switch; and without having gone any further with school or being a *mabhalane* after all. They had killed my interest in the only thing I had wanted to do with my whole being, and which might never have been rivalled by anybody; something I would have pursued with inflexible determination and perhaps achieved great heights in. Among us 'many a flower is born to blush unseen'. Many a talented youngster is brutally suppressed by parents who look upon their children as assets, parents who were brought up accepting that to be in the paid service of a white man is the only form of work, that as soon as the child reaches 'pass-age' he or she must leave school to 'work for his parents'. Those who do encourage the child make the mistake of wanting to choose what the child must be. This attitude of parents and many teachers, the forced labour regulations and a system of education that is moulded to train only 'servants' (imagine domestic science and agriculture at Matric level, and try to find the same implication that I find) and suppresses initiative, are the main reasons for the wilting of many a child prodigy, apart from the fact that it costs money to develop talent in many instances.

Yes, I found myself thinking that, seeing I had no talent, slaving for a pittance under the constant racist harassment of the Jan du Toits, or working out a plan to steal my subsistence from those who had more than me, were the only alternatives left. Neither appealed to me: not the first, with its concomitant degradation and lack of compensation; not the second, with the risks it involved and its moral unacceptableness. My future was a blank impenetrable wall in front of me. In the same way I had pounded down the granary wall for Koos de Wet I had to hammer my way through the invisible wall with a mental battering ram. All the time I was thinking these things my consciousness was gradually giving in to the slow invasion of my last sleep on Traanfontein. Bobby had been right. The experience would be worth relating to my grandchildren.

Three months and two weeks later there had not been a knock in the middle of the night and torches blinding the drowsy people at home. I had spent the three months sleeping out at the homes of relatives and friends; or at 'parties' over weekends — just in case Koos had reported. After a further two weeks I assumed that I could go to my former employers to be signed off in my passbook, get my E and F cards (I never could find out their significance) and anything that might have accrued to me from the wage deductions that had been made in my wages in the two years that I had worked at SA Electrical Wares.

I went into the lobby without having met anyone that I had worked with. The receptionist was sitting on her revolving chair trying to catch the sunbeam that filtered into her little cubicle and concentrating on her knitting, not aware that anyone had come in. I leant on the sill of the window that said 'Enquiries' and cleared my throat. She raised her head with a jerk to toss the long hair out of her face, then, seeing that it was a black person, she knitted a few more stitches before casually putting her wool and needles aside. She looked up slowly this time, removing a loose lock of hair from her eye and trying to look at me loftily, like Cleopatra. Recognition flickered in her eyes and she was slow to prevent herself catching her breath. She did not know whether to flash her hypocritical receptionist's smile or chase me out. From her reaction to seeing me still in one piece, I concluded that she had thought prison would gobble me up. I wondered what she would say if I told her that I had only served a week of my punishment for belting her dear brother Jan.

I came to her rescue. 'Is your boss in?'

'What do you want here?'

'Is your boss in?'

He was in his office alright — her eyes told me that, while her stupid mind creaked for suitable humiliating words. I pivoted on my heel and went further into the building. My duck was reading a 'Captain Devil'. 'Your boss in?' I asked.

He glowered at me and worked his mouth as if he wanted to ring the bell for round one once more. Experience rescued him.

First floor. A group of ten 'boys' with bowed heads and the expressions people wear when watching a loved one's coffin sinking into a grave. 'Hey't, gents! You look like a group of schoolkids waiting for punishment outside a principal's office.'

'*Hawu!* Is this you? When . . .'

'Who told you to walk into my office without being called?'

'Myself.'

'What do you want, work? You see all those boys standing outside? I'm just going to fire them all. Hey! Are . . . Are you the boy who assaulted your *baas?*' He glanced at the phone. 'You want to go back where you come from?'

'Relax. Discharge me and give me my cards and whatever you owe me.' I dropped the brown booklet on the table in front of him.

'Owe you? You want to start trouble, I'll phone "John Vorster" now.'

He signed, opened the drawer of his desk and removed two cards, one blue, one pink; he must have had them ready from the day I fought with Jan. Putting the cards between the pages of my pass, he tossed it to me. 'There's your dompass. Go!'

I caught the book and swaggered out.

'*Mfo*. Why didn't you let us know you were out? We would have bought you a lot of "beahs". If only you'd come here on Friday.'

If only you knew that after today you won't be able to buy any beers, I thought. 'Soory maan, *majita*. I'm in a hurry. See you around. Sweet.' And I skated down the stairs on the soles of my takkies.

Jan was waiting for me. I did not look at him. When I went past him I saw him out of the corner of my eye, glaring. 'When I meet you in the street I'm going to shoot you, kaffer!' he said.

I ignored both this ominous promise and Cleopatra in the reception cubicle, and went out into the clamouring Golden City.

A Son of the First Generation

1. *The Tune-in*

'What is it sonny?'

'A baby,' answered the one wearing a grey straw hat with a black band, and a tweed jacket with narrow lapels which was a size too big for him. He replied as from an empty and dejected soul.

'Hey, *ndoda*. What's wrong with you? Girl or boy?'

'Boy.'

The train staggered, heaved and swayed with its human load, and the hold-on straps hanging over our heads slipped in our grips as the weight of the passengers leaned heavily on us.

You might have thought that our destination was Pandemonium, capital of Blazes, and that we were fast nearing it. The way we were sweating! Streams of sweat tickled down the side of my ribs and cascaded over my brow.

Maybe it was the heat which vaporized the cheerfulness out of the young man's soul.

His friend wrestled a handkerchief out of his clothes and wiped his face: 'Shoo! Eight in the morning and the sun is already so damn hot! How the hell do they expect us to work in the frying heat?'

I couldn't guess who *they* were, but I thought how intransigent man can at times be. Never satisfied. Cold, rain and heat, conditions beyond his control, are all reasons for complaint.

'I reckon you're awed by your newly acquired fatherhood status, *mfana*. It is sometimes frightening to think that there's a new human being on troubled earth just because of you. To think that the new life is as delicate, as vulnerable and as mortal as yours; nothing permanent. I think death starts at conception, *mfana*. Growth is a slow death process. That's why people die naturally when they get too old.'

Great simple life concept, commuter train philosopher! His dome did not shine for nothing. Father of three, stable matrimony, social drinker, zestful worker, Sophiatown upbringing and four-room at Rockville. You can always tell the latter from the Afrikaans-sprinkled dialect.

His friend and co-worker, the younger man, was not listening. He looked as if a worm was gnawing at his heart.

Don't anyone say I was listening in on anybody. In the first place I never go around with earplugs. And then, you see, they were talking through my head, my ears and consciousness forming a sort of crossed-line telephone system.

I guessed that he wanted to get something off his chest. He wanted to get rid of the worm perhaps.

'No one would be excited by finding himself a step-father first try, Bro Zakes.'

Bro Zakes raised his eyebrows dumbfoundedly. He blinked as if he had got something in his eye. 'You want to tell me the child is not yours?'

'Ya.'

'How can that be? *Mos ub'umuskepa* almost everyday *uMartha* . . .' His eyes blinked some more and seemed more mystified.

The voice of the younger man told of the pain in his soul. I knew from the mention of a girl's name that it was a pain of unrewarded love; of betrayed emotions. 'I took her home with me every day, Bro Zakes, I admit; but nature can never lie.'

'Why? How can you tell a baby a few hours old from the lump of meat that it is? Those who identified it concluded too early that it's not yours. They should wait until that meat takes human shape if they have doubts.'

The train snaked around a bend and they all fell on us again, distracting us for a moment while we sought to maintain balance.

'They did go to identify the child and they returned with the gifts they had taken with them. That means . . .'

'You didn't go and find out for yourself; why?'

Bro Zakes had to draw the information out of the young man, as it apparently sat heavy and deep in his soul. He must have truly loved the girl; gambled with his emotions. Like Dr. Faustus, sold his soul to

Lucifer.

Before the lovelorn young man could reply, Bro Zakes continued: 'Hho-o . . . Kana, a child is not seen by men before it's ten days old and the umbilical cord has dried, fallen off and been buried.'

'I went, Bro Zakes. Couldn't wait for ten days and couldn't wait to hear from anybody else whatever it was that made them return with the gifts. Especially not from Auntie Abondabas.'

'Mhh . . . What was it?' Bro Zakes could not suppress the ring of intense, sympathetic curiosity in his voice.

I felt like aiding him to coax the answer out of his friend.

2. The Previous Day

His sister had welcomed him with the good news when they were passing the shops three hundred metres down the street from home. He had felt shy in front of so many people.

'It's a bonny boy, my brother. I knew Martha could never beat you to the winning post. When I phoned maternity and heard it was a boy I was so excited, dear brother!'

'*Ek sê* . . . come on Thembi, don't talk so loud. People are looking and listening. You're broadcasting to the whole world now.'

Those who had overheard had put on welcoming smiles of congratulation. He had experienced the feeling that had always enveloped his being when he heard he had passed a standard at school.

During his courtship of Martha it had occurred to him from time to time that he could never be sure how much he meant to her until she bore him a child. During her pregnancy he had lived for nothing else but pampering his 'ill madam'. She had been all his for all the period she had 'pushed the wheelbarrow', no other creature in trousers giving her a second glance. He had grudgingly parted with every cent for dire necessities while he was saving for *lobola*. They would marry when the baby was weaned.

'Aunt Nellie, Aunt Thandi and Aunt Nomvula have already gone to see the child. The presents that we bought for his reception! He's going to be the best dressed newcomer on earth, my mother's child, I'm telling you.'

'To think that it will be ten days before I see them,' he remarked dreamily.

The sister had gone into a friend's house and he had continued alone. Alone with his exultation! Nature had seemed so mysterious to him and he had thought it was wonderful not to know the why and the how come of everything. Only the other day they had discussed life and death during their lunch break. The topic had been inspired by the death of an old man who had worked with them. Bro Zakes had said that life was both a passing phase and a perpetual state, limited by death but perpetuated in birth. They had all agreed that Madala, as they had nicknamed the late old man, was not dead but still living in his descendants who would also die but remain alive in their own off-spring until the end of the world. He began to see Bro Zake's concept in a brighter light now that he had passed his life on to another human being.

Aunt Nomvula was the last to enter the house and the bundle of baby kits and the shawls which had been meant for Martha's mother were unmistakably still on her head as she sank low to avoid catching the top of the door-frame.

That was the moment he started feeling tremors deep down at the base of his immediate joy. They were supposed to return empty-handed, happily discussing a brand-new clansman! He had seen it happen around him for as long as he could remember. The birth of a normal human being was always reason for infinite jubilation, not the sombreness that he could make out four houses away. Was there something grossly wrong somewhere in the whole set-up?

The first thought to invade his throbbing mind was the safety of the mother and the child. His brain simply failed to register a possibility of such hideous proportions. He blotted it out, and the next thought seared through like a burning spear: had there been someone else, someone who had remained obscure until that final hour? At this reflection he felt the instinct to kill right in his marrow. If that were the case, he did not give a nip for life, existence or any of Bro Zake's hog-wash about these two states of being . . . he did not care for anybody or anything in existence, let alone his own life and the life of whoever might have wronged him! Then came a slightly more acceptable likeli-hood: perhaps they had not been discharged from hospital, and that had been the cause of disappointment to his highly expectant folks. It had been a long time since a son had been added to the clan.

He had progressed by no more than a few faltering strides while seeking an explanation. Then his inner self challenged his will to a tur-bulent tug-of-war for his body, and he found himself standing in the middle of the dusty track like one trying to locate a vital factor in the shadows of his memory. Until he heard the hoarse warning in Sotho:

'Out of the way, mister. You wanna be trampled?' followed by a whistle and: 'FIRE-E-E-WOOD!' like a lost dog howling in the middle of the night. He moved out of the way to the side of the street and for a short period of awareness watched the wagon drawn by a scrawny, dejected horse which seemed to have accepted ages ago that life was drawing a squeaky ten-foot wagon that sagged to one side on flat tyres, under the weight of firewood and a ragged driver, through sandy streets all hot day long. The animal hung its head almost to the ground and did not bother to look where it was headed as long as the driver held the reins.

Ten minutes later he felt like killing the dog that attempted to prevent his entrance to the yard, and at the same time announced his advent against his wishes. He picked up a stone, and before he could throw the canine had vanished around the corner of the house.

There had been a shady movement behind the front-room window lace before Martha's elder sister opened the door and let him in with a smile which immediately betrayed her strong desire for the floor to gape and consume her.

'Where's Martha? Tell me, Busi. She alright?'

Busi's eyes had flitted towards one of the doors. She had also stammered something which he had not even tried to grasp. His mind had been in that other room long before the rest of him had portered it there.

Busi had grown roots where she had been when she let him in.

3. Cupid's Targets

'Hey, sis . . . sorry, *tu* . . . ' The strange young man quickened his pace to catch up with Martha. She did not slow down to wait for him. Only one male voice meant anything to her and she could recognize it at a soccer cup final at Orlando Stadium. The man who was calling, 'Please, *sisi.* Wait for me. We're going the same way . . . ' was just blowing his breath to prove he was still alive as far as she was concerned.

He caught up and she felt his arm across her trim shoulders. She brushed it off as she would a fly: 'Don't touch me. You've no right to hug me,' she said without looking at him.

'Alright, if you think I've got leprosy,' the man said with mock pain in his voice.

'Oh,' — she looked up then, with big eyes that were as clear as a baby's — 'did that hurt you? I didn't mean to.' She smiled to show it. That soothed the hurt look in the young man's face.

They turned up Eloff Street in the direction of Park Station. At half past four the evening bustle was beginning.

At twenty Martha was a fullblooded black lass. Warm but not excessive. Sensitive and woman enough to welcome appreciation from more men than her Monde. She regarded the satisfaction she derived from her popularity with men as essential to her feminine ego, seeing no point in being a woman if one could not raise the pulses of men and attract love propositions wherever one went. However, she declined the latter advances courteously: 'I'm sorry, *buti.*'

'For what? Sorry that a man is attracted to you?'

'That I hear you talking but your words happen to be falling on barren soil.'

'What? You mean you're not interested? Then you're not woman enough.'

'Yes, I am. What brought you next to me if you think I'm not a woman?'

'I didn't know that you were an iceberg. A girl who does not enjoy being admired is not woman enough.'

'That's the trouble with you men. Can't give appreciation without expecting something in return. And I'm woman enough for a man in spite of your opinion to the contrary.' She thought of Monde and suddenly felt bored by the young man's company.

'What man? You mean I'm not one?' The young man felt really sore this time.

'For a man that's waiting for me at Park Station. And, you're also a man but, unfortunately for you, I happen to be engaged.'

'Hey, don't play that trick on me. Where's the ring to prove it?'

'I'm engaged at heart, brother. It does not take a gold and diamond ring for us to prove our love for each other. Those things are for whites and people with lots of money.'

The argument had carried on along those lines, until they descended onto the crowded platform where Monde waited for her at the same spot every evening. She suddenly stopped and reached out to slip her hand under his arm. 'Here's the guy I've been telling you about, my friend,' she said.

Monde grinned and greeted: 'How's it, *mfo*?'

The other one grunted, 'Sweet,' and sheepishly returned the grin. 'I thought she was lying about you. Anyway, so long — and good luck to you lovebirds.'

'Who is he?'

'Ag, lovey. Just another one of the Park Station playboys trying his luck.'

'How did he fare?'

'Oh, Monde. Why ask me that? How do you expect me to reply?'

There was a short pause.

'Sorry, sweetheart. I'm both proud and jealous that other men confirm my fortune by trying their luck with you.' He threw his arm around her and gave her an affectionate squeeze.

'I should be the one to apologize for allowing him to accompany me right up to you, darling,' she muttered softly, snuggling closer. 'It's as if I were showing off to you that there are always men trying to worm their way into my favours.'

They studied each other's faces like twins who had been separated for many years.

'When we first met you had lovers, but you took me on. No harm in another guy seeing what I saw in you. It's up to you to accept or reject them,' Monde said, trying to make her feel at ease.

'I never loved anybody before I found you — or was it you who found me?'

'It doesn't matter. We are one another's foundlings.' He gave her another squeeze.

'S'true, Monde! I never loved anybody else before you. That's why drink used to be a prerequisite in all my associations with men. I had to have something with which to lessen the pain of my shame at being intimate with men I did not love. Had to be "anaesthetised before I could be operated upon".'

'You talk as if you're the only person with a history. Always mentioning the past as if you lost something by dragging yourself out of a vicious way of life. What is it that you miss so much in the past, which makes you look back, hey sweetheart?' Monde asked, slightly disturbed at being reminded of the bygone days and the embarrassing lengths to which he had gone to convince Martha that one man was enough to make a woman happy and that *he* was the man. His friends had made him an object of mockery for chasing one girl when the hunting grounds abounded with easy game.

Jabu, his best friend, had been the wettest blanket: 'Yissis, sonny!

What has gone wrong with you?' he would ask, preparing to deride him.

Monde would not reply, knowing what was coming.

'You go on as if this girl has "dressed you in a heavy greatcoat," my friend. Look at Pinkie for instance. She is just plain crazy about you, but you turn a blind eye and keep running after this kid that anybody can make for a bottle of beer. I bet she feeds you all the love potions in the market,' Jabu would continue to rail.

'You believe in potions?'

'Of course! Why not, if there are cases like you for proof? Who would believe that you're the same guy who only yesterday, before you came across this girl, was preaching to me about the morals of drinking women?'

'That's exactly what I'm trying to discourage the poor girl from, Jabu. There's a lot of good in her but no one to appreciate it. In a way I'm trying to save a beautiful creature from the pitfalls of vice,' Monde would argue defensively.

'Oho. You're wasting your time, *mfowethu,* I don't want to lie.'

'We'll see.'

Jabu had seen for himself and even learned to appreciate Martha.

'No, love. You don't understand,' Martha explained. 'I don't miss the past. I'm always thinking how good my ancestors have been to me. What d'you think I'd be today, because of men who appreciated me only because I wore skirts and kept a promise of ecstacy underneath them? I'd be counted among the Soweto human scraps, I'm telling you, lovey.' She paused to look into his eyes and smile faintly, almost sadly. 'You came out of the blue and gave me all that a woman needs in order to feel fulfilled; you taught me to love.'

'I never taught you anything. I loved you in spite of everything.'

It was her turn to squeeze his hand. 'Thanks ever so much for that, papa. I wish all men were like you . . . '

The homeward-bound workers were swarming around them. The trains rumbled hollowly in and out of Johannesburg station. Stone-faced whites on platforms three and four. A youth in 'Lee' denim overalls, checkered shirt and perched white 'sporty' sun hat was teasing the whites: 'Hey, *baasie!'*

Some of the stone faces showed signs of response.

'*Wat sê julle, kaffers?* Ha, ha, ha!'

Some of the people on platform two chuckled at that. The stone faces snapped away, looking tormented.

'Hey, *kaffers!'*

Nobody looked this time.

'What's eating you? Why don't you make conversation, or at least smile to yourselves? Look at your faces . . . You all look like you drank poison . . . Or have you all been scolded . . . Or fired from work? . . . Tell us, we might be able to help . . . '

The nearby people on platform one and two had a refreshing laugh after a hard day's work. Those on platform three and four switched off their receivers and wished their train would arrive.

Our two lovers were swallowed in the buzzing life around them, although to them nothing else seemed to matter but themselves.

Their train clattered into platform two.

'Wait, lovergirl. Let me prepare to grab a seat . . . '

The middle coach they always boarded crawled past them and Monde dived inside through an open window and broke his fall on the dusty floor. Legs kicked in the air as men dived in and, before the train screeched to a halt, there were human clusters like rugby scrums at the doors.

Martha moved down to the coach Monde had entered and was caught in the whirlpool of jostling for some moments before she burst inside and rushed to Monde, who sat on the longitudinal seat with his legs wide apart, his hat next to him and a no-nonsense expression on his face to show that the seat had been 'booked' and any intruder was likely to incur his displeasure.

4. The Way to Perdition

When eight of them — three 'teagirls' and five others from the manufacturing department — were called to the general manager's office a few minutes before they were due to knock off, they were all of one mind.

Martha found Maria and Mme Thandi already waiting solemnly opposite the closed office door. The rest of them who had been called were still changing out of their work clothes. She walked up the carpeted passage with arms folded across her chest and the general appearance of a child summoned for a tanning.

'What is it now Mme Thandi?' she inquired when she came to the two women.

Mme Thandi was equally confounded: 'Who knows, my child? I was only ordered here without any explanation as to why.'

'Don't be frightened, maan. Maybe we're going to receive wage rises.'

'Yo, Maria. I wouldn't cling to that hope if I were you. What if *ba-yadiliza?*'

The prospect of staff reduction was too much for Mme Thandi: 'Come on now, girl. You're too pessimistic. The firm is doing well and they can't afford to chase people away — they'd lose business.'

'What can prevent them doing so? They might think that we have been working here too long and have developed ways to beat their security,' Martha replied, adamantly refusing to nurse any hopes.

Her fear was catching. Maria mused anxiously: 'Oh-h . . . You can say it again *sisi.* They can get rid of us at the bat of an eyelid and have us replaced by the first work-hour tomorrow. Just imagine how many women throng Polly Street, desperate for a job, these days.'

'Desperate for subsistence, my child. The fear of hunger is the driving force in our lives. Everything belongs to *them* and they hand out little doles for which we are forced to prostrate ourselves and lick their shoes or "bite each others' heels" to receive.'

'And 'strue, Mme Thandi. We might have been "pimped". You know, I don't trust that Sarah. The other day . . '

'Sh-h-h, here they come,' Mme Thandi cautioned when the others came into view at the end of the passage.

The three of them fell silent and tried to study the attitude of the five approaching women from a distance. All but Sarah wore stricken faces.

Sarah was reassuring them: 'You'll see. He's only going to remind us about the party. You should be smiling because that means overtime pay.' She was the 'head-girl', if that is a suitable feminine gender for *induna* or 'baasboy'.

On the last day of October, the end of the financial year of the firm where Martha was employed to make tea for the fifty-two white male and female secretaries or clerks, who had seemed to be two sets — one male, one female — of 'multiplets' when she first arrived, a generous party was thrown for the white staff and they received their annual bonuses. The occasion naturally called for the extra services of the three 'girls' who made tea, plus a few other girls from the predominantly black manufacturing department. From the size of the ceremony one could deduce that the garments and draperies the firm dealt in earned considerable profits: the firm could afford to give its employees a free treat several times a year, but chose to make one big celebration of it. No, two celebrations, for the white and black workers separately.

The whites took the first turn, and on this occasion drank like fish and ate like elephants. The blacks had their Christmas party when they received their 'presents' of towels and matching washrags, bed-spreads, tablecloths, glass and teacup sets; even teetotallers broke their resolutions and helped themselves to the 'free' booze.

These events at work were nothing special to Martha and her colleagues. You could even say they regarded them as part of their duties, which in her case, being only making tea and running errands for the white employees, needed no detailed attention. Every day's work was completed that same day and did not carry over to the next. Small wonder then that, as the end of October drew near, the evaluation of the firm's financial position, necessitating celebration, was totally out of their minds.

The office door swung open and a grunt from inside told them to go in. As the others hesitated, Sarah led the way. They followed and spread to the right and left of the door behind them.

'Mind the wall girls,' the general manager warned from behind an acre of gleaming mahogany with gilded ballpens jutting out of a cobalt blue stand, two scarlet and cream-white telephones and a brown leather table mat on top. The off-white walls of the spacious room would embarrass a fly, and the ankle-deep ocean-green carpet appeared not to have been made with a view to being trodden underfoot. 'Mister Merwe', with a double chin, a glossy over-nourished pink skin and well-groomed black hair starting to grow white at the temples, looked like a Prime Minister.

Dawie Steenkamp entered the office and went to rest his athletic figure on the low window sill so that he seemed to be an appendage of the skyscrapers behind him. The girls stood still and waited.

'You all look nervous. I'm sorry to have called you in this manner. There's nothing to it except that next week . . .' 'Merwe' spoke like a real Prime Minister. He proceeded to lay down what would be needed of the 'girls' the following Wednesday.

On their way home that evening Martha had told Monde about the arrangements.

'*Nxa!*'

'What's it, love?' Monde had asked with a ring of concern in his voice.

'Nothing. We've just been reminded that the end of the month is drawing near and there's going to be this party at work.'

'What's with it? *Mos* it's just part of your employment. Take it that way.'

She looked at him with disbelief written on her face: 'But that means I'll have to sleep at home to prepare myself. I can't go there dressed the way I like. I have to dress for a party, white style, it needs time to do that. I can't do it at your place. And you act as if you don't mind that we won't be together that night — why?'

'What difference does one night make, sweets? We'll be together the following night. Don't try to make me fret over it.'

'Actually, it's just that I didn't want to show up at home just yet. Wanted to show my mother that I'm a woman and can take care of myself. Last time I was there she told me about fornication and all that sort of old-fashioned morality. I'll marry when I like; not when someone else feels it's time.'

5. Dawid Steenkamp

May had been his nannie.

May had been so dear to him and he to her that he had evolved an attachment akin to an Oedipus complex towards May and not towards his natural mother.

May's broad back had been so comfortable, soft and secure.

They had gone shopping with Bull, the Great Dane. They had gone walking to the verdant, willowy and tranquil parks, all three of them together, although for some reason mysterious to his sprouting mind, May and Bull had confined themselves to the walks and would not go for a tumble on nature's carpet.

Their home, where they slept on an iron bed elevated with bricks, had been the servant's quarters of the large Steenkamp house. There they relaxed and listened to the radio in her language, which he was beginning to pick up in scraps.

The family could not take May to 'their' church on Sundays. So she and Dawie stayed behind and prepared dinner.

They could not go on holiday to the Natal coast without Dawie. So they had taken May along with them. She had remained knitting in the car when they had gone to cool off in the surf.

'Why won't you come, May? Please do.' His innocent eyes had twinkled with ignorance.

'No, Dawie. I can't swim and I have no swimsuit.'

'Oh, May!' His eyes had made May feel a tinge of guilt.

'Honestly, I can't, Dawie. Now go on to mommy.'

'No. I want to stay with you and watch you knit . . . my May . . . You're my May; aren't you, May?'

'Yes, Dawie.'

'Father says "maid". I tell him it's May, not "maid".'

The jersey had been ready on his birthday, towards winter.

Five years later he was ready to go to the Hoërskool in the Vrystaat. May and he had stayed closer than ever. At eleven years of age he had slept in his own room, though it had been difficult to move him from May's room. In spite of this the bond between them had never loosened. She had accompanied him to the busstop in the mornings and waited for him in the afternoons out of an almost maternal love. Her own children had been faraway in 'Zululand' and all the maternal care she might have bestowed on them had been showered on Dawie.

They had all tried all they could to treat her as one of them. But because of prejudices peculiar to this land there had been times when she had been reminded of her position in life — as in the instance of the family's churchgoing. However these had never rubbed off on Dawie, whose childish innocence of human evils had made him pure.

When the two older children had gone to the Hoërskool they had promised to write. They had neither kept the promises nor as much as sent regards to her in their letters to their parents. Only Bull the family dog had received greetings. Each time they had been home on vacation she had sensed that they had grown colder towards her. This had bled her heart but she had dismissed it as being part of life. Dawie would never change.

In spite of her trust in the little lad, he was leaving for the same Hoërskool and there was good reason to fear that the Hoërskool would do to him what it had done to the others. She had cried because of this and Dawie had cried because he had not been able to accept that he would not be with May for a long time.

At that time he had been a staunch believer in the cruelty of his parents. Separating him from his May! There were many schools everywhere in Johannesburg. Why did they have to send him to the Free State, many miles away from May?

They had taken him there by car and May had accompanied him to the gates of the Hoërskool. The gate-watch, an old white man with a mole on a big nose, had stopped her from going any further than the portals. Torrents of tears had marked the parting. Once the gates had clanged behind him and his parents, who had taken him to the tight-lipped boarding master, they had been worlds apart.

The other children had given him hell for crying over a 'Bantu maid'. Everybody at the Hoërskool had seemed bent on subtly scarring his love for May.

The change had been remarkable. When he came home on holiday he had adopted a reserved attitude towards May, as if his schoolmates and teachers had kept a close but invisible watch on him.

With each succeeding term of school he had drifted further away from 'his' May. The latter had excused him by convincing herself that it was all because he had grown accustomed to living without her. When he had been uncouth — 'Your *boyfriend* is looking for you, May,' he had said when her husband came to take her out on her day-off — she had only reacted in an admonitory tone: 'But, child . . . that is my husband,' and chosen to take it in her stride. 'Boys will always be boys. When they reach a certain stage of their lives they become incontinent of speech,' she had reflected afterwards.

Without contact with other people except his own kind at the Hoërskool, Dawie had become completely detached from May. He was now wholly 'on the other side' and inaccessible. What May had feared on his first departure had eventually been realised. The innocent little boy was gone and his place had been taken over by an almost callous youth who demanded to be addressed only in tongue-knotting Afrikaans and who seemed blindly to believe that all people of different descent from his were enemies bent on effacing his species from the world. He had become completely distrustful of humanity and himself untrustworthy — in that if this attitude were encouraged it could develop into an unshakeable prejudice which would affect his relationship with his human brothers, among whom he held the delicate position of self-appointed fashioner of destiny.

These meditations about Dawie had deeply pained May's heart. She could not quite accept the fact that all the love she had showered on the boy when he was younger, and which had been rewarded with a pure child's love, could be so completely erased by later teachings of hatred and contempt. For this reason she had clung desperately to the hope that maturity and more experience would later give her 'white son, Dawie' a more rational outlook on life, and the memory of a black woman who had tried to sow an all-embracing love in his soul would linger in his mind.

However, May's stay with the Steenkamps was at its end. She never saw whether her hopes for Dawie were ever fulfilled. Having brought up the three children and seen the first daughter married, she found that only a daytime cook and house-cleaner was now required. Having no stable abode in Johannesburg, she had decided to retire and be forgotten in the parched valleys of KwaZulu, the land of her birth, among those of her contemporaries who had never lost themselves in the cities, but had returned to the old land, making way for their off-spring whose turn it was to venture out to try and eke out a living in the promisingly glittering cities.

6. Party Day

The cheap alarm clock rang or rather rattled at exactly half past four that morning, disturbing everybody's sleep in the hollow matchbox. Martha, being the one who had set it the previous night, jerked painfully out of her dreams in the twin bed she shared with her sister when she was at home.

Still dazed, she blindly patted the floor near the bed to locate the irritation and stop it. Then she searched for the candlestick with the matches on it.

The light brought her closer to full consciousness. Yawning audibly and stretching her arms until she heard the shoulders crackling, she sat there looking blankly at the gloomy candlelight, fighting the urge to succumb once more to the welcoming embrace of slumber.

She won by swinging her legs to the floor, whereupon the chill characteristic of matchbox architecture sent a reviving shiver through her body. The next moment all her senses were a hundred percent awake.

After making the fire and putting the kettle on the stove she again had to resist the temptation of going back to wait in bed. The reason for her being up that early passed through her mind and she summarised her opinion of end-of-the-financial-year parties in her favourite three-letter exclamation: *'Nca!'* and went to sit on the bench opposite the stove like a sad soul, her hand supporting her chin on her knee. She thought: why do they always have to be waited upon by us? Sis! Those women are just ornaments! She tried to remember when she had last woken up at her chosen time, except on Sundays. That brought

Monde's encouraging image into her mind. When they were together it was not such a tough business to wake up and face a day of labour. If only he would pass at her place on his way to the station, so that they could go together as always. She knew he would come. It was one of the things she counted among her few blessings: to be in love with a man like Monde. There were few left like him. Everybody went to the shebeens.

By the time the kettle was humming she was feeling much more like a hard day's work. First rinsing the baby pail outside, she emptied the hot water into it, cooled it with two jugs from the *emmer* under the kitchen table and went back to her room.

Her sister was awake: 'Thanks for your sleeping home last night, Mati. I would have overslept.'

'Didn't want to disturb you, *sisi*. Thought you still had time,' answered Martha, placing the pail on the floor and removing her washing utensils from her bag.

Busi sat up in bed, yawned and sighed then said: 'You know Mati, I woke up as I was dreaming about you. I dreamt you and Monde were getting married.'

'Oh, *sisi*. How can you dream bad omens about me?'

'You're so superstitious, my mother's child. One would think you were born on the farm.'

After washing Martha dressed half-heartedly though with her usual care and without forgetting that the general manager had put it in no uncertain terms that they all had to appear in their 'Sunday best'.

She had chosen her favourite but rarely touched cool, sleeveless light blue silk maxi. The dress had been bought for big occasions and there were few such occurrences in her life.

After she had slipped it on her well-formed body she was not satisfied, but went ahead with matching accessories: a set of large navy blue beads, white earstones, a white belt and blue-and-white soft leather shoes with heels which had led Monde to ask her if it were safe to walk on them. She added the finishing touches by painting her long nails a matching blue and adorning her delicately plaited hair with a pale artificial rose.

All through these preparations her sister helped her. 'Now you look like the queen of Sheba, beautiful sister. *Abelungu bakho* are going to wish they were black.'

When she looked into the wardrobe mirror she saw that Busi was not flattering her. She wished she were a model and not a tea-girl. Making tea was burying a talent, she thought.

Outside, Monde felt a tightening in his midriff. He experienced the same sensation after every short period apart from her. He knocked. The door opened and her pretty face peered from the shade of the house. Monde stepped into her freshly applied floral aura: 'Hey, you outshine the sunrise, girl!' His eyes absorbed every minute detail of her beauty.

'*Awu*, Monde. Don't exaggerate,' she cooed, pretending not to believe the sincerity of the compliment.

Busi came out of the bedroom beaming all over: 'Oooh, hello squeezer! Where did you think you'd end up? You've promised a thousand times to pay me a visit, and you never did unless Martha was here. I've been waiting for a chance to tell you that you mustn't think I don't know that to you the only important person in this house is Mati.'

Monde waited smiling until Busi had finished chiding before answering: 'There now, *sis* Busi. This is exactly what I fear even when I've decided to give you a surprise visit. I haven't got the guts to come because I know you'll swoop on me before I draw breath to present my excuse. You're too strict maan, *sisi!*'

'What's the use? What's the use of an excuse when I prepare everything and sit here waiting for Noah's dove? Even now I'm not prepared to listen to anything except: how's life treating you?'

'Just fine "squeezer". Only that last night was the longest in my life. I've discovered I can't live without her.'

'Oh, that's beautiful! Mati, you hear that? Don't play with this poor child. If I had the choice I'd take you to the Commissioners right now, before either of you gets other ideas.' Busi winked at Monde before retreating to the bedroom and leaving them alone.

'How d'you feel about going to work this morning?'

'I woke up angry and missing you. But now that you thought of coming it's like any other day.'

'Good, lovey. Are you ready? We must leave immediately to make the station on time.'

'Yes papa, I'm ready, but first you have to say hello to my mother.'

'*Ag*, Martha. You know I'm so afraid of her. Moreover she's still asleep. Why disturb her rest?' complained Monde.

'Never. She cannot be sleeping at this time. She's the first to regain consciousness in the morning. Come on in. It's been a long time since you saw her.'

Monde was about to utter a stronger protest against it when the o'lady spoke from her bedroom. 'Don't let him escape, Mati. Bring him in here. Where have you seen a shy man?'

Not that Monde was shy. He remembered the days when he and the o'lady were arch-enemies, and he was always promised a charge of abduction for taking Martha out. But the o'lady had since given up, and learnt to like Monde when she realized that the two were so inseparable that the tradition she meant to uphold was of no account to them.

He braced himself and went to meet her.

At work — despite all the slit dresses, transparent blouses and bare backs on view — they buzzed around Martha like bees around a flower on a spring morning when she arrived. The incidence of accelerated pulses transcended the race spectrum. 'Men will be men, in spite of the Act,' she thought when she caught them eyeing her hungrily. If people could be charged for 'illegal' thoughts all her white male colleagues would be guilty, beyond any doubt. For the first two hours the ladies did nothing but make their rounds of the offices to admire, envy, show-off, privately criticize and secretly hate one another. Were it not that she was only a black 'tea-girl', which disqualified her from competing as far as the white women were concerned, Martha would have been the mark of the most poisonous glances and asides.

Like most social gatherings the party started in low key with people chatting in subdued groups all around the large room (the 'Council Room' was its pretentious title on other occasions) while Martha and her black co-workers made endless trips to and from their kitchen which served as a bar. Martha regretted the high heels, and even her dress was largely covered by a white pinafore which fitted her snugly into her role in the party.

As more liquor was served it began to have its effect on the merry-makers and their initial reserve started crumbling. Male-female pairs separated themselves from the milling crowd and took to shady corners where, first cautiously, then boldly, they began to chip away at the bounds of conventional modesty.

Martha began slightly to enjoy the day when the men paused mid-sentence in conversation to scan her contours with laser-beam stares, earning the disapproval of their female partners. She was not pleased because the men were white but because they were men, and it amused her to note that no matter what kind of restriction was placed on them or what mode of behaviour was expected of them, they still could not be prevented from exercising their right to respond to femininity, in spite of a woman's colour. *Legally* she was not a woman to them, but *naturally* there was no way of excluding her from consciousness.

In the kitchen Mme Thandi and the others had appointed themselves 'tasters' and thus managed to keep up with the party spirit in the council room. Only Martha felt a bit bored, which Sarah quickly noticed. 'Come on, Martha. A little champagne wouldn't harm a baby. Just so's you don't feel out of place — come on, maan.'

'I wouldn't touch it in a million years Sarah, my darling, honestly. When I called it quits in this field I meant it.'

'Hawü? Don't say, my baby. People have said that and broken their resolutions as easily as the devil sinning' said Mme Thandi, jovially, drawing beer out of a can with a straw.

' 'Strue, Mme Thandi. I wouldn't like to let the man in my life slip out of my hands because of drink. He made me stop, and as long as he loves me I'll remain as dry as a desert.'

They laughed appreciatively at that: 'Yoo! Martha and that boy! But would he be so strict on you as not to overlook this one instance?'

'Oh *Nkulunkulu wami,'* thought Martha. 'No one to support my floundering will power. Instead they are all begging me to take just one sip for the sake of the party. I would understand if that were the case.'

'They have their party in the other room and we have ours here in the kitchen. It's not that we are gatecrashing. We can't just sit and watch other people having a good time. We must partake somehow.'

She wished Monde had been with her to prevent her from doing what she was finding it hard to resist. 'If I had never started drinking in the first place! This poison must have a permanent effect on one's will to resist it. How long is it since I last took a strong drink, and here I find myself with my will power going brittle. *Aga* maan, as if I couldn't measure how much it would take to make me drunk. What? *Kenna* Mati, who is thinking this way? *Nca!* Why is the time dragging so slowly today? I wish they would finish. The world is easy to face without drink, but a sober world, not a drunk one. Lord! They're all so drunk and happy, getting happier by the moment and there's still so much left ...'

They heard a man's footsteps approaching the kitchen and with amazing reflexes everyone found something to do — rinsing glasses, packing empties, emptying crumbs — but their general manager, though also plastered, had noticed, for when he went into the kitchen he said:

'Mm, such diligence, girls. Nice loud party talk, and then sudden industry at the faintest approaching footfall.'

No one said anything nor turned to face him, including sober Martha. No one ever said anything for herself when 'Prime Minister Merwe' accused; nor did anyone ever look into his over-nourished face and icy eyes.

He did not know what was meant by good humour: 'Take off those aprons and come with me.'

They responded like a pack of trained dogs. Martha was the last to hang her apron behind the door, while the others were already in the passage following 'Merwe'.

The glass that stood half-full on the sink was irresistible. Without a second thought she snatched and gulped it as in the old days, at one tilt. It was too late to stop it going down her gullet when she realized that whisky, for one thing, was included in the mixture.

'What could it be now? Even during a party!' She searched her mind for an answer as she went hurriedly after the others. 'With his endless accusations the bastard should have been born a prosecutor.'

She caught up with them.

'Merwe' led them to the party hall where he clapped his hands once to freeze his subjects to pole-like attention: 'Er . . . ladies and gentlemen. I thought there was something we were forgetting . . . '

'Yeah, yeah!' everybody agreed boisterously, although they did not know what the 'Prime Minister' was going to say.

'Our hon'rable waitresses here. The party they are waiting on is going so well that they deserve an on the spot invitation . . . '

Martha felt a courageous warmth in the pit of her stomach. It was her opportunity to show off what kind of black stuff she was really made of. They'd stop seeing her as a 'tea-girl' that day and look upon her as a woman, as Miss Stevens and Maggie, both white, did.

While many of the intoxicated minds present reeled, trying to decide whether they had any choice in the 'Prime Minister's' decision to relax South African white convention, Maggie was making her way to Martha. The two were genuine friends. For some reason known perhaps only to her Maggie couldn't understand and was disgusted by her people's racial prejudice. However, it was not to demonstrate this that she became friends with Martha. They just became friends: two beautiful girls admiring each other, seeing the beautiful side of each other.

The two friends started talking and giggling as soon as they came into contact. Martha decided that another drink, something light this time, would do. Together they went to the kitchen bar. She took a half-glass of champagne and smacked her lips: 'I didn't know his prejudice was soluble in alcohol. Whatever made the Prime Minister decide to invite us, Maggie? Surely it was not solely his decision.'

'Miss Stevens hinted, and you know that she's the only one in this firm whose suggestions are worth his consideration.'

The sweetness of the champagne lingered distastefully in Martha's mouth and for something to neutralize it she opened a can of beer and took a sip. Long abstention made the effect greater. Her head felt pleasantly light.

Engrossed in a lively conversation and wishing to keep it that way, Martha took a drink each time Maggie did.

When they returned to the hall dauntless Sarah was sharing the middle of the floor with a white lass, each dancing to the rhythm of a pop song in a fashion peculiar to her background. Everybody, especially every man, was cheering heartily.

Maggie said: 'Let's go, Martha. The one you showed me the other day.'

The latter did not hesitate. Amidst her frenzied gyration with Maggie she heard Mme Thandi cheering: '*Awu*, my children!' and adding to the entertainment with a motherly version of the dance.

The song over, Martha felt like another drink. 'Damn,' she thought hazily. 'I'll take as many as I can hold and Monde will understand.'

Miss Stevens, a beautiful middle-aged spinster and the 'Prime Minister's' secretary, was serving a round of drinks. When she came to them Martha took one.

Maggie looked at her quizzically: 'Why, Martha? You're taking too much.'

'Oh never mind, Maggie,' she answered, 'I know my dose.'

'What'll your boyfriend say?'

'He'll be cross, but he can forgive.'

They laughed.

Towards the end of the party, in the afternoon when many people had left but those who remained were still feasting, Martha had needed to visit the ladies. The passages were full of couples desperately clinging to each other. Habit led her to the black workers' toilet one floor below the one where the party was held.

The right-angled, tunnel-like staircase was gloomy. Only the light reflected from the passage made her descent visible. She switched on the passage light when she came to the lower floor.

'I followed you. Felt lonely in that crowd without you.' He was speaking from the top half of the flight around the corner.

'Yoo!' Martha exclaimed with surprise. 'You frightened me.'

Dawie filled the whole tunnel end, towering above her like the colossus of Rhodes. She felt like a mouse trapped in a dead-end hole, with a starved feline waiting with characteristic patience at the opening. She started trembling like the poor mouse, too.

'So that's why,' she thought, realizing for the first time that she had taken much more than she could contain, 'so that's why Mister David Steenkamp unnerved me so much when I was serving him drinks.'

Dawie had always been a loner at work. He was everywhere. He personally attributed it to the early days of his life when he had been torn away from the one person he had ever loved, and been taught to hate. It was only as a grown-up that he had got to know that they had never been able to destroy the love he had held towards May. That was when he began to notice his 'weakness' for dark-skinned women. That love which should have been eradicated systematically from his being had only hibernated deep down inside for a cold season, while the waves of hate, contempt and selfishness swept over it. And because this revived emotion had no object towards which it could be directed, May having vanished into the sea of black skins that covered the land, he hunted blindly and tirelessly for fulfilment. The law did not allow him an outlet. But his reasoning was that it was an immoral and inhumane law that prevented him. So he felt no qualms about breaking it. His main hunting ground was Swaziland, beyond the borders of the country he so loved, yet so hated for its laws. At home it was the dark alleys of Hillbrow and the glittering streets of downtown Golden City.

The only part of it which left him unfulfilled was the financial ingredient. It was so impersonal that it made him yearn for the day when he would find one black woman with whom he could form a real relationship and give to her what he was not allowed to give openly. That is why he had continued to hunt.

It had not surprised Martha when she found him alone with his thoughts when she was serving drinks. They all knew that he kept to himself and this obvious loneliness inspired a feminine sympathy in all the women at the firm. What got them all where it hurt most was that although he was the right hand of Van Der Merwe he was such a gentleman and so impartially considerate towards everyone that Mme Thandi had once said of him: 'This one is lost. He has forgotten that he's white or he never knew it.'

When Martha was handing round her first tray of drinks, even before the whisky he insisted on had gone to his head, he had said: 'Thank you very much,' in such a warm voice that Martha had almost tripped when she walked away from him.

On each of her subsequent rounds he had tried to look deep into her eyes. She had looked away each time, afraid that if she allowed their eyes to meet and lock something might happen which would necessitate a cold brush-off for poor Dawie.

Poor Dawie! Yes, that was it. His eyes, so full of longing, looked at her, searched for her, like eyes from a different but equally human planet. They held a need so great that it spanned light-years, arched across a whole inhuman universe of wasted lives. Her love for Monde, based on respect for him as a man, instructed her to have nothing to do with this message from outer space, this strange and compelling appeal to the roots of her human sympathy. Monde's effect on her was to make her feel responsible for *herself*: their love was a triumph over a world in which neither of their lives mattered until they mattered to *them*, at which point the power of the oppressor received its mortal blow. Yet here was this other voice crying across a wilderness wider even than the one she had wandered in before she met Monde. In the moment that she had turned her eyes away she had experienced a short struggle between the equal forces of disgust and compassion that Dawie evoked in her. The disgust, in a strange way, reminded her of the person she had been before she met Monde. The compassion told her of the person she now was. And in that moment she had known that she, as the person she now was, felt responsible for this white stranger. Even though her compassion threatened the very basis of her new self, her love for Monde! Poor Dawie!

The drinks she had taken had braced her nerves and now a romantic element attached itself to Dawie's following her into a secluded spot. In her semi-drunken state what might have shocked her earlier excited her now. The appealing blue eyes looked straight into her soul. Her drugged mind tried to find out why she was so excited and defenceless. Was it habit? Had she grown so used to a man by living with Monde that one night without, plus a few drinks, melted all her resistance? Neither was it a habit of the old booze parties and shebeens, though prior to the drink she had felt no urge . . .

The voice of those teachings which had controlled their feelings towards beauty in others not of the same skin became fainter in their minds, until it went totally silent. Natural laws took over and offered no option but obedience. The cat stalked the mouse.

'No. Mr. David. No. We'll get into trouble!'

'I cannot resist you. You are so beautiful, Martha.'

She reacted in the natural manner of a black maiden to a compliment. 'Oh Mister David — a plain person like myself? I don't believe what you're saying.'

Her boldness had given her a pleasant surprise. She had not expected herself to be so much at ease.

'I prefer to be called Dawie by people I like.'

'I'd never get used to calling you that.'

'Ja. You will when we've struck something human and not the baas-servant acquaintanceship, the rubbish.'

She heard that from afar and it made her fight to maintain control of her faculties. 'Damn the drink!' she thought. 'What? What did you say . . .'

'I long to take you where the fact that we're South Africans of different colours and rights will be of no account.'

'Why Dawie? Why choose me? There are so many white girls. I can't. I don't want to get into the papers. Oh God . . .'

Her anaesthetized mind tried to resist.

'The white girls bore me. It's as if they are all my sisters. I want a girl from another family. God made us one human race but different families. The adventure of life lies in the families discovering the beautiful human characteristics in one another. And sharing them.'

Her mind searched for something to say: 'But the laws made by you white people say it's wrong. You get arrested.'

'I see things differently from the rest of my family. That is my right.' Thanks to the whisky he was able to state his outlook on life without wracking his brain. The situation demanded that he be completely free of any fears he might have had about stating his case. He felt natural and the days of old washed back like the sea into his consciousness, those days with May abroad in the green parks, before the first black woman had ever said: 'How much are you prepared to pay me?'

7. *Face to Face with the Truth*

> *Life floats away with the wind of time*
> *It is temporary*
> *Yet eternal*
> *Limited by mortality*
> *Yet eternalised by birth*
> *Its origin not felt*
> *Not known*
> *Until it is there*

If he did not commit a double manslaughter, or a suicide, or both that early evening, it must have been because his will to live was harder than alloyed steel.

His heart had pumped so hard that the blood vessels all over his body had threatened to burst, and the sweat had been wrung out of his skin until the shirt he wore was like a second skin. The irises of his eyes had thumped in unison with his heart. Breathing had become a problem and his bowels had shrivelled inside him. First a haze as dark as the darkest night had blotted out everything before him. Then slowly it had been replaced by one as red as the insides of the eyelids when the face is turned towards the sun on a cloudless day. But all the time he was looking. The following haze was a silver one and the last, the natural light seeping through the window.

At this stage he had awoken from his hallucinations and seen her on the mattress on the floor, weakly holding the baby up to him with trembling hands. Her naturally big eyes were bigger and rounder, and glassy and frightened. The very recent throes of bringing forth a child had made her gaunt, and the pink night gown she wore looked like a rose petal.

'He cannot be yours, Monde . . . I have prayed every second of the nine months that he should be yours . . . but now I know that the only prayers I can say are for him . . . I am beyond redemption . . . For one moment I wanted to kill him . . . but forgave him . . . How could I expect mercy if I could not give him the basic right of life, like the millions of other babies born into the world? Give him a chance too . . . I know I have betrayed your trust and I deserve no less than contempt from you . . . But do not perform what you're thinking on either of us for he has not betrayed anybody . . . ' Her voice sounded millions of light years away from him. It was some super-natural, omnipotent reason that spoke through her. The reason for life. The reason why he lived and why they lived, and a reason he could not fathom but simply had to accept for its infinitude.

'If nature has approved of the baby, who am I to dispute it Martha?' Tears were welling up in Monde's eyes. 'It is myself I feel like killing now, because I should never have been born.'

'Simply because nature has taken her course, Monde?'

'No. Because you shall never be mine again. You betrayed my feelings. Even if it had been a black man I would still feel the same way about it.' The tears had not rolled out of his eyes. They just dried. He felt an unexpected surge of courage rising from the trough of his feelings. 'You did well to wait till the last moment, Martha. It shows that you wanted to save me from the shock for as long as possible.'

'Yes. Also because I was not sure. I met the white man only once, when I was drunk.' The sexual myth was that one intimate meeting between a man and a woman was harmless.

'Your guilt was not the birth of a child but your betrayal of my feelings. There are many like him in our midst, and nobody hates them because they were fathered by white men. Remove the thought of killing him from your mind, Martha. He will survive like any other child in the black community, whereas in the world of his father he would be a bad omen. He would not go to kindergarten without a question being asked. He would not attend school without a question being asked. He would not go to church without a question being asked. He would not be allowed even to enter the house of his father's people. He would not live in their neighbourhood without permission from the lawmakers. But among us he will live like any other human being. He will be given a name and I hope it will be Sipho, because he is a gift from God as all babies are.'

He stopped, and Martha's eyes met his in the light of the same understanding.

'And it shows that despite the laws which divide people according to race, men are equal and related to each other in their natural context. Every animal species reproduces within itself, with those of its own kind. He, the first generation 'coloured' child, my child, links us in direct relationship with the people of the white skin. If they reject the relationship, we accept it. I accept my child with all that is in me of a mother's love.'

Epilogue

Dedicated to my 'Coloured' brothers and sisters.

Yes, a child is born; a new human being comes into the world, and the worldly gods have the audacity to call his natural conception an immoral act, insinuating by that that the child's very existence is immoral!

But I do not see what can be immoral in the mere existence of a human being. Even the child born after an act of rape cannot be stripped of its right to exist, once born.

Martha's child was a first-generation 'Coloured', a direct fusion of the races, a natural bond between two people of a different skin pigmentation, and in his descendants this human bond shall be represented until the end of time.

To me a so-called 'Coloured' human being is a brother, conceived in the same black womb as I. Child of a sister robbed of the pride of motherhood by the man-made immorality laws.

White father, black mother, coloured child. Marriage of the races, above man-made laws. Black man and white man married in the blood that flows in Martha's child.

A Pilgrimage to the Isle of Makana

1. The Letter

The day it arrived, the brown official envelope with a red Prisons Department stamp had set my heart at a gallop, and my hands shook like an alcoholic's as I started to open it.

According to an admittedly blurred memory I had never in my life even dreamt of making penpals with anybody to do with prisons. What could it be? It was addressed by hand, an arrogant-seeming scrawl which probably reflected the writer's indifference as to whether the missive reached its destination or not. My name, without the bare courtesy of a 'Mr.' . . .

Forgive me, friends, if I happen to sound prejudiced, or attach importance to small matters. After all, which of you can tell me with a straight face that he regards prisons without any bias? Especially when someone is trying to involve him in prison affairs?

When I had opened it my heart beat still faster, but with sudden relief now, and a new excitement.

They came back to me, those days when they had come to my beloved kennel to make sure that I was the man who had applied.

Twice they had come, both times scaring me out of my wits. The first time they had not found me in. A white man and a black man had come looking for me: the kind of news that goes straight to my bladder. The second time I was cornered, in the room I share with my two brothers when they are both at home. You know how it is: you want to crash out of the window and run for your life when you hear a white man's voice in the other room — asking for you in Afrikaans!

I went out to meet my fate. There were two of them. One white and one sellout, black and burly.

They asked me if I responded to my name. Who could deny it? Their eyes told me that they already knew. Perhaps from a mugshot they had picked up from the pass department. Had I applied for a visit? I answered, 'Yes,' and to my huge relief they left without another word.

Now the letter in the brown envelope told me when my pilgrimage had been set for, the departure time of the boat from the Cape Town docks, the time of its return. The rest, I presumed, was left to me.

Another memory floated across the screen of my mind — the day they took him away. It was a bolt out of the blue for everyone, his colleagues at work and the folks at home. For me it was not, because I have long since accepted arbitrary arrest as part and parcel of the South African lifestyle. They took him from work, after assuring the people there that it was only for half an hour in their car outside. His employers suggested that the interview could take place inside their building. While a room was being prepared for them, they slipped out with him to the car, and that was the last time anyone at work saw him.

A friend — can't remember who it was, there being always a guy hanging around with me (I reckon I hate loneliness) — this guy, he brought my mind back to the Prisons Department epistle. 'What is it, Chuck?' Guys'll always have a better tag than the original for you.

I told him. Ya, I remember now. It was Joe. I gave him the letter to read in case he should think I was lying about getting permission to embark on a pilgrimage to the holiest of holies.

Over the next few days everyone who happened to get wind of my destination wanted to talk of nothing else. What I found interesting was how the talk always embraced all the people at 'the shrine'.

'Will you see *him* too?'

'What do you actually want to know, *ndoda*? In any prison you only see the person you've visited. Or would you expect everyone to be paraded before you?'

'Naw — I mean you might see him by chance.'

'Well, I don't know.'

Another one: 'How many people are kept there?' Another: 'Do they do hard labour?' And another: 'Do they wear the same uniform as ordinary convicts? And how many to one cell? They eat well? Sleep on beds?'

'I'll find out,' I would say although I had no idea how.

'Greet all those you'll see.' Plural. Not only him, but the others too.

The preparations were not anywhere near exhausting, thanks to the mother of one of the inhabitants of the Isle (for six years he must remain there). She introduced us to a practical, humane association of people who care, called the Dependants Conference. I had never heard of these people and the first time that I made myself known to them I was greeted with a helping hand. They provided me with the fare. Eighty-four rand for a second class ticket and three rand for provisions!

The little that one gives grows manifold in the heart of the recipient. The recipient, not me, but the man incarcerated. The Christian saying goes something like: when I was in prison you visited me. It may be hard for those whom the imprisoned man desires to see most, his folks. But because the Conference is there, there is no need to go without or even steal (that's possible, you know?) in order to travel more than one thousand and five hundred kilometres to give strength to those removed from life, and with your smile, if you can still manage one, show them that life goes on in spite of all the injustices that drove them out of it.

2. A Journey Through South African Life

The fourteenth of December had come and there I was, setting out on a journey that was to open the eye of my mind to truths I'd never pondered before.

I had discovered that people bound for my destination, either as prisoners or visitors, carry with them the wishes and desires of many others. It was good to know that so many people cared. My friends, their folks and friends, the friends of the incarcerated man, their folks and friends. It was good to be going there for everybody.

I had this small black bag, a blanket and a paperbag of food prepared for me by the old lady, all ready, and I sat on the stoep counting the minutes before the actual take-off. You see, I prefer to travel with my hands in my pockets because, in the first place, I'm scared of long distances. More so if I am going to be confined by two parallel rails. I get this eerie feeling: I'm a stiff in a coffin, en route for the grave and the unknown.

It was my first visit to Cape Town and there'd be time, soon, to compare those images of the city stored in my imagination with the real place.

Were it not for the Conference people I would not even know what to do with myself when I got there. I felt like a *goduka* going to the Golden City for the first time in his life, afraid it may swallow him, afraid he may not return from the dark earth's entrails of gold. Up to that day I had never known the fear of being lost in a city: after all, I was born and bred in the one the *goduka* fears.

Was it a fear of Cape Town, the unknown city, or was it a fear of something else? I tried to analyse my feelings. That was where they landed, back in the seventeenth century. That was where it all started. This life of endless warring; of massacres; of detentions without access to the law; of maiming and death in detention; this railroad to prison; this denial of millions of people, guilty of only one 'crime' — the pigmentation of their skins.

That must have been what was rattling me. It had to be more intense in the Western Cape, at its intensest in the Peninsula, the westernmost Cape. Only recently the papers (not the papers, the laws reported in the papers) had been declaring that blacks would not be tolerated there. They were to be excluded from even the minor concessions granted to urban blacks. *Crossroads* . . . where was I going? To the holiest of holies.

We would see. The spirit of adventure relieved some of the tension in me. I guess we all have a bit of this, and I guess most of us need all we have. The train would leave at ten thirty from Platform Fourteen.

My friend arrived in his little blue van to take me on the first leg of my pilgrimage. I could have gone to Park Station by commuter train, but because this was a pilgrimage and not just a jolly trip, he had offered to burn a few litres of invaluable petrol to take me there. At least that's how I thought he saw it.

Joe accompanied us, folding his Herculean figure in behind until he could scarcely breathe. As the little van zoomed away, taking the 'Soweto highway', I felt as if I were leaving my dear location, dear old Mzimhlope forever. I thought with a weight on my diaphragm: they say it is rough in there. They fear to go there. They call it *'Slagpan'*. Yet I do not see what they fear — to me it is home, and no place is better than home. There have been stabbings, tragic 'factions', *inkunzi* (muggings) and rape, I concede. But where else, in a land of hate, haven't these things happened?

Orlando East. My friend, 'Chicken'. Wonder why they gave him that one? Noordgesig on my left. So-called 'coloured' township. So-called because I bet you my skin to flay, they never gave themselves that one but somebody else did. And I'm positive they would have preferred to be known only as human beings, South Africans, nothing more, nothing less, further details to be kept in the file of life: if you get what I mean. In case you don't, let me try to explain my words: one thing that goes a long way towards impairing human relations in our fatherland is the fact that South Africans have had it deeply ingrained in their characters to place emphasis on physical features (race) in the evaluation of human nature. Even a moron will tell you that this is a negative and destructive attitude which feeds the flame of many antagonistic nationalisms within the borders of one country, which the moron will also tell you is not healthy . . . *kodwa ithemba alibulali*. Yes, it is hope that keeps us going, that makes the difference between the will to survive and despair. This living hope that one day we shall all overcome these divisions and live as South Africans. No! As Azanians, because South Africans have been divided for three centuries. This living hope is the driving force.

The freeway is also the physical division between Orlando East — 'Plurals' — and Noordgesig — 'Coloureds'. Ridiculous!

Diepkloof. *'Eyi* sonny!' And were it not for his many years' experience behind a wheel we would have crashed. Because that cry came from my friend the wheelman who, instead of fixing his eyes on the road ahead, had them pasted on some delicately contoured creature thumbing a lift on the roadside. Joe was wriggling his huge frame to peep through the rear window. One right no one can take away from you — to appreciate the beautiful things with which the world is adorned.

Past an old mine compound, the gum trees and mine dumps, towards Booysens with its rusty factories, ahead.

'Seems we're going to wait nearly an hour at the station,' said my driving friend after glancing at his watch.

'If there's one thing I hate, it's waiting for a train. You don't mind if we cross over to Braamfontein? Some guys I'd like to say goodbye to there,' I returned, feeling ashamed of taking advantage of a friendly offer to get more out of the giver.

'Naw, I don't mind. How can you say that when I'm at your service, *ndoda*?' He had always been a generous fella, that one; so much so that at times you just felt like refusing because you were always the recipient and seldom the giver. But to refuse generosity is to kill an endangered virtue on earth. So seldom did I refuse.

The city was bustling with mothers who reminded me of hens with newly hatched chickens, leading the little chicks all over the fowl-run, scratching up the dirt, pecking here and there as if showing the young crowd what to pick out of the rubbish, to subsist.

'Christmas shopping has already started, huh. Only the fourteenth and the scramble is on,' observed one of my friends.

'By the time Christmas arrives they'll all be penniless. Better if they waited until the last week,' the other one said. 'Rather take the peak of the rush than face the big day with nothing. The food's got to be used immediately. Not every house has a freezer, *phela*.'

'Ya, sonny, say it again. The whole year's sweat squandered in a single week,' I added. 'No. One day. Few can afford a double shopping spree. Christmas ought to be renamed "commercial season" instead of festive season, or season of joy. Or, even more frankly, "spending spree season", the time when the owners of the means of production rake back the pittance that they've been paying the workers for running the means.'

We found that tickling. Different visual stimuli divided our attention. Mine hung onto the Christmas plunder. One single swoop and the thing is done — by taking advantage of the suckers' superstitious instincts. The extra lights, the artificial Christmas trees hanging all over the commercial heart of the Rand. The Christmas carols blaring all over the Golden City. All the trimmings. Because Jesus is coming you must buy, sucker. If you don't celebrate the anniversary of his birth you stand a chance of frying in hell. So the suckers go all out on their 'savings' and 'backpays' for Thanksgiving. Thanks for what? For mass exploitation, for brutalization, evictions, forced bantustan citizenship, unemployment, bannings, Tabalaza's death, hostel life, mine deaths, the wars in progress and those looming over us. Thanks for the great cause of racism euphemised as apartheid, separate development. Thanks for Damien and Lucifer's presence in Africa. Never! That cannot be. Thanks for survival — maybe!

May be something to it, however. Those young ones are sure worth a little candy after a laborious year, a taste of the crumbs that have been scraped together, plus a new set of clothes to last them through the coming trial. 'Backpay' time is the only chance to buy more than just mieliemeal. But apart from this, it's all an unreasonable fuss. Hire-purchase — bedroom suites, diningroom suites, hi-fi sets and instalments the whole year round, repossessions, smooth talk and psychological anaesthetics. *Nxa!* Pawns, but pawns in an international chess game.

Don't fall for the hypocrite who assures you that he will argue your case fruitfully with your exploiter. They're all in the conspiracy against you. It's your baby, black boy. All the hollering is just to ease their consciences. Your hard toil is an American magnate's investment. The rape is as subtle as seduction . . .

'Give me the directions, *mfowethu*.'

'You know where Race Relations is?'

'*Awu*. I know this city like the back of my hand, boy.'

'Okay, you go just there.'

Having forgotten that I had already told them that I wanted to salute friends, I expected him to ask what I had to do with Race Relations. If he had, I would have answered: 'I am concerned! They gotta improve in a positive direction. Otherwise the whole country is in danger of sinking to an animal degree of savagery!'

Mark and Motsamai bade me farewell and I could tell it was not the kind of parting salutation that you make to someone going on vacation. No 'have-a-good-time', or that sort of stuff.

At the station we walked down the platform past many white people going on holiday to the coast or seeing others off. A maudlin scene, fifteen coaches long, down to the first three 'non-white' second-class coaches. A few farewell-bidders there. I was glad to note that 'our' part of the train was relatively empty. I had travelled hundreds of kilometres in 'third class' coaches with two people to a compartment bunk, one or two on the floor and people as well as baggage in the corridors.

The reservations list said Mrs. Myself, among five other matrons and misses. Call my reaction chauvinism or sexism, whatever you like: but one thing you must know is that I don't like silly mistakes which provide my friends with hilarious entertainment at my expense. I did not like this mistake at all.

I decided to ask the guys working on the train what to do, seeing I was not a Mrs. but a Mr. This bushy-haired guy in a blue denim uniform, sitting on a trolley on the platform, was sorry that he could not help. *'Gaan maar net in die trein in, my bro. As die inspekteur kom vertel hom jou moeilikheid.'* I took his advice. Rather than stand in the corridor with my little baggage I thought it better to keep it in another compartment, also full of aunties and a 'coloured' lass who made me wish I were one of those guys who fall in love instantly.

My two friends bade me farewell. Again, not the sort of farewell you bid a holiday maker. 'What now?' I thought when they left. Stand in the passage and watch the guys offloading mailbags out of a mail coach onto a Railways truck. Tireless brutes, they are. Remind me of anti-aircraft gunners in the heat of battle, although I've never seen, nor do I wish to see the said gunners at work.

Another man boarded the train. A big man in a grey suit who might have aroused my wariness were his face not familiar. Sellouts seldom go around with familiar faces. Not that he looked like one; not by any means. But wisdom says that any stranger may be a sellout.

The man stood a few paces to my left down the corridor, his travelling bags in both hands as if he did not know what to do with them. Just then Bushy Hair came in dragging a mailbag.

Almost the same problem as mine. Booked, but his name did not appear on the list. So what was he supposed to do? Same advice. The single compartment was empty. Why couldn't he park there while waiting for the inspector to solve the problem? Bushy Hair obliged without question, although he might have to explain later who had empowered him, a black worker, to allocate space on the train.

He dragged his mailbag past me. Then something struck his mind. He turned to me with an angelic grin. *'Hoekom wag jy maar ook nie daar binne?'* He did not wait for me to say thanks.

The familiar man came out into the corridor and wedged himself between the two walls, looking outside like me. He turned his eyes towards me. They remained on me just too long to be those of someone who had never seen me before.

I ambled over to him as the train ground into motion.

If you've been to school long enough to master 'the language' to a communicative level but have none of the hallmarks which place you on the rung of the gentleman, you know enough to compensate for the latter with the former: so you use 'the language', when the person addressed happens to be wearing a suit.

'Say, mister, haven't I met you somewhere?'

'Oh, Thandi. Were we not together *eDikeni?*' That's Alice in the Eastern Cape.

'Ho, ya! Now I remember.' That place. That hell of my mental strife. My refusal to conform to a training aimed at raising me above the grass-roots level of life to pioneer a 'middle-class' or help make the Bantustans viable. Seventy Six, and my loss of interest in academic pursuits that had come to seem selfish. The many others who wanted to go on with 'their studies' as if the nation was not undergoing an upheaval. Death did not mean anything, as long as they lived in dreams of 'comfortable futures'.

Soweto sprawled to the horizons like a reposing giant. I could not help feeling something like awe, a clutch at the heart of my being. With due respect, the train decelerated to a crawl as it left New Canada station behind and crossed Noordgesig towards Mlamlankunzi station, below Orlando Stadium.

'There, near that high building which is Mzimhlope station, is where I stay. This is Phomolong, beyond is Killarney. Further up is the hostel — the one that engaged in the faction of Seventy Six. The horizon is Meadowlands. The school with a green roof to the right of that ridge, is Orlando West High where the first bullet of Seventy Six snuffed out thirteen-year-old Hector Peterson's life.' I pointed it out to my companion, thinking that perhaps one day when Bantu Education and all the black man's other ogres have been defeated I shall suggest that the school be named after Hector Peterson, for reasons well understood.

My friend looked attentively at the living map I pointed at, like a determined school child in a geography class. Trouble was, our class was moving and we missed some landmarks. 'And that there should be Dube,' he said, pointing. 'Ya,' I agreed, stopping short of patting him on the back, 'Nancefield hostel: didn't know they were still enlarging those human sties.'

'And this?'

'Kliptown . . . Lenz, for the Indians. And on this side a military camp or base or something.' The lesson ended as I took a last glance at Chiawelo, as if to absorb a last snapshot of my home. Chiawelo, Dlamini, the two locations I had traversed so many times to Avalon to bury the faithful departed.

Having seen what we could of Soweto we went into the compartment.

'A long journey ahead of us, huh?' I prodded for information which would help me to estimate how long we would spend together in the coffin.

'Ya. Cape Town is faraway. But fortunately this is a fast train. Otherwise we would be bored stiff by the time we got there.'

'How many days on the rail?'

'We get there tomorrow afternoon.'

I felt some relief at that, because I had braced myself for three days' continuous motion. And, as I have said, I am not an easy traveller.

Then I could settle down and allow my mind to drift with the motion.

'Why don't you bring your parcels in here,' the man offered before I asked him if he would not mind.

'Ya. I think that's better. You know . . . ' I told him my reservation joke. A common plight united us.

We had hardly warmed our seats when the inspector showed up, grunting his 'Tickets, *gou, jong, gou.*'

We took them out.

'*Naam?*' and his fat lungs expelled a gust that would have blown out all his birthday candles at one go. It went 'hiss-s-s' out of his thin nostrils, with a jelly-like motion of his neck — I could not tell where the face started. Where it was supposed to start was a blue patch on his pink flesh, which made me wonder why his friends, if he had any, never told him to leave the beard on. His eyes directed an indifferent blue stare into my face.

'Mrs. (Myself),' I told him.

A gust of wind and a look which told me that jokes from our kind didn't tickle his humour, if he had any.

'Mrs. (Myself),' I repeated — seriously this time. He studied me, seemingly to discover if I were really a Mrs., or what. 'Look it up on the list.'

The stare wandered over the paper as if nothing was written on it. I rose to help him find it. Life sprang into the blue pebbles. '*O ja, nou sien ek wat is jou probleem. Hoekom sê jy nie?*'

'*Hoekom* is because I wanted you to see the humorous side of life, fatty, and you failed to do so. You're surely a disappointing specimen, you are,' is what went through my mind at that question but I let him be.

My ancestors! This penguin. Exactly! This seabird complete with white shirt, black epaulettes and ellipsoid shape. Good old penguin. His left paddle reached out for the ticket which he clipped and handed back. All the time sending down jets of hot wind out of his lungs, he scribbled on the list and grunted: '*Kompartement B,*' and stood there waiting for me to grab my baggage and light out to crowd the 'coloured' youths and an old man I had seen down the coach.

'Later. I'll go later. *Ek sit nog so 'n bietjie en gesels.*'

The last part got him where it counted. He melted like ice-cream on a hot day into a sweet fat Afrikaner boy: '*Ja. Jy kan maar sit en gesels, jong.*'

My companion explained that he had reserved a first-class compartment, but his name did not appear.

'Why did you come on this train then, if your name was not on the booking list, huh?' Penguin left his little red beak open in what ought to have represented a sneer and was nothing but a little red 'o'.

My black mate seated himself firmly and launched his counter-attack: 'Look,' he said, 'I confirmed my booking at both stations, Pretoria and Johannesburg, and was told that I was on this train — the ten thirty a.m. to Cape Town from Platform Fourteen at Johannesburg station. Whose mistake? Mine or the S.A.R.'s?'

Penguin rested his obesity on the doorframe: 'You want to say it's mine now?'

'You are the Railways' official in charge of this train and, I believe, your duties include seeing to the well-being of passengers, black and white alike.'

At the mention of 'black and white' Penguin fluttered his eyes incredulously. He sucked air with effort before saying: 'The trouble with you people is you don't want to understand. I am not the one who allocates the bookings . . . '

'But you are here to see to it that passengers travel comfortably. That's why you're called inspector — to inspect and ensure the passengers' welfare.'

Penguin was angry, the way fat people get angry: 'You want to tell me what to do with my work? I've worked for the Railways . . . '

'I don't care how long you've worked!' Two workers flinging their frustrations at each other across the colour line. 'All I'm doing is presenting you with my problem, and as highest representative of the Railways on this train I expect a solution from you and not your biography. This train is empty. All the compartments are used by the staff. Where should the passengers travel? In the corridor?'

'Listen, I don't allocate places on the train. That is done at the office where you booked. Those people give the staff these *kompartemente*. I only . . . '

'What do I do then? Because I want to get to Cape Town and I've paid for it.' He had been to Pretoria to mark external examination papers and I bet he was missing his family.

'The trouble with you people is you don't want to understand . . . '

'That you have no initiative, neh? Instead of clearing space for passengers who've paid their money, you tell me you don't allocate. You can stop the train at the next station and phone back to head-quarters to find out if I'm on this train or not, if that'll suit you,' said my companion.

'Okay, give me your ticket,' and the paddle shot out to receive the white piece of paper which served the same purpose. 'But this is a rail warrant. You didn't pay anything. Your case is just paperwork. You didn't pay a cent!'

'My department has paid all my expenses! If other means of service exchange are a miracle to you, I'm not about to start explaining them.' My friend was losing patience.

'Okay, then. I try to explain things to you and you don't want to understand. I leave you just as you are,' said Penguin, sensing it. He clipped the ticket and left.

'This was getting interesting, you know? It's a pity it ended so abruptly,' I remarked to my mate.

'The whole trouble in this land turns on the question of attitudes. There can never be any inter-racial personal communication without hostility becoming the medium. And always they start it.'

'It is because they believe hate and contempt to be their salvation. How? I can't tell. All I can say of them is that it's a strenuous effort to strike reasonable contact with them.'

While my friend's tension diffused, I tried to find the logic of hate, but my mind failed me. I could only deduce one negative aspect of it, namely: that it was a self-destructive life philosophy. If I hate another human being, being human myself, it means that I hate my own image. I hate myself. The same applies to contempt. And oppression; if I despise or oppress my own image, it means I despise and oppress myself also. Practically, I see it this way: when I start hating I do not expect the reaction to be love. I expect a reaction equal to my action, a relationship of hate for hate. So if I hate, the same hatred boomerangs on me with the same intensity.

Now, hatred breeds distrust and consequently insecurity. I hate someone else. Therefore, I know that he hates me too. And because he hates me I do not trust him. I do not feel secure against the one I hate. What shall I do to feel secure? There are two alternatives. One: replace the hatred with love and receive love in return, then trust, then security. Two: remove those objects of my hatred who try to resist hate with hate, and railroad them to the Isle of Makana.

Which of the two is the more lasting? The first, obviously: replacing hatred with love, learning to trust and feel secure. The second is a futile attempt at establishing security because, for every object of hate who responds with hate, and whom I remove either by termination of life or incarceration on the Isle of Makana, ten more arise to cry out the injustice of my second alternative. They rise and overwhelm me with their call for justice and in the fury of their call I hear my name. Shivers through my nerve tree render me a raving wholesale slaughterer. Power has rendered me insane. There must be some means, some power to counter this crushing power. For every action there is an equal and opposite reaction, the physicist states undeniably. I can't stretch a spring infinitely. Somewhere it has to break. I think this applies to people too. Yet I go on hating and feeling insecure. There is no turning back for fear that the ghosts who lie on the roadside behind may rise in retribution. To reverse things is to bring the ghosts back to life, for it is like reversing time to a time before they died at my hands, my chains and my guns. Yet there shall be no retribution on the backward road if it is a road to love. For, in the way of love one finds only love.

Plains to the right and left of our train. Fertile farmland for the chosen to grow sunflowers, potatoes and maize. Acres of it that stretched to infinity. Convicts (black of course) at labour, who greeted us. Little insignificant stations I hardly had time to read the names of before we swept past. A tractor droning far away and raising a dust column to the blue heavens.

And a revolution!

Three lovely little white fairies peeped into our compartment down one side of the door one head above the other in order of their ages and heights. Three most innocent pairs of questioning blue eyes, most sincere little smiles, most melodious child voice from the tallest toothless one: 'Excuse us, please mister. Haven't you seen Angie?'

'Oh no, girlie. Try next door,' I said.

'Thank you.'

Two little boys, apparently their brothers, followed. They looked at us with the indifference of little boys to old people, busy discovering the train.

'Innocent little ones,' said my companion with a paternal voice.

'Ya,' I agreed, ashamed of myself for thinking, 'Innocent little whites growing into guilty big whites.' *Nxa!* This racism is infectious.

'They know no other mother but Angie.'

I peered around the doorframe. They had found her and she was uttering maternal sounds, ruffling hair, kissing and fondling. I pulled myself back, relaxed and felt good. It made me feel good to come across rare innocence.

'Mother gave them permission to go over and see Angie on the black side,' I said, 'gave them permission while varnishing her nails.' Damned sceptic, I thought.

My mate chuckled: 'Even the innocent cannot cross the line without permission.'

'Which goes to show that racial prejudice is an acquired and not a natural attitude. All racists must know that they're nothing but a bunch of brain-washed zombies.'

We laughed at that.

'The worst part of it is that these are fanatics that no one can simply ignore — the common fate of other cultists. Maybe it is because should they attain power over others, the lives of millions are placed in jeopardy. They are in danger of a racial catastrophe. A separatist cannot be tolerated in any position of power because he is a divisive force against the unity of the subjects over whom he wields authority, obsessed as he is with colour and ethnicity. A flame of destruction burns him and threatens to burn everybody. What can one say on his behalf?'

The penguin tried to play hawk but the chickens might not have known anything about hawks as yet, because they did not scatter or crawl under the nanny's wings. '*Wat soek julle hierso?*' came his growl.

The kids continued playfully with the black ladies, apparently because they did not see anything amiss. They thought the growl was directed elsewhere.

'They have just paid their mother a visit from their other mother, *oubasie*,' replied Angie with a smile by way of explanation. I could feel that she was praying against an outburst that would embarrass her before the children. But because those were white kids in the midst of blacks they loved, there was none. They were not harried out of there as black kids would have been if found on white premises. The scene closed with a gentle reprimand: 'They need a special permit to come here.'

Whites can go anywhere blacks can go. But blacks cannot go everywhere whites can go. The law of the country I was traversing in my train.

I went down the coach to the toilet, past that compartment I was supposed to cram myself into. The 'coloured' youths looked at me with such open friendliness that I found myself obliged to greet, and ask for matches although I had mine. While I shared a smoke with the only one who was hooked on the habit of lung-busting we chatted about life in general — where we came from, what it was like, where we were going, until I forgot about the excess water in my body.

Judging by the angle of the sun it was now about three hours past the meridian. I'd rather have a hazy idea of the time when I'm travelling, because I don't want to know how much longer I'm going to be confined. 'Damn!' I thought. 'They ought to show movies in long distance trains, or at least allow blacks into the saloon so's everybody can wile away the time making friends. It's not like we were prisoners, *mos*.'

Klerksdorp. No one left or boarded the train. Nothing to that small town. Unlike what a friend wanted me believe. Each time he went there you'd think he was going to Wonderland. But maybe in the location there was life. Never a dull moment in a location if you stay awake. I was beginning to long for home, I guess.

When the train pulled slowly out, as if disappointed by the vain wait, I felt better. More rich and flat lands. I wondered if they were flattened at the beginning of time or by man. 'Part of the eighty seven percent that belongs to the chosen.' So it did not matter whether I solved that one or not. I did not care who had flattened the land.

One good thing about that pilgrimage was that it took me out of the quicksand of location life for a while, to open plains which allowed me to think about just anything which entered my mind. For even the liveliness of a location turns inwards, is of itself and no other place, chaining the mind.

Warrenton. Plains cut up into fields, thornbushes. Riverton. Both moss-growing stations reminded me of old western movies we saw at Mahala bioscope on Mondays when we were kids. So dead there was no need for the train to stop.

The little white girls (the boys having left long before on an adventure) promised us they would see us again at Kimberley. The emptiness of the plains again filled me with a deep longing for the city. The women next door sang church hymns and, after a lengthy wailing, paused to laugh like banshees. The sun slipped behind dark rain clouds. Sunbeams shafted through to illuminate patches on faraway plains. Iron wheels skated on iron rails as we hurtled into infinity. A man with a bicycle next to him knelt by the side of the railway clasping his hands in supplication over a pile of stone — his shrine or the grave of a loved one.

A greyish patch of dried marshland towards sunset. Plants, shrubs, crying out to deaf and blind heavens for rain. A golf course. White golfers and black caddies. A human habitat looming ahead. Kimberley: life and relief from loneliness. Tin shacks. A civilized 'coloured' residence. The light-skinned family men sat barebreasted in the shade of their verandahs. Matrons watering gardens.

Platform One. Kimberley, Kimberley, Kimberley, confirmed the luminous station signs. Strange faces looked at passing strangers.

An old 'coloured' man, accompanied on the platform by his son, daughter-in-law and grandchildren, was the only passenger to join the train. One grandchild stood out among them with her arresting beauty draped in a white frock, her black hair reaching down to the middle of her back. I thought of a friend who used to say: 'When God makes a woman he's in real earnest.' I thought he had been right. Nature knows that without beautiful things to admire life would not be worth living.

It made me feel quite sore to think that by the decree of the powerful I was supposed to look upon her only as different, not as beautiful. Blast it! Was I going to conform to that sort of lowly thinking? What was beautiful was beautiful, black, white, 'coloured', Indian or whatever. To hell with all differing opinions!

The train was jolted. Goodbye kisses and handshakes for the old man. A few minutes and the locomotive was into its stride.

Carboniferous mine dumps — charcoal-coloured compared to the gold mine dunes — moved slowly back towards Kimberley.

It became unexpectedly dark. The locomotive was making a fuss of it. Pounding with such enthusiasm one would have thought we were going at well over a hundred kilometres an hour, when all we were doing was dragging with jerks and jolts across an ink-black Karoo.

The little white children paid us another visit as promised, and this time they brought their 'mother' along. The ladies next door had run out of hymns and hilarity.

A full moon materialized and hung up there like an ominous silver ball. A station, its name has slipped my mind. Three 'coloured' youths who might never have been out of the Karoo in all their lives, went up and down the platform greeting everybody who was peering out of the windows for the duration of our stop.

Our neighbours came to our compartment and asked why we did not make travelling friends. We told them we were shy and that tickled them. We talked about this and that until we arrived at the reasons for our journeys.

'I'm going to Cape Town with my master and madam,' said one.

'Oh? All expenses paid by them?'

'Of course. They are going on holiday, not me. I had asked my madam to give me the money instead, so that I could also go and spend Christmas with my people, but her husband would not hear of it. Said he was not prepared to eat tinned stuff.'

I thought: 'Because you're black, you shall not do those things which it is in your heart to do.'

'So the wife can't cook?'

'*Awuwa!* What else can a white woman do? I'm her physical extension. Her housewifely chores end in bed.' We laughed at the joke.

'*Wena?* Where are you going?'

'Also Cape Town.'

'To spend Christmas?'

'No. To visit someone at Robben Is— land.'

A hush fell over the compartment. The locomotive gave a shrill whistle in the night.

'Was he one of the "Power" lot?'

'Meaning by that that he has some areas of disagreement with the government, or what?'

'Mh.'

'Well, yes. Otherwise he would not be there.'

'Do they allow you to visit them?'

'Yes.'

'So he's there with *bo*Mandela *le bo*Sisulu *le bo*Mbeki? Tell him to say *bayethe* for us to all the great men there who have sacrificed themselves for us. *Molimo!* I remember the days of the Congress. I was this small then.'

'For the sake of justice,' I corrected. 'And justice is not only for black people. There are also whites on the Island for similar reasons as the blacks there.'

'*Awu?*'

'Ya.'

We talked for a while and they said goodnight.

Out of the blue the war in Zimbabwe came into my mind. Up there Africans were carrying their homes on their heads and moving away. The sky was burning.

It was late and we decided to sleep. I went out like a lightbulb and, in spite of the braggart dragging us, I slept like the dead till dawn.

I woke up to ragged and uninhabited country. It seemed that God had forgotten that part of the earth, for he had apparently sent no rain to it for centuries. The shrubs were widely spaced like the hair on the head of a black child suffering from malnutrition. Perhaps they survived on mist and frost — where from I did not know, because the rivers had dried up long ago and on some river beds I could make out car tracks. They had become natural roads.

The scrub began to undulate and I guessed we must be nearing mountainous country.

I was right. The mountains rose high to shoulder the heavens. Clouds formed halos around the peaks and the majesty of the whole sight gave me an impression of holiness although, truly speaking, I've never known what holiness is, having been caught up in evil since I was born.

Touwsriver. While the coaches were being shunted everyone left the train to stretch legs on the platform. Blatant apartheid! The station bridge was divided in the middle with another wall for obvious reasons. 'This is it,' I thought. 'You're getting closer to what you feared. This was where it started.'

Vineyards, acres of them stretching towards where we were crawling precariously on the mountainside. Damn engineers! There was the valley down there where we could be travelling safely, and they chose a railway on precipices, if only to show off their building skills. A great boulder diminished the train to a toy and the other mountains to mere anthills. De Doring. I saw no ebony-skinned people like myself but golden men who smiled and greeted us welcomingly.

After dusty Worcester I could feel it in the atmosphere that I was nearing the end of that part of my journey. Anxiety was building up as the distance to Cape Town shortened. It was my travelling companion's turn to give me a geography lesson, in a voice that told me he was happy to be home again. While he pointed out the landmarks and I appeared to be listening, my mind tried to conjure up what it was like to be him. To be told that you do not belong to where you were born and bred. Obviously his mind or his very being did not believe a single word of that. So I thought he did not pain himself thinking about that aspect of his existence. Which is one main shortcoming of the black man. We are concerned only with the immediate, as if we believed in *manana* — never doing today what we can do tomorrow — while the conspiracy against our human rights goes on: or, we simply lack foresight. Yet tomorrow, when the fact of our uprooting has grown to its true proportions, we may find it too late to voice our protestations against laws that nullify us.

In the other cities blacks may at most be tolerated, on leasehold, or for ninety-nine years — *ag*, that sort of stuff, maan. But why should these people here be counted out? Are they not urban blacks? Or simply South Africans worthy a stake in their fatherland?

Ho-o-o . . . I see. The labour. It's the labour that counts. In the Western Cape there is enough of it in the so-called 'coloured' form, so that 'blacks' are not needed except as reserves — which deal has been fixed with the bantustan puppets. So you see how it is the labour that counts more than a black person's being? The 'coloured' blacks can stay in the Western Cape because they provide enough labour. Nothing but units in the apartheid machine. I just wonder how my dear brothers see themselves. In the other cities, too, they can stay and work: because they are so few, relatively, they pose no threat to white property. It is not because they are 'related' to the white man, as some maintain, if they are anything to the white man they are rejected 'relatives'.

We were moving in some kind of natural trough — jagged grey mountains faraway, rising unexpectedly out of flat land all around the horizon.

The avalanche of impressions entering my mind made me feel a bit faint. I decided that the best thing to do was just to look and not register anything for a while. But one thing I could not ignore as we passed many crowded little stations was the railway labour gangs composed totally of 'coloureds' and the railway constables on the beat: set one 'coloured' to catch another. Where I came from and in other places I had been in all four provinces, workmen and policemen were mostly black.

Acres of graveyard with skyscraper tombstones. One sweep of the eye tells you thousands of the faithful departed are spending their eternity there. Would be really interesting to wake each one and ask what they did with their lives. Wonder how many would confess to racial prejudice.

Cranes rose into the sky like giant steel claws. 'That's where the docks are,' my mate said. 'On the other side of the train, Table Mountain. You can see the Island very well from up there.'

'The top?'

'Yes, but not necessarily. You can also see it from other vantage points uptown.'

The top of the Table was covered in clouds. 'They call that cloud the tablecloth.'

A dome-shaped concrete monster stooped to our left. 'Good Hope Centre.'

'Where they have the big fights?'

'Ya. It's on permit.'

I lost interest in the Centre as soon as I head that.

Table Mountain was green. The cranes clawed at the sky. A shade. Cape Town station. A cave of more than twenty platforms supported on a forest of concrete pillars. We went into the last platform. The anxiety was back with me. Would those people be waiting? I had expected the journey to last three days, which would have meant arriving the following day, Saturday, and that's when they expected me. How were we going to make each other out? Not that I feared getting lost, or that I might have nowhere to sleep. If there is one thing black people can give, it is a roof over a stranger's head. I thanked whatever Power was behind my being born black. A taxi to the nearest location and the rest would happen naturally. Even my travelling companion, from what I could gather from his disposition, was not going to part with me until he was sure I was not stranded.

When the train stopped I got out on the platform to receive baggage through the windows. In no time everybody was down and I stood there not knowing which way to go, waiting to follow my friend, at least to the taxis. At the same time my eyes were scanning all the faces on the platform, looking for two people I had never seen. I shall call the man Martin, after Luther King Jnr. and for the love of people I was to discover in him once we had met. S'Monde was the woman I was looking for.

Two 'coloured' porters pulled a trolley, loading all the baggage. I wanted to stop them taking mine. You see, I did not trust having anything of mine out of sight. I would carry my own load.

'No, never mind. They are safe,' my companion tried to assure me.

'Is it an apparition or what?' I asked myself. 'In Cape Town there are porters for everybody. Even blacks don't have to carry their own baggage out of the station.' That might have been nothing to you but to me it was quite striking. Not that I enjoy having someone else carrying my load for me; that is a privilege of the rich, to have others do everything for them while they do nothing for anyone . . .

I wouldn't mistake a black man or a black woman anywhere in the world. I mean a black woman and a black man, not 'non-whites'. There is something about a black person which tells you at a distance what he or she is. Something about the 'auras' of those two people drew me towards them in a way I could not resist. Maybe it was the way they appeared to be looking for people just arrived in the train that made me notice them. Anyway I approached the tiny woman. So tiny in a very feminine way that I immediately felt like offering her some kind of protection.

'Er, sorry, *sisi,*' I said to her.

I was not so sure about the protection anymore. Little serene eyes which made me wish for her protection in a strange city looked into mine. She looked no more than a teenager. You may have your laugh at a guy wishing for a girl's protection, but that was what I felt and I was not going to suppress my feelings.

'Sister, are you looking for people who have come to visit, er . . . the Island? My name is . . . ' and I told her.

'Oh! We were only expecting you tomorrow.'

That was how I got to know Nomonde in person. Our friend, the mother of the man incarcerated for six years on the Isle of Makana, had said: 'And I hope you meet that girl and all the others.' So I had known all along that it was not an ordinary skirt-dangling girl I was going to meet. I was glad that that was confirmed. I would not have liked to meet a disappointment first thing in Cape Town.

Martin came closer. His head was crowned with brownish curly hair, neatly combed into the shape stylists call Afro, that set off clearly what I thought to be a dauntless face. Strong cleft chin, unwavering eyes and a golden brown complexion that reminded me of a Red Indian brave. A man I could trust with my very life.

S'Monde acquainted us in a woman's voice that did not need to sing for one to listen to it.

I shook hands with Martin.

'Thandi is the first name.' I don't like being called Mister as if I were some member of a community council or something.

'Good, Thandi. Aren't there other people who came down with you?' S'Monde asked.

'If there are I didn't meet them.'

My travelling companion came over. 'So you've found your people, Thandi? That's great,' he said, as pleased as I was about it.

No other new arrival was on a pilgrimage. My two parcels and a blanket were on the trolley. When I wanted to follow the porter I was told not to worry, we would find them outside.

I followed my people to the staircases past ticket examiners who did not ask for any tickets. Three or four entrances to platforms. Neat architecture, nearly the same as the black section of Park Station. Packed with people coming and going for Christmas festivities. Light brown people mostly.

Near the main entrance with a U-shaped car park outside it we found the porters waiting with the trolley. I removed the parcels. Martin took the small bag and I took the paperbag and the blanket. We said goodbye to my travelling mate and left.

The Kombi was parked on the far side of the U. My people went in front and I behind, and we drove away. We turned to face the docks and the clawing cranes, the city to our left and behind, then right onto a highway.

'There's the Island,' said Nomonde, suddenly turning in her seat and pointing above the docks. 'That black patch on the sea's horizon.'

Everything else melted out of sight as my vision transmitted my mind's whole attention onto that isolated little country surrounded by a natural moat of lapping green waters. 'There they are,' I thought and something happened deep down in my soul. All those men of clear conscience imprisoned for intolerance of injustice. I was about to take off in my imagination to the Isle, when it dipped out of sight.

'Quite near — heh? I always thought it was a bit further out in the sea.'

'The ferry takes about fifteen to twenty minutes to get there. Comes to the mainland three times a day, morning, midday and evening. Fifty cents a return trip.'

All the anxiety that I had had in me up to that stage of my pilgrimage was fast seeping away. I have always been that way — I feel good in the company of good people, and have an instinct which warms me or warns me when it comes to picking the good from the bad. Not that I'm good myself but neither do I consider myself a hellish villain. It's just that in my life I have experienced more evil than good, that being the state of affairs in the world into which I was born. Good being a rarity, I find myself naturally searching for it in both other people and myself: it needs to be shared, and if one is on the lookout for it and prepared to give one cannot miss it.

'Groote Schuur,' said Nomonde, pointing.

We turned left and went down a suburban street. The greenery, trees, hedges and creepers overshadowed the dwellings. It's the same in all white residential areas, anyway. Nothing new to it. We crossed a busy street. A bus terminus. 'Buses to the black townships,' said S'Monde and I believe her 'blacks' embraced all but the whites, because I saw mostly light brown people. 'That's Mowbray station.' A train was just pulling out, as packed as ever, township-bound.

Martin swung the Kombi into the last street and about half-way down it we stopped. 'Institute of Race Relations.' I prefer 'Institute of Human Relations' to the present title. Anyway, Martin told me to leave my parcels in the car.

We went in, down a passage past a door open on a room with books and African crafts, across another room and out into a small square with walls on which were painted black figures — mothers carrying babies, children clinging to their long skirts against the background of a dog-kennel house. On one wall of the square one saw rows of dog-kennels on both sides of a street, with a group of men being herded into a kwela-kwela. The office door was diagonally opposite the back entrance to the small yard, in a corner. Another door in the same wall, with a young white woman working seriously at her desk in the office.

Our office was very small. Too small for the immeasurable work that was done there. Martin and Nomonde shared a single medium-sized desk, working on opposite sides. An automatic telephone that looked out of place in the simple room rested on the table. The rest of the space was taken up by a filing cabinet behind the door, a small table in the remaining corner and two chairs on adjacent sides of the table, one between the table and the cabinet and the other in front of the table on Nomonde's side of the desk.

By way of decoration there was a picture with portraits of the peoples of the different continents. Some young and jubilant, others pensive and one striking age-wrinkled face. 'Togetherness irrespective of race and creed, and the burden of life feels lighter: the message in some of those faces,' I thought.

We all took seats; they at their respective places across the desk, and I on the chair in front of the table and facing the door.

It was hot.

After my arrival was confirmed and the time of my visit noted, we left the way we had come, to the Kombi and god knew where — if it were not for Nomonde who told me: 'We're going to *kwa*Langa now.' I nodded as if I knew where that was. We descended onto a freeway that ran under the railway-line from Mowbray, towards a power-station, past it, turned left: and it needed no one to tell me that we had arrived *kwa*Langa. 'You prick up your ears when you come to your own kind of environment, bastard,' I said to myself when I got the same sinking feeling that I always experience after being out of a location environment for some time. Nothing attractive but the human inhabitants. 'Administration Board offices.' Nomonde pointed to our right, turned left and pointed again to a prefabricated structure: 'Pass Offence Court.'

'May the permit to the shrine save me from them,' I thought. 'If they don't want Cape Town-born blacks in Cape Town what will they say about others coming in from outside?'

We turned and went into a narrow street lined by continuous 'houses' which reminded me of Meadowlands, only they were delicate-looking. As everywhere, people try to enliven their environs; even if it means growing flowers in sand. We stopped outside two adjoining houses, behind a simple cream-white car. I could not make out exactly which one of the two doors with a common doorpost was ours. It was the one on the right.

And whom did I find there, if not a lady from Mzimhlope! One of those women who have had to face life without their husbands; mothers of fatherless children; fathers crushed under the juggernaut of racism. Her husband is on the island in perpetuity, by decree never to return, and it was this that had brought her more than a thousand kilometres to *kwa*Langa. And with her a much younger woman, a girl by comparison, who had also come to visit her husband — on the Island for I don't know how long.

They were sitting on a very small and gloomy verandah, the younger lady spinning a plastic ball in her hands, perhaps still nostalgic for the days of play, the other one knitting pensively. Mother and child facing the same plight silently.

Most probably there was still hope in the younger heart, in the elder only a prayer for a miracle. Many people in this world, but very few to cry to. Woman and child who could cry no more. What would it help, because tears would melt neither prison walls nor their makers.

A fresh tot of about two came bouncing over to Nomonde with unrestrained gaiety. They had a short chat while I hesitantly took a seat, trying to avoid a visual exploration of the new surroundings, and Martin crossed into the kitchen to greet the people there. The little girl was now through with Nomonde and trying to pull Martin down to her little height. 'Martin, Martin *ndiph'icent,'* which the latter would not have understood but for the last word. Nomonde lovingly reproved the little one for the root of evil.

The people of the house came out of the other two rooms to greet. The owner of the house, his young matron and the two women on the verandah. I'm ashamed of my memory when it comes to names. When I came to the one who was from Mzimhlope I noted recognition in her eyes but she did not know exactly where to place me or who I might be. The generation gap. I bridged it by telling her exactly where I stay in Mzimhlope and who my people are. She knew me then through her contemporaries and neighbours. The young woman also came from

Soweto.

Everyone was smiling. Somehow the common purpose of our meeting so far away from home brought us closer together, and bound us to the people who cared and helped. And our confidence in each other's trust was reflected in our smiles which vanquished all the sadness that might have been in our souls.

The matron of the house offered us cool drink. She had sent a child to buy it from the shops. But we had to rush off, with due apologies for turning down her generosity.

We transferred my two parcels from the Kombi to the cream-white car, said so long to Martin and then the three of us — the owner of the house we had just visited, Nomonde and I — got into the small car.

As our new friend started the car someone came out of the door that shared a doorpost with his. Our driver peered out of his side window.

'Let's go, man,' he shouted amicably.

One good thing about friendship is: a friend seldom asks 'where to' before he has joined you. It was only when he had got into the back seat next to me and greeted everybody, giving me a handshake and his name, that he asked where we were off to.

I reckon that I am most concerned with what I call the character of life, the impressions that life leaves on my mind. Names, though I do honour them once I have grasped them, do not come first in my consideration of life. I mean life would still be interesting even if everything were not known by name. I believe in discovery and then naming rather than memorizing and applying names already given.

We had driven for barely fifteen minutes before I discovered that the man sitting next to me was the kind of person that is good to have in company irrespective of how long you've known him: his soul overflowed with conversation and mirth.

The only snag was that we were on different wavelengths. Same humour, but his mind was filled with the Information scandal and mine with Smith's burning skyline. He talked about 'Info': 'It has proved to everybody, including the staunchest supporters of the government, that we're all a flock of sheep that cannot do anything about being sheared.'

'*Awu,* thank you Judge Mostert!' grunted the driver.

'Yes,' I said. 'It shows one cannot give one's support blindly. Look at Smith right now. I wonder what all those who backed him when he led that country on its first steps to disaster are saying now. *Phela,* the destruction of Rhodesia's biggest fuel dump is the greatest setback yet for his side's already futile war effort. Man, fuel is life.'

'Ya, too much power in the hands of a few is dangerous.'

It was Nomonde who brought our attention back to something closer to our souls. *'Ilele phaya i* first victim *yethu ka* Seventy Six.' The graveyard consisted of sand mounds with dust wreaths.

A brief pause in our thoughts to pay homage to the memory of that year of repression. No black man who survived that indiscriminate massacre will ever forget it. I can still hear the bullets whizzing past my ears, and smell the gas.

We stopped at a butchery that did not look like one because it was a township butchery. Nomonde pointed out to me where she lives. No different from other locations I had been to on the Rand and elsewhere, except that this was another place. Boys with nothing to do lay on the grass patches on the sides of the street. Others were dribbling a flat plastic ball. 'Black child, nothing to do but await your calling to labour,' I thought.

A minute later we were on the way again. Two ragged young soccer teams were kicking it out on an equally ragged pitch opposite the police station on our right. I could not have missed the police station for the kwela-kwela that was parked in front and the tattered *vierkleur*. We stopped and Nomonde got out to deliver a Christmas wrap to a destitute family.

After that I noticed that we were moving out of *kwa*Langa. Who was I to ask where to? We drove on a highway full of buzzing vehicles on a late Friday afternoon. We followed a maze of roads. I saw many light brown people. Suddenly we stopped in front of an old Dutch-style house and everybody got out and went in.

3. The Enlightenment

It was homely: nothing there that made you feel like dirt. A carpet that did not reach the walls, a stereo with many buttons, an unused fireplace, an old wooden couch with big home-made cushions, and in the middle an old rocking chair. The walls were animated with cloths, brightly printed in African styles.

We made ourselves at home on the cushions.

'This is where my friends stay. I always come around to listen to their music,' said Nomonde.

'Where are they?' I asked. Our friends seemed not to be worried about whose house it was.

'Should be somewhere around the neighbourhood. The house was open.'

'Who are they?'

'Phil, Rachel and Sally.'

I pricked up my ears. Did this mean that people in Cape Town still delighted in 'slave' names? Personally speaking, nothing embarrasses me like being called by that other name I got from church, and which was my 'school name'. To be honest with others is not to hide one's true thoughts from them. I made my disapproval known. Far as I knew, it might provide a good subject for discussion — and we all know that discussion is the easiest way to mutual understanding and honest friendship. 'They assimilated to western civilisation, or what? How did they lose their heathen names?'

'You didn't say that about Martin. Or were you thinking the same but remained silent?' asked Nomonde in that voice of hers that made me want to listen to her talking all the time.

'No, with him it does not matter whether he is Martin or Sizwe. The choice is his and he would not lose face anywhere if his name were either. His dignity would not be affected. But what about the three you've just mentioned?' I was all the time convinced that they were as black as I am. 'Calling themselves that completely nullifies their identity. Unless they too are a "higher" shade of black.'

'No. They are white,' said Nomonde and watched for my reaction.

'Wha . . . white?' According to me all people who befriended whites were sellouts except myself where Mark back home was concerned. We communicated in the neutral realm of art which transcends all the stupid barriers and allows people to view each other as nothing else but humans . . .

'They are good people.'

The way I always felt on an escalator with whites came back into my mind. I nearly asked what did she mean, whites were good people. Okay, I agree: it is, in fact, my creed that judging people by their skins is an evil prejudice. But this is South Africa, and the whole world over knows that this is the in-thing here. To whites blacks are 'bad' and to blacks whites are 'bad'. The whites being the ones who started it, of course. The quiz in my mind was: how on earth could whites ever be 'good', when all they knew about was money?

'Well, there's always a first encounter,' I thought. I prepared to meet my first human whites excepting Mark. I looked forward to it without the wariness I usually adopted when about to come into contact with white people. Maybe it was because I had placed my trust in Nomonde and was inclined to believe that she could not deliberately mislead me. The only thing that worried me was the humid heat.

'The bathroom is at the back outside. If you feel hot you can fetch your washrags and go in there to cool down.'

I jumped at that offer. The next minute I was splashing and scrubbing. Very seldom an ordinary black gets a chance to have an ordinary bath or shower. The portable bath that doesn't give one a chance to relax is our thing. You keep the kettle hot and shout for more hot water as your bath cools down, or perhaps go to the public showers at the hostel. Ha!

When I came out, having changed into fresh clothes and feeling much more at ease, there were more people in the house. Two white girls and a youth. I guessed that they were the 'good people' from the way they appeared pleased at the sight of the others in the house. I approached the introductions with a measure of scepticism, smiling only because they were smiling, otherwise without any care for them in the world, and getting the escalator feeling back. A friend of mine has his own simple policy to deal with life under present circumstances: 'You smile when they smile and fight when they fight. Their attitude towards you should determine which is the enemy and which the friend, not forgetting of course that the brightest smile can hide the worst intentions.'

I agree with my friend, because if a person is human enough to smile at others, even if they are not of his colour, at least he deserves some goodwill in return.

But the image I had in my mind of white people was what concerned me. It was too beastly to be improved by meeting one exception in tens of thousands. What is the value of The Star of Africa if it is lying unknown in a trash dump? But wait till we've looked at it more closely . . . If The Star were by chance discovered, what then would the value be?

I let the new names run through my mind several times. Good, I knew them. I noticed that I didn't have the escalator feeling anymore, although I did not know exactly what to talk about to show Nomonde that I had declared a truce for the time we would be together with her friends. To be honest with myself and thus with you, I was not excited at all as yet by the contact. They 'left me cold' as one of their fathers had put it once. Which will show you how this racism smears all those exposed to it. I have been smeared, for my whole life. My very existence is determined along racial lines. So, normally, if I see a white I see a white and not another human being. I see an image of the man who plunders my humanity.

I'll put it straight to you as I see it. After all, no one can tell you better how I feel than I. My own prejudice can be described as reciprocal or reactive prejudice, as opposed to an active prejudice by which my whole life has been directly affected. That makes it an acquired reflex, perhaps a defence mechanism built on unpleasant experiences. And it does not take a genius to know that the best form of defence is counter-attack, that means an offensive defensive stance. I hope that explains my attitude clearly enough. It is a reaction, a conscious reaction.

The two friends who had brought us in the car were in a hurry to leave, but I was not ready to part company before I had proved to Nomonde that whites could never be good, even if God was apparently on their side. They would hate the black man even in heaven. Why did she think they had separate graveyards? So's we might not rub shoulders in heaven too! It didn't matter, my being superstitious, because she happened to be that way too. *Hawu*, good whites in South Africa!

'Nomonde,' said the owner of the car in the authoritative manner of true African men. 'There's business to settle in the township. We should be leaving now.'

My eyes told Nomonde that I would not be leaving if I had a choice: 'By the way, Thandi. I didn't tell you we're having a get-together here this evening. Just a little braai and music. Maybe you'd like to stay and meet more Capetonians, if you're not too tired.'

I thought there was nothing to learn in a township except what I already knew, in a different version. 'I'll stay for the evening, if taking me home will not inconvenience you.'

'No, it won't.'

You may be wondering why this good lady was so openly disposed towards me. Being the kind of person she is, acutely aware of the black man's lot and the causes thereof, she happened to know about a sister of mine who had been kept in gaol without trial for nearly two years. And you see, Debs, my cousin, was once like a sister to a friend of Nomonde who is like a sister to her.

Our two friends bade us so long and cleared out.

They were talking about getting provisions for the get-together. 'Thandi . . . ' she said to me, 'come along with us to see a bit of the place.'

Shirley remained. The four of us, Nomonde with the small well-formed limbs and serene face, Rachel with the lively eyes, Phil with the ruffled hair and myself with a sceptical approach to the whole outing (but trying to act as naturally as the others seemed to be) went out to a green Beetle that was parked in front of the gate.

Holy Apartheid! Trying to be natural in a situation that is considered unnatural in the land of my birth!

The girls went in behind and Phil and I in front. The tough part of it all was the communication. Spoken English is a tongue-knotting affair to a person not used to expressing himself that way. Things I would have liked to say refused to translate into words. But I guess that their not attempting actively to make me feel at ease was making me feel really natural. I looked at Phil next to me and asked myself: was that indeed a white man going out of his conventional way to make friends with black people? What had prompted him?

'Here comes Soks,' said Rachel. So it was not only Nomonde they knew. A guy wearing a black overcoat that went down to his ankles greeted us with a smile and went into the house.

We drove to the local shopping precinct, passing a police station that looked like a hotel on the way. Nomonde and Phil went out to get some table wine and a few beers. Rachel and I remained in the car.

She tried to strike up conversation. I say 'tried' because for some inexplicable reason my mind seemed to have locked up all my ideas in its strongroom. Maybe I was trying to play the part I'd learnt to play all my life towards white people. Never to give them the smallest hint of my capability if I wanted to maintain communication with them or to remain relatively free. The reason is simple, and reflected in the way in which blacks are raided daily, slammed into prison, banned or even killed as soon as they suggest an insight into the negative workings of racism upon their existence.

We talked about what I was doing in life, to which I answered that I was trying to write about life but did not let her in on the fact that by so doing I was trying to rid my mind of all those things which went towards making my life miserable. In other words I was struggling against the chains of racism in my mind.

'For how long was he sentenced?'

'Only two years. One of which was suspended.'

'He was lucky.' So she knew the brutality of her people's laws. 'The others get sentences ranging from five years upwards.'

'Ya. Seldom you hear a guy gets less than that for a political "offence".'

'I understand there are also children kept there. It must be terrible!' Her eyes told me that she meant it.

Having noticed an honest touch of human compassion in her I presently warmed to her, although I still withheld the best part of me. We went on about how it was in Cape Town and such matters until our friends returned.

Next we went to a supermarket where the girls went out together and let us grow 'seat-sores' and run out of conversation. Being men (no offence aimed at the fairer sex of course) we had this in common, and it was easier for us to talk.

I was amazed at the way the trash seemed to vanish at the discovery of the diamonds. Those were human beings with a conscience and everything, like me! The feeling of the escalator was rapidly going. Racism was crumbling fast before my eyes without a single bomb or life being wasted. There I was sitting in the same car and talking naturally to another son of the fatherland. That mutual respect is all I'm asking for in life. People must live in equal and mutual obligation on earth. This is the one cause for which I will lay down my life.

Did it have anything to do with my pilgrimage? Did it mean that I had first to understand what the reasons behind the presence of prisoners of injustice on the Isle of Makana were? As far as I could see, at the root of all the thoughts and actions which took them there was this burning desire to see justice and fairness in their lifetime. After all there is only one life per person and in that unstipulated period one surely expects to see some of one's ideals taking on the flesh of reality.

Eventually the women came out loaded with the whole supermarket. I bet they had resolved before going in that they would not come out until their common purse was empty.

'We did not keep you too long, did we?' they had the nerve to say.

When we drove back home I kept my eyes peeled for other motorists' or pedestrians' reactions to the four of us, two blacks and two whites in a car. There were none discernible. Nat Nakasa's words rang in my mind: 'The best way to live with apartheid is to ignore it.' In other words be natural, be yourself and not what some political fanatic says you must be.

Home again, I went straight into conversation with Soks who had arrived when we were leaving for the shops. He had been sitting on the rocking chair talking to Shirley, who left to join the other girls and Phil to make preparations.

Soks was a typical South African urban black youth — trying to find a niche for himself in a hostile world. As such we both lived in the world of tomorrow. We foresaw Azania, where ability and not the colour of a man's skin or his creed would be the criterion, where no laws would prevent any human being from living naturally, from being human.

Soks and I know very well that there is no place for us two black boys under the sun. We've heard tell of this, seen for ourselves in Seventy Six, and later developments have been nothing but a fading hope. One other thing we are clear about is that no one can give us the happiness we long for. We must bring it about ourselves. We cannot expect Phil, Rachel and Shirley and those of their people who still have a conscience to give it to us, because they haven't got it themselves. Our unhappiness tarnishes any happiness they might have derived from their own existences. Moreover happiness is something that cannot be bargained over since it is a conditional state. Certain conditions have to be satisfied.

Happiness eludes even the potentates of the world, it's often said, since they have to spend all their time guarding against the loss of their power and financial 'security'. The same fallacy drives the criminal to murder. And the same fallacy leads the racist to exclude all others from the fruits of the fatherland.

It was comforting to know again, sitting there with Soks, that I was not alone in my awareness of the potential within ourselves for changing our lives.

Each one of us needs only to keep that flame of life burning — a flame which may one day grow into an inferno of sufficient magnitude to melt the chains of prejudice. Remember, an inferno is made up of many little flames . . .

'Thandi, Soks. So engrossed in your subject. You must be thirsty. What about something to drink? Coffee or anything?' The woman's instinct for the maintenance of life is what makes her the most admirable creature on earth.

'Thank you Sis'Monde,' I said after finding the courage to state my longings. 'A beer if you don't mind.'

She looked at us disapprovingly: 'But you haven't eaten yet.'

I did not know how to put it to Sis'Monde that in my young life I had drunk until, deriving no more excitement out of it but trouble, I decided to call it quits. I tried this line: 'Oh, one beer between us won't do us any harm Sis'Monde. It'll whet our appetites instead.'

She brought the beer. People started arriving. So it was not only the few I had met who were natural in Cape Town. There where it had all started more than three hundred years previously, there, people had forgotten or were forgetting race.

When the sun had finally set so much later than at home, I decided to go and buy myself cigarettes before the shops closed down. There was a shop nearby. Outside it was drizzling, a very fine drizzle that would soak you without you knowing it. I borrowed a raincoat and went out with Soks.

The neighbourhood did not look 'white' as I had expected. If it was, it must have been the poorest of white people who lived there. Some houses looked dark and deserted. I was only to learn later that this was a 'coloured' area which had been declared 'white': always the dark-skinned man making way for the light-skinned man.

Back at the house we found that people had poured in while we were away. When I say people I mean a whole spectrum of South Africans. A get-together that anticipated Azania.

There were people from all over Cape Town. People from the white suburbs, two from a 'coloured' township, and the others from the locations. The music was blaring and our chairs had been kicked out of the way because people were happy and felt like dancing, trying out all the rhythmic bodily contortions that their minds could conjure up. I flopped onto a cushion, watched the dancing and listened to the music. I have never been good at dancing except when I am alone, when I reckon that John Travolta would come second.

The meat was passed around on a tray. It went very well with the beer while the beer went very well with the music. I chatted with the guy next to me who came from some 'coloured' township. Next Rachel came to sit next to me and we talked pleasantly about life in general. When she asked me why I would not dance like everybody else I made a flimsy excuse. In the pauses between the records others came to sit at my side and we talked like the South Africans we all ought to be, and not like South Africans who are obsessed with colour.

There was an abundance of happy sisters and brothers of all three shades.

Everybody wanted to know whether the stranger was enjoying himself. Who would not be happy to have the evil image of a white as an oppressor cast aside for a while? Where were the haters then? Doubtlessly barricaded in their hatred and waiting, shotguns in readiness, for a *swart gevaar* onslaught on their identity and civilization.

Thinking that way made me check everybody for the slightest sign of a change in their features. Roy, Phil, Rachel and Shirley were as white as when they had first come into the house. I checked myself, Nonkosi, Vuyani and the others. As black as ever. Nor had anybody's manners changed for the worse. The laughter that filled my ears was like part of the music, from the core of our souls as the musical notes were from the core of the musicians' souls. Nobody was drinking too much — except myself: I sat there and each time Sis'Monde danced close, plucked her leg and asked for a beer as if I was a thirsty athlete asking for water.

I could not help celebrating the moment of my temporary triumph over racism. Who could give us guns at that moment and order us to go for each other simply because we happened to be of different colours from the same human spectrum? I am sure we would have laughed him to scorn, knowing that togetherness and equality in each others' eyes made South Africa a better world to live in than guns would.

We had forgotten apartheid. The mere existence of statutes aimed at keeping us a cold distance apart did not mean anything to us during those moments: because we knew that thinking of them, just remembering that there were such restrictions, would prejudice our whole thinking and make us subconsciously uphold them, even if we were aware of their intrinsic injustice and insult to humanity.

What was supposed to be a little braai turned out to be a party as people kept on arriving to replace those leaving. The tirelessness of youth was remarkable. Everybody, including myself after some beers, was dancing as if it was a marathon.

After midnight people started trickling out. Those who had come by public transport were invited to stay until the morning.

When dawn began to infiltrate the eastern horizon Nomonde played 'The Best of Nina Simone' which went right through my ears to the roots of my soul. 'Suzanne: between the garbage and the flowers is a child lean and leaning out for love.' I had never heard anyone like Nina Simone. Nothing like well-sung music to soothe a scarred soul. I forgot everything for a while and let the black lady's voice speak to me.

Most of our sisters surrendered to sleep in Sis'Monde's room. She was among the tough sisters who kept up a running conversation and brought us black coffee towards daybreak. The lounge floor reminded me of the Guyanese cultists' mass suicide. I cursed myself for comparing the living and the dead. I put the remaining cushions together in a corner that seemed more private than the others and tried 'poison' to the accompaniment of Nina Simone's voice.

The 'poison' of slumber wouldn't work on me. I thought the best thing to do was to lie there and let my mind wander. I let my eyes go over the room: 'Sleep black child, the white child has gone back home to sleep, sleep black child, sleep where the sun sets on you, yesterday the sun set on apartheid.' They were all sleeping so peacefully, my black brothers.

What would they be doing at that time at home? Doubtless already awake. One thing we have in common at home is waking up very early . . . like prisoners . . . a prisoner's day starts long before the world wakes up . . . maybe on the Isle too it is like that.

The Isle of Makana! I had gone down with bitterness in my soul. Against all white people and their black sellouts. But that morning I rose with that bitterness qualified. I said to myself: 'May the sellouts rot in hell and the white people purge themselves of the racists that have marred their human image, sending all those sub-humans to join their sellouts in the flames. Those who trade in life are not fit to live among other human beings. Nat Nakasa did not hit the nail directly on the head, he just glanced it. Ignoring apartheid is not the best way to live with it. The best way to live with apartheid is to destroy it. The people I had met overnight did not want to live with apartheid. They hated it. I had felt this aversion in their manner. But it was impossible to ignore. They could reject it in principle but not practically. They could ignore it in theory, but as long as it was entrenched in the law they would be living under its rule.

Again I wondered whether it was a coincidence that before I embarked for the Island I should be in a situation that would make me think deeply about such matters. Was it intended that I should be cleansed of whatever blemish racism had left in my soul?

Nina Simone was singing 'In the morning of my life . . . ' Was I in the morning of a new outlook on my world, this world of racism? Why were there men of all the shades of the human spectrum that comprise South Africa on the Isle? My mind gave me an answer: 'The army for the defence of the rights of man, or the deliverance of the rights of man from the monster that threatens to devour our fatherland, consists of all the true people of South Africa! Our gesture the previous night had simply meant that if it had been left to us to decide, we wanted no war. We wanted to live in peace and brotherhood in God's world. But I noted with pain that most, if not all, the nations of the world were united by the tragedy of brother against brother. They only discovered the wisdom of humanity after having treated one another inhumanly.

When I thought of an army I did not necessarily have a belligerent force in mind. I was thinking of that army of men and women of our world who see the outrage being perpetrated on mankind by an insane ideology and resist it in different ways. This army is also not necessarily black, should not be. To define it along those lines is to make true sons and daughters of the soil of other shades believe that they have no place in the ranks of the army of justice.

Four, five hours' sleep did me some good. Phil, Rachel and Nomonde woke up feeling like a cool sea breeze. The day was not hot enough for a swim. I gathered from the way they spoke about it that those three were in love with the sea. The overcast day would not prevent them from driving along the shore to Sea Point and beyond. There was no need to ask me if I wanted to go. In any case, if I had refused my friends would have thought that my spirit lacked adventure.

As we left I was eager to see what it was that was so impressive about a great volume of water. Up until then I had seen the sea only in passing. And I had never been drawn towards it as my three friends seemed to be.

Both my bitterness and my discomfort in the presence of white people had completely left me Yet I sat there next to Phil devoid of speech, absorbing and digesting with my whole being a passing respite from the life of hatred and wariness that I knew. Tomorrow, with others unnatural and unlike my friends, tomorrow hostilities would resume and intensify. Events would take place which would compel *me* to invoke again the only effective means of defence against hate and contempt: hate and contempt. Tomorrow *he* would go to the army and learn that the enemy he was being trained to defend himself against was the black man in the backyard who was stalking his household and abundance, day and night. However, regardless of all these likelihoods, to know that we once tried when everybody else was not trying would give us reason to say we once lived; we were not stillborn in the struggle for a truly human life.

After some meandering among dwellings and buildings of all sorts we rolled onto a highway from the crests of which the Isle was a blurred dark line in the grey of the drizzle. I wondered what they would be doing on a day like this. Their thoughts would migrate to all corners of the mainland, perhaps. Except for those, maybe, who had no hope of ever getting back there except in coffins. Possibly they thought only of matters affecting the Isle, and waited for death's deliverance. Yissis! Should they die there! Who would be held responsible for their deaths?

I did not want to think of that while my friends were carrying on a lively conversation.

On our right the sea was close, and the way the aroused waters were lapping at the shore like infinite tongues caught my eye. If the oceans were left to go on like that forever they would lick the firmament out of existence. Near Sea Point a lawn grew next to the sea. Hundreds of people, some walking dogs, nannies walking mesdames' kids, others sitting on park benches or hanging over the rail that ran along the shore, all entranced by the rhythmic splash of the breakers. A small boy running in the surf, followed by a big brown dog with tongue hanging out ecstatically. Those sights of human happiness with nature gave me the reason for my friends' love of the sea.

Then the reality of our world came back to us in the form of a question from Sis' Monde:

'By the way, are blacks allowed here this December? I see no beach constable hunting for dark skins, and there are many.'

We drove to where houses, carved out of rock faces or perched on top, apparently at a fortune's cost, represented the most enterprising architecture I had ever seen in my untravelled life. Entrances and garage doors like sesames. 'So this is the material aspect of your father's relentless hold on power, heh?' I nearly asked Phil and Rachel, but not knowing how they would have taken it I kept it to myself.

We drove down a steep incline to the very edge of the sea. A group of white youths stood at leisure near where we parked, got out of the car and descended stone steps between two wooden cabins. 'Coloured' youths were busy tending the surroundings.

Large smooth boulders on the shore, gleaming as if they had been soaked in oil, suddenly emphasized our microscopical presence on the beach. We froze on the last stone step and watched the first wave start as a ripple and gather momentum as it surged towards us, finally exhausting itself at our feet. It retreated like a dog with the fight bitten out of it. The second one gathered and made another futile grab at us.

The boulders to the left were covered with black sea birds, also gleaming as if dipped in oil. About fifty metres in front, where the water was really irate, was one rock with a cave-like aperture at the uneven water level. 'Surely there must be something which lives in there,' I thought. Diagonally in front to the right was another that dwarfed the others around it. Men stood on it and took photographs. I stood there with my friends looking at the magnificent natural turmoil without words to describe it.

Then the most beautiful sight I had ever seen in my life occurred in front of us!

A wave must have accumulated with the strongest resolve to annihilate the unshakable caved boulder, once and for all. It was high time, counted in aeons since the beginning of the world, that the rock should be disintegrated and swallowed. With such a resolve and a surprise strategy it had crept upon the target unseen by us, among countless other waves. Suddenly: splash-sh! And a wondrous spray radiated into the sky out of the unperturbed holed boulder, leaving it shining like a gigantic diamond. I caught my breath and someone remarked: 'Ah-h, that's beautiful.'

Out of many more seconds spent at the foot of the stone steps at the brim of the spectacular ocean, speechlessly waiting for the phenomenon to repeat itself, came nothing.

'Let us go to that side,' suggested Phil and immediately darted away among the small rocks strewn over the beach sands. Rachel hesitated for just a moment, then took off behind him. As we two laggards, slowed by my distrust of the overwhelming ocean, left our pedestal, a snow white form started forming a stone's flick into the sea and swept towards us. We ignored its innocent volume and approach, and continued after our friends. Before we decided on the path to follow among the rocks a green liquid wall five feet high tried to ambush us. You should have seen us bolting for our lives in front of it towards higher ground under the beach cabins, making it just in time, the lunge of the living waters barely touching our heels. That decided us. No more adventures. We went back to our stone step and watched the sea birds bobbing on the breakers and diving.

Our friends used another route to return to us and we all laughed at the ambush. We went back to the car and Phil took us in loops and turns through a residential area which made me think: 'There is no difference between our two white friends and us. The sea did not wait for us darkies to turn our eyes away or absent ourselves from the 'white beach' before it gave us the spray display. Only difference is that they have human rights, and we none or very few. They live like human beings ought to live — no, that's not right — they live in unfair abundance, while most of us just manage to survive. Look at their homes and think of our dog kennels! But would you say they enjoyed human rights when among their people it was regarded as shameful, even sinful, to exercise their right to love indiscriminately? Was it this right that they were trying to claim, or was it just that they were nonconformists, that they chose to share their lives with us?' I ask myself these questions now, yet I know I cannot answer them. Only they could answer them. Why did I not ask them that day? I hate embarrassing other people unless they are out to do it to me. Those three were my good friends.

We did not talk much, more precisely I did not, because I found myself in a world foreign to the one in which we all exist, but still on the same soil. Only then did I realise the real extent of the damage that apartheid had done to my life. Through its draconian legislation it had divested me of the essential beautiful reasons for life, like friendship (where can one survive without friendship?) and left me to wallow in my depravity.

As I have said, I did not know whether it was a coincidence that I found myself meeting 'different' peoples of my country in a friendly, human spirit before the last part of my pilgrimage over a stretch of sea; whether there was something behind it all. The question whether it was not a precondition of my setting foot on the Isle of Makana that I should undergo a mental and spiritual revolution kept sneaking into my mind. I thought, however, that to consider it would be too great a concession to superstition. The idea of a limbo, of a purgatory, had never fitted in with my convictions.

Soon I noticed familiar surroundings and guessed that we were driving back to our friends' home. Nomonde showed me the University of Cape Town at the foot of green Table Mountain draped with the 'tablecloth'. When we skirted Groote Schuur she showed me the Rhodes memorial. Ha, Rhodes's memorial? Rhodes's memorial has more recently come to light in Zimbabwe.

Returning from the drive I felt a completely new man. Perhaps the sea breeze and the free spirits of my friends had something to do with it. I felt a calm in my soul I had never felt in my life, not even in a church. Nothing like nature and natural people to reassure the soul.

And not wishing to disturb this peace of mind with further thinking that second evening in Cape Town, I went to bed early after a bath and a light supper with my friends. My mind switched off, filled with anticipation of the following day, the greatest day in my life when I would take the last fearful steps towards that shrine of human sacrifice, the Isle of Makana.

4. The Island

The seventeenth of December was a slightly drizzly morning in Cape

Town. I was the first to get ready through Sis' Monde's conscientious urging, and became impatient as the others took turns in the bath although, by the time they were all through, we had more than half an hour to get to the docks by twelve thirty.

Meanwhile many young people, black and white, came into the house for brief spells loosened their limbs with the music that was always gracing the atmosphere of the house whenever there was someone in, and left.

We left. The weather was not promising.

'How would you feel if you were turned back on account of bad weather? Y'know, it happens sometimes.'

'Mh! I'd cry like a baby, S'monde.'

Phil drove fast to the docks, Quay Number Five.

We arrived long before the ferry docked and parked behind a corrugated iron structure which, I discovered, passed for waiting rooms, segregated of course, and the office where papers were checked. We all got out of the car and Sis' Monde led me past the two waiting rooms, the first of which was full of black people, to the office with a counter that kept us at the door, three at a time.

All I could say of the man in a prison guard uniform who checked my papers was that he was withdrawn, in direct contrast to my friends who had brought me. Maybe because he was past his youth, long past it, he enjoyed making the world uncomfortable for the young.

Back in our waiting room almost all the benches were fully occupied. Thanks to a light brown man who chose to stand, I found a little space between two ladies and squeezed in.

S'Monde was happy to see some of the people in the waiting room and they responded radiantly, forgetting the short voyage across the 'moat' for a while. There were four ladies and myself going to the shrine. Also, there were four light brown people, three young ladies and the gentleman who had chosen to stand. I did not have enough knowledge of their affairs to know whether they were visiting common law prisoners or 'politicals'. If it were the latter, it occurred to me that segregation might keep us in mutual ignorance on the Isle — the 'different' races kept apart. Very likely. I was thinking of the blacks — African, Coloured, Indian . . . *nxa*, dark-skinned South Africans, I mean!

The room was full of cigarette smoke. Also wishing for something to do I lit one and vainly tried to enjoy it. It tasted like burning cowdung, so I nipped the glow — economy, y'know. My legs itched for movement. Hey! My friends. I'd forgotten. I went out to them.

'How d'you feel?' Phil asked.

'Okay,' I said, omitting to add that 'okay' in this instance meant very anxious. It was not like the ordinary everyday jail visit all black people know. This was a visit which held a great significance in my life. I think Phil had noticed this. That was why he had asked.

S'Monde came to join us

An ambulance with white men in lily white uniforms waited with the usual impatience of ambulances. I reckoned that they were perhaps waiting for someone injured out at sea or a sick person from the Island, white man most probably.

Presently we heard the rising drone of something like a diesel engine to seaward.

'That should be the boat,' said Nomonde.

She was right. First there was a strong ripple which spread in the still waters of the dock. Then she appeared and swung gracefully to starboard towards us. Her name was *Dias*, a sky-blue and white affair. She stopped, then drifted sideways like a crab, while the crew (some wearing green uniforms, and others white) stood at the ready to fasten her against the cushioning tyres on the sides of the landing stage. When she was secure they placed two gangways fore and aft.

I watched all this with the childlike interest of a stranger to harbours. A few people came ashore from the boat. I hardly had the time to study their features before a scene that made everything else recede to the margin of my attention was enacted before my eyes.

The man was old and sick. So sick his limbs did not respond to his mind or, if they did, the pangs of his ailment would not allow it. For all my eyes could see he might have been paralysed. The canvas stretcher was borne ashore with extraordinary care, which meant that he was in a serious condition. I went as close as I could towards the stretcher bearers without causing inconvenience. The face was set, resigned to an unfortunate fate, and the eyes indifferent to life. What I wanted: a glint of life in his eyes to acknowledge that he saw what I wanted him to see in mind, namely that his fight for the acquisition of a human status had not been in vain, had never been in vain, could never be and was not forgotten even if his limbs could bear his life no more, for as long as Africa could bear sons and daughters. This which I sought from him I never found.

Whenever that scene is re-enacted in my memory I refuse to think that the man's resignation could represent defeat. I believe he was saving me from what had slipped my mind at the sight of him. Maybe if he had paid attention to me I might have been encouraged to communicate, say ask who he was or what was wrong with him, and perhaps that might have landed me in trouble and robbed a man waiting for me on the Isle of a visit. I had completely forgotten that one was not supposed to cast even a glance in the direction of a brother, in his case a father, in chains.

The sight touched me to the point of crying inwardly because a man does not cry so that it shows. If there was any sight purposed to greet me on the last steps of my pilgrimage, that was the one.

The man was transferred from the portable stretcher to one that was wheeled out of the ambulance. Why were they denying him the right to pass out of this damned life of suffering? For what purpose, when they had already usurped his right to live among his people, on his fatherland?

These questions may appear to come from some advocate of euthanasia, but if you had been standing there at Quay Number Five with me on that overcast day, maybe you would have asked the same questions too.

I suppressed the bitterness that started to fill my whole being by peeling my eyes off the ambulance. Only to find that everybody was looking, as if bound by a spell, some with tragic expressions on faces that had learned too well to portray grief, others with nonchalant features that had learned only too well to depict apathy.

All the light that had shone in my soul for the past two days was immediately transformed into unbearable darkness by those regards which were passed to us from the Island. I hated those who had done that to that man. I hated them! I hated God for condoning it. 'There is no God,' thought I. 'How stupid and superstitious I can sometimes be! Whatever phenomenon brought about the universe *occurred,* and that was that. No omnipotent being was appointed to run the affairs of man. Man *became* as part of the phenomenon and was left to his own fate, like all the other existing things. That's why man destroys man. Otherwise this Being would stop it. To hell with the idea of Satan too, there never has been such a thing from the beginning of everything up to now. The whole earth's trouble is the making of man himself. The savage in him makes him kill another man, that is all. Absolute civilization or, in my own concept, human refinement will be attained only when man ceases craving blood, and desires only to kill the savage in himself. The savage. The instinct to kill. When man kills the instinct to kill which is in his nature, we can start thinking of civilization and a greater chance of peaceful co-existence on earth . . . '

Had that scene been enacted to remind me that all was not well, in spite of the past few hours' relief from the evil that engulfed my life? I might have civilized thoughts, but while the world was in the hands of savages my soul would never rest. Why did it have to coincide with the beginning of the last lap of my pilgrimage? Was it a trial to prove whether my mind had been completely weaned of racism? Would I still see my friends as friends after that?

Yes, I still saw them as friends and would not condemn them simply because they wore white skins. I knew very well that there was a special kind of white, the racist, who killed people.

'Thandi.'

'Awu, they are going aboard already. So long, people.'

'Go well, Thandi.'

I left my friends for the gangway that was fixed aft on the boat. A paper that I had been given at the office was torn, one piece of it handed back to me, and I went to stand in front of the cabin directly below my friends who were on a second platform one metre above the one level with the deck.

All the time my friends were standing there and looking at me and I could sense from their semblance that they knew how I felt and were with me in spirit. They stood close together, one girl, Rachel, on Phil's right and the other two on his left, S'Monde next to him.

I can still see them standing there. I remember S'Monde in a black overcoat that hung close to her. None of them were smiling. After what we had seen a minute previously there was nothing to smile about. The sight had spoiled everything.

The engines of the *Dias* purred and roared into life after the gangways had been removed and the securing ropes hauled aboard. She crawled away from the landing stage, again like a crab, pushing giant ripples ahead of her.

My friends still stood there looking at me. I waved at them. They waved back and stood still. The *Dias* began to swing around to point her bow to the seaward entrance of the dock.

We started to bob and lurch as soon as we cleared harbour. I secured myself on the bench fastened to the deck, surprised to find the ocean such an uneven surface. Imagine a desert with high dunes and you have an idea of what I mean.

Swimming being one sport I would cherish if I had time for sports, I weighed my chances in that sea and marked them at nil. I was not so brave as to challenge the ocean. Only the brave . . .

Yes, only the brave. He who had sent wave upon human wave of warriors against the very gates of the barracks at Fort England in Grahamstown on 22 April in 1819. He who had led one of the early nationalist movements against colonialism. His aim was to restore the people's unity by pointing out the danger of the white intruders rampaging into the fatherland. At once soldier and prophet, by name Makana. It is supposed that he died by drowning trying to escape from his prison on Robben Island. He died a free man, out of the walls of his prison, going to his people.

Yes, only the brave like Makana. 'The Left Hand'. For a long time the people believed he would return to lead them.

The 'coloured' man wearing a golf cap who was sharing the bench with me was smoking a cigarette. I lit one from his butt to overcome the unusual salty smell of the air. The sun found a gap in the clouds and held on to it. A rusty-coloured ship ploughed its way uniformly, unlike us, to the docks which were becoming smaller and smaller as we bobbed and lurched away from them with the roar of the engines making a great fuss over our negligible pace. My eyes hung onto the docks and Cape Town in the background. Table Mountain. Everything was shrouded in a misty grey, and seemed almost holy. A few sea birds of the kind we had seen on the boulders the previous day followed the ferry in the water with determination as if fated to follow and accepting that fate. The sea was brightly mottled with many little triangular sails on a flotsam of tiny boats, with white people lolling in them. A cluster of seaweed made me think of myriads of octopi floating towards where we were sailing.

The sun did not leave the gap it had found, which became wider around it, clearing a vast expanse of the skies. Its rays glanced off the apices of the uneven surface and flooded our eyes with a silver sheen. If only the damned tin-can would stop roaring so monotonously, switch tone at least, maan. Small wonder seamen are renowned for cursing. I was yearning to do something along those lines too, only my vocabulary was limited. But I did have a little practice for a short while. Going up on the summits and sinking unceremoniously into the green valleys of water was not by any means comfortable. The ocean had no respect, tossing us humans about like lousy flotsam. None of my companions wore happy faces, either. The buildings of Cape Town, sticking up at the water's distant edge with Table Mountain behind, were like a miniature city in some architectural art gallery.

I was beginning to get really bored when one of our 'coloured' sisters shouted, 'The Island!' with an unmistakable ring of relief in her voice. I immediately came back to life, out of the sea doldrums.

The Island! The Isle of Makana.

It was coming at us like floating land that had broken off some continent and was being swept by the Atlantic Ocean towards Cape Town; or an unimaginably colossal monster surfacing in the green, blue waters, its back silhouetted against the cloudy sky. The outline was rugged, the foreground bushy and dark.

The Island rushed at our helpless *Dias* and suddenly, to my untold relief, it stopped and we were bouncing towards it.

Holy ancestors! There was a whole community staying there. I could tell this from the residential buildings to the left of our course. How did they manage to live with it? I would rather die than willingly share common ground with people imprisoned because they deplored a system that stripped the majority of a society of its human status. For, whichever way you look at it, political prisoners always represent one side of a human rights controversy. In other words they are spawned by injustice. *Heer!* I would never live on Robben Island willingly, knowing it was notorious all over the world as a place of human sacrifice for a racist ideology. Some people really have no principles. Do they derive excitement out of notoriety?

The single dock was made of large concrete cubes and I got a sensation of being swallowed as the ferry passed the small gap which was the entrance to it. 'Common Law' prisoners, all of them coloured and probably working as dockers, formed the reception party.

Do you love, hate, despise prisoners or do you understand some of the reasons for there being prisoners in every capitalistic society, which is said to give every able-bodied human being an equal chance with all other persons? We do not know about other societies, but what is it that makes our prison population so high?

With particular reference to South Africa, what is it that drives black people in such great numbers to prison? Have you ever been to Leeuwkop, that city of the outlawed north of Johannesburg? What is it, if our system of government is fair and just to all the peoples of our country and therefore the most suitable? Not to say that there is no crime among white people. They do commit crimes too, but mostly crimes of passion or those crimes which it is not wrong for them to commit — crimes against black people.

White jails are sparsely populated while black jails are overpopulated.

How many black people are waiting in Central Prison for an appointment with the hangman? And, how many white people? What circumstances imposed on him and beyond his control led Solomon Mahlangu from a high school classroom to a cell in Death Row? Why? Think of this. Maybe one day we will get a chance to exchange views on this. I know quite a number of factors beyond a person's immediate control which reduce black people to victims of government-determined circumstances.

Back to the Island. As the *Dias* went through the same motions as when she arrived in Cape Town, several white prison guards in shorts suddenly materialized out of the few buildings, one holding our old friend the Alsatian on a leash. When we had docked the gangway was positioned and we went ashore.

My first step on The Isle of Makana, though light and tremulous, jolted my whole being. To me that ground was as holy as the kraal of the ancestors, where none but those admitted to holy orders ought to set foot. That, of course, excluded all the other prisoners, the guards and the community. I was thinking of the men who were there for the cause.

I know some sceptics will start saying that many were there for crimes of violence, for reasons like rioting, arson and sabotage — in an attempt to insinuate anarchistic tendencies. But to me it all boils down to one thing which I have already stated, namely: the rioters, the arsonists and the saboteurs were spawned out of the injustice that is inherent in our society, coupled with the intransigence of the rulers of the society when their attention is drawn to their wrongs. People therefore resort, are compelled to resort to extreme ways to achieve attention.

'Kom.'

We followed him. Our 'coloured' sisters and one gentleman remained, and I never found out where they were led to see their people. We were led along a high slate stone-coloured wall on our left, towards a gate through which I could make out the corner of a strongly-fenced yard.

Impatient to the extent of not being aware of my pace I found myself ahead of our escort, headed for the gate, when one of the ladies said, 'Hey, *ngapha*,' with unbridled excitement in her voice. She was rather young to have already been robbed of a son. Later, after I had marvelled at his youth, she told me that he had only turned eighteen that year, in jail for a 'political offence'.

I turned to the right and moved with the others towards this flat building which formed an L with the slate wall. It was constructed of the same stone. Into this official-looking house we went.

The waiting room had benches all round the walls and was about twelve by twelve, with two doors to very foul toilets on one side. I regretted having felt like going in there because after one glance into the basins I felt like throwing up.

This guard with a moustache came in to check our permits against a piece of paper he had with him. Then he grunted to clear his throat before asking us what languages we chose to speak to our people and, with an expression that was meant to convey the seriousness of the 'crime', instructed us not to mention even a trace of 'politics.' After that he left us waiting. It was hard for the women to remain silent, apparently because of anxiety. They talked about the people they had gone to see as if they were already in front of them. I smoked. My lungs must have been like an old soot-clogged stove by the time the ten minutes or so of waiting was over.

Our friend who did not want us to 'talk politics' came back. He called our names one after the other and we filed down an L-shaped passage with a steel door in the corner. In the upright part of the L it was like a post office counter, or a series of telephone booths. Telephone booths they were too, because in every cubicle was a telephone hooked on one side.

I was fortunate to get the last cubicle in the line. So I was able to see all the people who had visits that afternoon. I walked slowly, like a sinner approaching the holiest of holies and, as I passed each cubicle, I saw a black son of the fatherland attired in the cloth of sin and shame, the prison uniform that is designed for society's banished.

But, in spite of this outward semblance, there was not even a flicker of shame in the faces of those warriors of our generation. Wanting to see more than just their mothers from the outside, they each spared a second to look at me as I went past them. From the way they looked I had the impression that they knew me from the photographs I had sent in.

And you know what, brothers and sisters? Their eyes were bright (one wore sunshades) and their faces were lit by brilliant smiles which shone right to the core of my soul. I nodded to each and they nodded back. And I knew that defeat was infinite ages and distances from the heart of Africa.

'Prison, where is thy victory?' Huey Newton had once asked. If you don't know him it's your own funeral because he is one of the writers a contemporary black person must know.

Truly, where was the victory? If I had had the faintest expectation of finding it, there was not even a sign of it in any of the men that I saw. The cloth of shame failed dismally to conceal the vibrant vitality of Africa in my brothers' souls. They were strong. Their pride in their humanity was inexhaustible. The chains, the bars, the walls and the cloth of shame were ineffective. The victory was theirs, ours.

I felt stupid that the idea of going to the Isle to give solace had ever entered my mind. And I was taken aback to discover that I was the one who needed solace and courage which I found in abundance in the semblance of 'the prisoners'.

'Hi, son,' I said into the mouthpiece.

'Hey't,' the device crackled back inaudibly. I guessed the last part of the sentence to be *'Kunjani?'* (How's it?)

My eyes shifted from the face, moulded in the same womb as I, three years apart, to the guard who had a double brain — he held two telephone receivers to both his ears like a music recorder wearing earphones and analysing the electronic sounds. Or maybe his brain hemispheres worked independently.

He got the message but lifted his shoulders to show that there was nothing he could do or was prepared to do but listen to whatever we said.

I raised my voice: 'I came on Friday. I was dying to get here.'

'Mh?' From behind the double sound-proofed glass partition he was studying my face for expressions that would animate the 'dead' telephone communication.

I grinned out of the sheer delight of seeing him still in one piece. When people fall into the hands of bad-tempered captors they become accident-prone. Everybody knows that. 'Very well, sonny. And excited to see you also so well. I mean physically.'

'Nothing's the matter there. All I can complain about here is the weather and that's no use, ha.'

You see? Prison, where is thy victory? Physical confinement does not amount to the imprisonment of the whole being. As long as one has the imagination, one can pass through castle walls two metres thick and wander wherever one likes on earth; even to the stars. He had nothing to complain about in man-made circumstances, perhaps because if they were made by man they could be overcome by man. So the only thing he could complain about was what was beyond man's control, the natural elements: but he did not because that would be a futile exercise.

'Already used to the place, neh?'

'Well, one just about gets used to everything.' Nothing as adaptable as human nature.

'Even the work? Are you forced to work?'

'We like it. It is to our advantage because it keeps us fit.'

'Otherwise what do you do to while away the time?' I wanted to form a picture of their world in my mind.

'We think. Because one has got to think, brother. Use your spare time to think and read anything you come across if you're not studying. Develop your imagination to the point of being able to get out of here whenever you like.'

You see, again? I told you. He confirmed it too. We talked about my side of life — a few family matters, friends, sport — and evaded all the vital issues of life as our double-brained 'superior' desired us to.

I was beginning to imagine the latter as a waxwork piece and talk freely when he cut the line without warning. The . . . the . . . I could not think of a suitable word to describe him. Was that all we had travelled thousands of kilometres for? I had no watch but I estimated the duration of our visit at fifteen minutes, twenty on the outside when I had expected at least thirty.

We grinned at each other as we reluctantly replaced the receivers on their hooks, delaying the parting as long as we could.

No one escorted us out to the quay.

The *Dias* was at anchor, a bored bitch. The convict dockers were bored too. There was a strong impulse in me to address them and I could tell that they also felt just as I did. However, we resisted this temptation and sat viewing each other from a safe distance. I knew that they were 'common law' prisoners and I vainly tried to guess what they had done to be taken to the Isle. I checked myself. That was wrong. How could I try to pin 'crimes' of my own mind's making on other people? That was a prejudice caused by the fact that they wore prisoners' garb, which I was not supposed to allow to determine my opinion of other people.

There was no guard in sight. We sat on the slate stoep because it was hot in the still waiting-room atmosphere, while outside there was a slightly cool breeze from the sea. I remembered what I had been taught at school about evaporation causing cooling. They had been right.

All that we could see of the Island was the dock and the wall that formed an L with the visiting house.

So the house where we had 'met' our people was where Mangaliso Sobukwe had been banished to after serving his sentence.

Where could Nelson Mandela be staying on the Island? Definitely not with the other sons of Africa. Holy Makana, Maqoma to be exact! Were these people really resolved to let him die slowly on the Island? Were they aware of the possible consequences? Did they know that he occupied the holiest of holies in the heart of many a black man? Perhaps they did not know. Maybe they thought we would forget him and all the others if they banished them to the Island. Maybe they thought we would forget the pangs of our lives.

A guard with a cruel face came from the direction of the prison. I wanted a souvenir of that momentous day. When he went past us I followed him: *'Ekskuus meneer.* Where can I pick up some pearls around here.'

'Everything here is government property.'

A necklace of pearls from the Island would have been invaluable to me.

The hours we spent there waiting to get back to the mainland could have been spent with our people. I tried to imagine what Maqoma must have looked like. My mind created a vision of a brave African warrior with a spirit that could not be suppressed by man but only by natural elements. I wondered which direction he had swum in on his escape.

The voyage back to Cape Town was rougher but I refused to go into the entrails of the ferry and enjoyed the sight of whites throwing up in their compartment, plus conversation with a little white girl who told me that she was down in Cape Town with her parents for the festive season. They had gone to the Island sightseeing. Her mother had thrown up too. Her father was seasick but she did not feel anything.

My friends stood waiting for me as if they had never left the quay. The only difference was that one of the girls was sitting cross-legged on the landing stage and S'Monde was no longer wearing her coat. They waved while I was still far away.

'Nothing to declare,' said Phil to a penguin at the entrance to the docks.

'So how was your brother, Thandi?' asked Rachel as we turned at the robots to ascend the highway.

'Encouraging. Being there is no more than just a physical inconvenience to them.'

'Oh, that's great!'

I cast one last glance in the direction of the Island. It was like a monster stooping in the blue waters.

'*A luta continua,*' I thought.

Three Days in the Land of a Dying Illusion

> *The illusion was uhuru:*
> *in the minds of its originators*
> *it survives in sickly form,*
> *hospitalized in materialism's walls,*
> *medicated with the roots of greed.*
>
> *In the minds of those upon whom it was imposed*
> *nothing but the cadaver remains,*
> *shorn of flesh*
> *by the vultures aloft in the azure*
> *when the venom of death was injected*
> *with shameless lies and false promises:*
> *ready to swoop down and scavenge,*
> *for them*
> *death brings sustenance,*
> *death means life.*

I set out with a feeling of great relief from the sometimes — after a few months in there — unbearably vibrant conditions of my Soweto. On top of looking forward to a long-desired reunion with close friends whom I had not seen for two years there was also a measure of curiosity. It was a chance to observe, from another angle, the changes that never cease to mould my environment, one of which has been an upsurge in the exodus of a landstripped peasantry from the bantustans to the Rand. Transkei, Umtata to be precise, was my destination.

I chose a simple means of transport, the people's, which means public — a train and a bus, third class, people's class.

A friend of mine was going to Port Elizabeth on the same train, which meant that I had a companion for starters.

The train was full of migrant workers, boys and men with all sorts of baggage and many with the inevitable and regrettable radios. Regrettable: it is through this medium that the minds of my people are stolen. Let me explain how the mental outrage comes about: the system denies the black man enlightenment by subjecting him to an inferior and expensive education. In other words the rural black masses in this land have little or no education. Neither can they read or write, and if they can they are conditioned to empty materialistic values. The thirst of the illiterate masses for knowledge about the world at large is quenched by the mass media. To them, the radio is still one of the technological wonders of the world — a box that speaks many languages, including their own. And there is absolutely no suspicion in their minds that the box may tell lies in their languages. The rest you can figure out for yourselves.

The baggage of the *godukas*, all *godukas*, consists of their sweat and blood in the migrant labour system. They work hard for meagre incomes with which to buy little gifts and useful implements in an attempt to make their folks' lives a little more bearable in the forlorn wildernesses that are said to be their homelands. One comes across heavily loaded tin and wooden trunks and drums (apparently for water storage and other purposes), packed with basic groceries like sugar, salt and tea, and bound in cloths with straps to make them easily portable.

Apart from my friend I had three other travelling companions. One was still a teenager, playing his mouth organ and whistling playfully all the way, enjoying a train ride like any other kid — despite the heavy burden of supporting himself and his people which had been placed across his small shoulders at so early an age. The second, in his late twenties, wore spectacles and a sincerely humble smile. Together we downed a few 'dumpies' of beer which we got at the extortionate price of fifty cents from the Railways waiters. Amusing people, these. When we came to Vereeniging station the one who sold beers and cigarettes said: 'Oh, how I hate this station! The most hateful place in the world to me.'

I asked: 'Why?'

And he replied: 'Because my wife got off the train at this station and I never saw her again up to this very day,' to our hilarious sympathy.

Our third companion was a man whose age was hard to estimate. He looked in his forties but seemingly life's hardships had added their own independent wrinkles to his face and bent his back somewhat. He came from some labour camp in Germiston and was on his way to King-williamstown for the Easter weekend, while the others came all the way from the coal mines of Witbank and were going to the Queenstown district (for that was where I lost them), also for the weekend.

One disappointing aspect of their company was that they tended to reserve their personal opinions of migratory labour — victims perhaps, of the chronic fear (among the oppressed) of arrest for original views. Or perhaps their silence reflected the characteristic distrust of the poor for strangers. Or was it simply that they had accepted their lot?

The train inspector was an old friendly man, patient with the passengers as they dug in their baggage and pockets for misplaced tickets. In spite of his amicable approach to his work he had two uniformed black policemen as bodyguards. One of these tried to show tough by growling at us, until I told him that I knew him. After reminding him where we had met, which was at Mzimhlope station where as teenagers we used to make him earn his money the hard way, he gave up the act: I had known him to be on the timid side.

When we boarded the train at Johannesburg station, I had seen about four women in their thirties carrying heavily loaded bags, and taken them for migrant women going home to give a few days' motherly love to their children. They turned out to be itinerant shebeen queens who opened up shop after the Railways waiter had done his trip.

I was surprised: that had been a man's occupation in 'seventy-six, when I last travelled that way. From the look of it the women were already proficient at black marketeering for they had ways of coaxing the passengers into buying. The one I have in mind, who had a big bust and wore a wedding ring, knocked at the half-open compartment door and when she was invited in said: 'Shoo! So hot in this train that one needs something cool to drink. Here's a beer and a brandy, *bafowethu.*'

'But brandy's a hot drink,' I thought. Aloud, and only for interest's sake because I still had some , I asked: 'How much is the can of beer?'

'It's not a can, brother, it's a "Long Tom".'

'I see, *sisi,* I see. How much?'

She was focusing my interest as a prospective customer on the 'Long Tom', making sure that I clearly understood the unusual capacity of the can she had in her hand. The attention of all the other compartment occupants was also glued on the tin, and they were following each word of our exchange. At last she announced the price: 'Eighty cents.' She wore as honest an expression as one had ever seen on a pedlar's face.

I also reckoned that it *was* honest, though rather expensive. Between these two considerations my mind swung like a pendulum, and finally settled. 'No thanks, *sisi*. I've still got some as you can see,' I answered, no longer allowing our eyes to meet.

My friend must have seen the disappointment on the woman's face, for he said: 'Wait, let me buy it for you, Mtu,' and he paid for it, wiping the treacherous stain from my soul in time for me to see the grateful glint in the woman's eyes.

As soon as she left the sale became our topic.

'You pulled me out of the mire there, my friend. If my funds were not limited I would not have hesitated to buy. I know what it means to buy from her rather than from the Railways.'

My friend nodded in agreement.

The fortyish man from the Germiston compound joined in: 'She needs that sale. It's not as if she was trying to make herself rich. You can see she's a family woman.'

'Ya. Her children must eat and go to school,' I added.

'Of course! Some children are at boarding schools and universities because of such efforts,' the man from Germiston concurred.

'Wonder how much they sell per trip,' I mused aloud.

My friend speculated: 'Not much, I should say. Hence the high price.'

'True,' I agreed. 'You can imagine the cost in time and fare for one who has to travel all the way from Johannesburg to say, Bloemfontein and not make a single sale.'

'But they must be making enough to get by, otherwise the exertion would not be worthwhile.'

Such stratagems to keep famine at bay are ingrained in the very lives of black people. Let me not limit this to blacks, but extend it to embrace all the poor of the world.

The third class coach surrounded me with all the sensual impressions of close-packed humanity. How apt the 'third class' connotation! I wonder if it is only coincidental with the social stratification into the Upper (rich), the Middle (fairly comfortable) and the Lower (simply, the deprived) classes. I wonder because we, of the third denomination, always find ourselves in crowded conditions. You need only look at the locations — dog kennel cities — buses and trains of poor people in order to grasp my perspective. We are always lost in our crowds, our individual human value nullified. Lately the rich do not even bother to count us, to give us, at least, digital value. When they detect increases in our mass, they simply stir us into turmoil, whereby we reduce our own mass or give them excuses for massacres. Just you look at the wars all over the world, fought by the poor, set ablaze by the opulent, in many instances remunerative only to the latter and costly in dear life to the former. *Sies!* These lucrative wars. Anyway, it is not for me to prescribe what is the right manner in which humanity should conduct itself; as if human justice is not instinctively known to every sane person though it happens to be buried under heaps of selfishness and hatred in others, the trouble-makers.

Our young companion was blowing a thoughtful tune on his mouth organ. We all sank into a contemplative trance for a while.

Kroonstad at late sunset and, two to three hours afterwards, Bloemfontein. At this station the itinerant liquor-sellers left our train in a hurry that brought from my friend the remark: 'They know the train schedules better than the timetable planners themselves.'

When the train pulled out we settled back in our compartment. I read *Africa My Beginning* aloud to my friend and felt that I was going to 'sleep courage' that night. There was courage in other passengers too, for as we lay on our chosen bunks we heard singing in the corridor. Two or three sisters led a traditional lyric of joy, which became movingly voluminous as brothers picked up the tune. I wished that I had had a tape recorder or that I could write music. I wrote the song on the tablet of my soul.

We were boring through the cold night of the land that had been left barren of populace and ready for occupation by the first tribe to blunder upon it, long ago. Left barren by the Mantatee Hordes and the Nomads of Wrath.

I cannot look back at the rattling train nosing southwards around the hillocks of the northern banks of the Orange River, known to our forefathers as Igqili, without the simultaneous impression of a burning arrow searing backward through history. Every hillock, etched against a clear but moonless sky in which millions of stars formed part of the milky way, was to me like an historical cairn, which had stood there to mark the beginning of time, witnessing every form of life that ever passed over, below and around it; every event . . .

Three Days in the Land of a Dying Illusion

The Mantatee Horde

Fifty thousand people uprooted by imfecane,
led by that formidable chieftainess Mantatisi,
rolling aimlessly in a circle of destruction and pillage across the plains.
Tracks marked by human and animal skeletons;
cattle penned inside a constantly moving, circular human wall;
council held on the move: to destroy is to survive.

Clouds of dust and doubt during the day,
glowing campfires dotting the still hillsides at night.
Whither tomorrow?
Whither, to sow fear and death?

When the first rays of the sun pour over the eastern margin,
they shall move;
theirs is a policy of motion aimless and doubtful.
They believe in the swift, rash decision for survival.
Why?
Regina belli, Mantatisi believes so,
so they move like a juggernaut, mixed and stirred black clans.
They kill and they die.
Regina belli is dead,
Sikonyela now leads the Horde.
Later there is an implosion;
the Horde crumbles under its own weight,
its own strain.
How much like a laager!

The Nomads of Wrath

Shaka's all-consuming empire was spreading, a wildfire over dry

grasslands.

Matiwane,
hitherto content with vassalage to Shaka's mentor, Dingiswayo of the

Mtetwa,

knew what that meant for him.
When Shaka's superior warriors reached his parts,
he would provide meat for the hyenas and the birds of the sky.

'I will take my people far away,
out of the reach of the spear.
I will swallow other clans in turn.
So that by the time the armies of conquest reach me,
they will meet with conquest!'

Council was convened;
the warriors were to sharpen their spears,
the kraals to be cleared and burnt to ashes,
the women, the children and the livestock to follow the warriors' path,
in blood discernible.

The chieftain's word was the order of life.
From the time it was spoken the warriors moved in swift arcs of
                                        devastation,
soaking up the small clans strewn in their path like a giant sponge.
Resistance met with annihilation.
The whisper of the Nomads of Wrath sent ripples of fear across the
                                        plains;
the ripples became waves of panic unleashed
as fury upon the next unsuspecting neighbour.

The face of the earth was marred with smouldering, burnt-down kraals,
where clans on terror-inspired rampages had passed on paths of
                                        destruction.
Small numbers broke off and lost human compunction,
Became man-eaters,
Hunted humans in order to survive.

It was impossible for the Nomads to dislodge Moshoeshoe from Thaba
                                        Bosiu,
the fortress of the rock avalanche.

The vast lands south of Igqili promised peaceful settlement.
There, to the banks of Umtata Matiwane led the Nomads,
With dissipated Wrath.
There, a Major Dundas galloped upon them,
and sent to Somerset for reinforcements.
Shaka's empire would not be allowed to infringe on colonized land.
There was no time to disclose that

this was Matiwane and The Nomads.
Clouds of musket smoke marked the end of the Nomads' road.

Matiwane,
chieftain without a clan, took off northwards,
towards Thaba Bosiu.
'I shall leave only my sickly wife and her offspring at your mercy,'
defeated chieftain said to chieftain at the height of his rule.
'The land of my ancestors beckons to me.
Dead is the conqueror that started my flight from it.
Perhaps, at last, I shall find peace among the bones of my fathers.'
Peace,
everlasting peace, Matiwane found.
In blindness he went to his fathers
In painful suffocation he went.
Dingane ordered that his eyes be gouged out;
his nostrils be staved like a wizard's.

All these remembrances of an uncertain past flooded my mind like kaleidoscopic dreams re-enacted on the hills, the natural monuments stooping out there in the grey darkness. Many other eras had passed over them since time immemorial and they had just stood there, as immovable and unperturbed as when our train tore across them, now silently testifying to an epoch of oppression.

One of my friends began to snore. The rattle of the train, the singing of my brothers and sisters in the corridor and the discomfort of the people's class coach gradually and unnoticeably faded from my consciousness, leaving me to the mercy of a fitful sleep.

I was the first to be woken by the morning twilight. We were at Burghersdorp. The name took my mind back by about three hundred years: to those people history called the burghers, colonialists who came to South Africa during the era of the first white settlement. They would stand on an elevated spot on a piece of fertile land and let their eyes roam the horizons, all the while declaring everything in sight theirs — the land, the people and animals within the radius of their sight.

Please pardon the interpositions, dear reader. I find it hard to look at a country without its historical background looming over it. Maybe this is because of my belief that what is today is determined to a great extent by what happened in the past.

The arrival of our train in that cold, small town was an event which had caused loss of sleep to a number of young people who had risen early in order to honour its passing. Many of them studied our faces as if they had expected to recognise long-lost and returned kinsmen. When they realised that we were only some of those countless faces they saw once, at the station, and never again, they put on masks of disappointment. Their faces, however, told me that the following day or later, when other trains went past the station, they would be there, determinedly waiting for people to arrive from other parts of the country to add some change, no matter how insignificant, to the Burghersdorp scene. I added my urban origin, though nothing to put much store by, to my short list of blessings. I also found an explanation as to why the human drift is more towards the cities than in the opposite direction; why men prefer being brutalized by urban hostel existence to spending their lives in the countryside. The latter might be a healthier environment according to scientific argument, but my heart will never be par ted from my polluted, rat-race city background. The country was too dull and therefore mentally unhealthy. How could one develop a keen and creative imagination where the cow set the pace and the silence and loneliness of uninhabited spaces buzzed in one's ears?

We started moving and the faces of the country people sagged even more.

After Sterkstroom, which was practically the same as Burghersdorp, we reached Queenstown, bored nearly to death by women hawking: 'Dresses and *voorskots* for your loved ones at only five rands, brothers.' I was going to switch to a bus for the last leg of my journey, and I cheerfully welcomed the change as it meant that I had arrived at the threshold of country into which I had never ventured before. And now, perhaps, I would personally find out why the system and its cronies — black and white — were so eager to have me 'volunteer' as a citizen of a land so many mountains and valleys away from my birthplace.

I alighted from the train and bade my friend farewell from the platform.

You would never have said it was the same *amagoduka*. So meek and docile to the point where it caused one to despair, on the Reef! Fearing their baases like death. Perhaps a whiff of home atmosphere just beyond the horizons had something to do with the explosive excitement.

One in an overall was describing in detail to another just what he would do to him if he ever tried to get into the queue in front of him: 'I will remove my axe from my baggage, chop your thick neck and, while you're jumping around like a decapitated chicken, finish you off with a stick to teach you some good manners!'

The other dared him to try. From the look of their magnificent physiques, I decided that the duel would not be easy for either. Poor brothers, fighting among themselves, little aware that the congestion had occurred because we of the third denomination were fenced into a quarter of the platform area, too small for our great numbers, to buy our bus and train tickets as well as weigh our baggage. I'm telling you, the queue to the bus ticket office was like a rugby scrum consisting of more than a dozen teams. The bus would leave long before I reached the window. A little imagination, involving the men who were weighing the luggage in a slightly corrupt scheme, got me a ticket in no time. The Info Department would have given me a top post, then and there.

An hour later the bus rumbled out of the station, filled to capacity with us people of the third denomination. My sympathies went to those who had come in last and had to stand all the way to wherever they were going. Nevertheless none of them showed any dissatisfaction with their lot. I reckoned that they were only too used to discomfort.

Out on the tarmac road which had told me before we'd gone far that it just rolled and rolled, on and on for eternal distances, conversation started rising to a volume that swallowed the thunder of our machine, subduing it to a monotonous hum.

I shared the back seat of the bus with five others, one of them about twenty years old but living up surprisingly well to the men's discussions. I concluded that the labour camps had doubled the rate of his maturing.

'*Tixo!*' exclaimed the man furthest from me, in the other corner of the back seat, next to the manly youth. '*Tixo!*' he repeated. 'I'm going to see my wife, the girl for whom I sacrificed *izinkomo zikabawo.*'

'I bet she has forgotten that you gave up your father's cattle for her and is still making you pay for her being at your home,' the man-child responded.

'What you mean by that, *kwedini?*' asked his mate.

'She's going to demand money as soon as she gets the chance to be alone with you. At least she's expecting it — *anditsho?*'

'*Tyhini! Unyanisile kwedini.* The truth in your words cannot be denied. And to think that I had to leave her to seek work *eRawutini* as soon as we got married. To work for her! Although I scarcely enjoy her companionship.'

Another, wearing a heavy coat in spite of the heat, interjected from the seat in front of us: 'Hayi, *madoda*. Don't say that about the good wives. They keep the families together while we are away for months on end, even for years. Otherwise what would we return to find where we were born?' His voice reached a crescendo: 'Ruins! *Anditsho?*'

This caught the imagination of a few others within earshot.

'Here's a man who knows the facts of life, the facts of existence,' assented one who had been concentrating on a carton of sorghum two seats in front. *'Bamba ndoda, sela wehlise unxano* while I elucidate the meaning of your words. I can see they don't understand,' he continued, stretching his arm over heads to hand the carton to the man whose opinion he appreciated.

The other one received it with both hands, removed his hat and held it in his left hand before he took a sip. He smacked his lips and said, gratefully: *'Awu, camagu!* As if you knew how parched my throat was.'

While he took slow gulps from the carton, the owner went on: *'Umfazi yintsika yekhaya.'* (The woman is the pillar of the home.) *'Ikhaya yintsika yesizwe.'* (The home is the pillar of the tribe or nation — tribe in this instance.) 'So the woman maintains the tribe alive. She bears the children and brings them up while you drink *utshwala* and sleep with concubines *aseRawutini ezinkomponi*; sometimes forgetting or simply omitting to send her the money with which to buy even a sack of mealies. But when you return you find her there, the children alive and growing . . . '

'Mh, mh-h. *Ewe. Yinyaniso leyo,'* some of the listeners agreed. A young lady showed a bright smile. I felt that if it were not a men's discussion she would contribute.

'Kodwa, uthini ngale ndawo yamakrexe, mkhuluwa? They also have lovers. Don't they? Would you defend them with the same breath with which you are accusing us of having concubines?' asked the man-youth with an indomitable expression on his face.

The man who had been addressing us from a standing position looked down thoughtfully at the young man and said: 'Say, *kwedini*. Do you already have a wife?'

'No,*mkhuluwa. Asoze ndithathe futhi.'* (And I never will be betrothed). 'Marry a woman and leave her to the mercy of *amahlalela* (the loafers)! Never!'

'Whether what you're saying about marrying is a childish dream or not, you must know one thing and that is: *Ikrexe elingaziwayo alikho!'* (An unknown adulterer is as good as non-existent). 'The important thing is that you find your home still existing because of your wife. Your mother in your case. She does not ask you anything about your city concubines. She knows they are there — men can't exist without women — but she never asks. The little maintenance you bring back to her after being fleeced by concubines she accepts without question. Don't she?'

'She should, of course. Why not? If she doesn't I ask her about all the money that I've been sending her. I want it back!' The one who had sparked off the discussion spoke with typical chauvinist arrogance, as 'libbers' would see it.

The woman who had smiled at their conversation earlier could not suppress her views in respect of manhood anymore. Her retort corresponded with my own silent viewpoint: *'Uxolo, buti,'* (excuse me, brother) 'but what have your children been eating all the time? You think she's been tightfisted with your money when your children wanted food from her? *Ninjalo nina madoda. Ibe nifana nonke kunjalo nje!'* (You're all like that, you men. Moreover you're all the same!) 'You enjoy being referred to as family heads. Father, father, all the time, but you forget the very tummies of the reasons for your father-hood status.'

'Suka, woman!' returned one who seemed to care little about wo-men's views. 'You would never be able to start and support families without *amadoda*. What makes you think that you're the more respon-sible parties?'

'Of course we are! *Lo tata,'* (this family man) 'has just been telling you that we are the pillars of the tribes and you did not dispute it.'

'Madoda, this woman! Whatever made you jump into a men's dis-cussion? Because now I'm going to show you just how inconsiderate you black women are: Xhosa, Zulu, Sotho, all those that I've come across are nothing but selfish creatures.'

'The same as you black men who are so eager to start families which you end up failing to support, or grousing about.'

'Say, *mfazi.* Do you know that *singamakhoboka nje,* it is partly be-cause of your self-centredness?'

'How, *buti,* how are you slaves? *Cacisa.'*

'In this way:' (he cleared his throat to enable his voice to come out smoothly) 'you forget that it is no longer like when we were born — when there was maize aplenty and cows with bloated udders to milk, and all our fathers had to do was plough the fields and keep their stock in good shape. Today those luxuries are all gone and because you insist on families, children all the time, we, the reluctant fathers, like this boy here, have to travel across hills and mountains to sell our labour cheaply *esiLungwini*. Don't you see that we would rather be slaves and stay like animals in those compounds than watch you and your children starving? You use your birthgiving nature to make us slave for you, and when we give you the little that we sweat blood for, still you're not satisfied. You call us failures as if *ilizwe* was governed by us and not the white man.'

In other words we're being blackmailed into slavery by the children they give us. Interesting. True to a certain extent, when one thinks of most of our sisters who regard matrimony as their sole ambition and salvation. Leave everything, education, government and work to the men. Fold your arms and watch with hawks' eyes for the one that'll flounder into the pit of the rapture of your companionship, thus limiting the scope of his thinking to work alone, slaving in order to feed, clothe and house an ever-growing family, without any chance to pursue the very natural virtues of justice, prudence, temperance and fortitude. Fock! I'm also not getting married until I come across a sister who does not conform to that base expectation!

'*Kodwa ke buti,* both we and the children are yours. You can say "your children" to your wife but you are equally answerable for them. Even you would not be here damning womanhood were it not for the man-wife arrangement of life. It is only a matter of accepting one's end of the responsibility without any grumbles, in order to make life bearable under present conditions. Under the present conditions of men's making! *Andithi?*'

'Eh! Er . . . what do you mean "of men's making"? Did men create the world?'

'We don't know who created it, for sure. But the present state of the world is definitely of your making,' the lady answered vociferously, sweeping her arm in a semi-circle which showed that she meant all of us wearing trousers in that bus.

'*He-e, madoda!* This woman. In the first place why did you enter a men's conversation?' said the man and turned his eyes towards us for support. But none was forthcoming.

The lady retaliated: 'Your father could ask your mother such a question. So could my father, my mother. But I am a woman *wesimanje-manje* (of this time). You can't ask *me* such a question.'

Everybody burst out laughing at that. The man looked like a cornered rabbit.

'*Ndiyabon'uba awanelanga, mnakwethu.*' (I can see that you're not satisfied, my brother). 'Let me ask you a few questions that may throw light on what I was saying . . . '

Indomitable Xhosa woman! Small wonder my friend 'Terror', Xhosa by birth, vows always never to marry a woman of the same extraction as his. 'They always have an argument to put up against men. Our mothers were the last disciplined lot of Xhosa women. My sisters — boy!' — and he ends up by wincing.

My answer to him is always that they are all like that from East to West and North to South of this globe, irrespective of ancestry, and that we need to mobilize in time to defend our divine right to make war and reduce the world to rubble.

As if she had been with me before the bus trip, she was saying: 'You allege that you are *ningamakhoboka* (slaves) because of us. Now answer this: is your state of subjugation not a result of your, er, how shall I put it — I'm sorry to say, your cowardice? Or your inability to foresee disaster? Of your own making? Where were the men when the land and cattle were lost? Something closer to our present reality: is it not your own so-called chiefs, men mind you, who have destroyed our very last subsistence by accepting *lo Zimele-geqe wenu* (this independence of yours) which removed even the faintest hope of developing the land?'

What she actually wanted to ask was, in simple terms: why did men allow other men to impose premature, tribal *uhuru* upon them? Or why did they accept 'self rule' without any economic structure to start with? What did they expect to live from? Where did they expect to work except where they had been working all the time, that is, in white monopolized industry?

Which reminded me where I was bound. I nudged the man next to me and asked: 'Sorry to divide your attention. Say, how far are we from the Transkei? When are we going to reach Umtata?'

He pulled his left sleeve up to look at his watch. 'We're almost in Transkei now. Qamata will be our first stop. Umtata is still far, far away. You'll reach it by sunset. I'm getting off halfway at *eNgcobo.*'

That was not good news to me at all. Sitting crammed up in a violently vibrating vehicle from twelve to five or six in the evening was not my idea of a pleasant journey, despite the interesting conversation of the people whose *uhuru* I so ardently wished to witness.

'*Hayi, madoda. Iyathetha le ntokazi! Imibuzo yayo iyahlaba.*' (This maiden can surely speak. Her questions are also thorny.) This was all the men could say in reply — a concession, perhaps, that they had made love whilst Rome was burning. I also interpreted their response as reflecting a subconscious fear in the men to speak against their chiefs. For the lady had thrown the gauntlet before the men: to take it up they would have to criticize the rule under which they lived.

How right I was with my latter interpretation, as I would soon discover! However let me not douse your interest. We shall go on in the bus to Umtata before I give my exposition. A signboard said 'Qamata' and indicated that we turn right, which we did and then took a loop to the left. I felt nervous at that stage, not knowing whether we would encounter a travel documents checkpoint.

I had nothing on me of that kind. When I had phoned the Plural Affairs Commissioner to ask him what I needed to visit the Transkei a few days before my departure, he had referred me in honeyed tones to the relevant offices next to Faraday station.

I was not that surprised by the Commissioner's amiableness when I reached the place. It was full of plurals, and as a black I stopped myself just short of turning at the door and forgetting my planned visit to Daliwonga's domain — Daliwonga! What a name! He who creates respect. He should visit the labour camps to see if he has acquired any respect at all for 'his' people. What kept me going forward was that the people I was going to in the Transkei were already informed of my coming and were waiting.

After some elbowing and shouldering I had found myself at Counter Two, face to face with a plural employed by the Plural Administration Board for our purpose.

'Yes, what can I do for you?' His tie had reminded me of a leashed dog. I am not swearing at him. I don't know why, but that's always the thought that enters my mind at the sight of a tie — conventional bureaucratic leash.

'What must I do to visit the Transkei?'

'What? Go there,' he had replied impatiently.

My knuckles had itched for impact. 'I want to know your red tape. Do I need some kind of travel document?'

'You know that. How can you expect to cross from one sovereign state to another without one?'

'Because I don't think Transkei is a separate state from South Africa.'

'Heh, heh,' he had chuckled at my ignorance of the present world. 'You don't know that Transkei is independent?'

'Independent from what, of what?'

'Of South Africa,' and his eyes had completed the sentence with 'bloody fool!'

'That's news to me,' I said as sincerely as I could.

'You must have been in jail. Were you not in prison when Transkei got independence? Or maybe you were mad, at Sterkfontein.'

'Maybe. If that's what you want — your fellow blacks to be in prison. What's the red tape?'

'Give me your pass.'

Fortunately, for once I had it for identification purposes. What with everybody looking for 'terrorists' under every stone. I gave it to him and he paged through it before throwing it back at me.

'You're Xhosa, neh?'

I nodded.

'Then go and apply for Transkei citizenship at Counter Six. Next!'

I could not suppress my indignation anymore. 'When you look at me you imagine I could make an ideal Transkei citizen? When you arrive home this evening you tell your mother to apply for it so that she can go and learn witchcraft if she is not a professional already.' I turned and stomped for the door without waiting for his reaction.

So there I was, rolling into Qamata with my third denomination comrades. The discussion petered out to a noticeable hush as everybody was diverted from the articulate lady by the crossing of an invisible Iron Curtain.

The soil was red, ironically reminding me of Avalon and Doornkop cemeteries back home, the land parched and scarred with erosion. In the first fields that we passed the maize had grown hardly a metre high. The weeds, blackjack outstanding, outgrew it. A woman in dusty traditional attire with a baby strapped to her back and two boys in inherited clothes following her, was searching for stems that might have been overlooked at harvest time.

We passed two cows shaving the roadside of sun-scorched grass.

'*Kakade*, what's the use of buying cattle that end up short of grass?' remarked one of my travelling companions.

'*Imfuyo* (stock) is no longer an investment these days,' added another.

I had thought the animals looked acceptable. Perhaps that was due to my inability to judge good beef. However you looked at it, some of the animals that we saw were scrawny and others well-nourished. Probably the latter belonged to people who could afford to buy hay.

The mountains rose high, solid, silent and motionless until they melted into blue-grey and hazy horizons, the only sight that appealed magnificently to my eyes. Below them there were picturesque villages of perfectly circular, thatched rondavels whitewashed for about a foot just below the edges of the thatch and around the windows and doors. This architecture dotted the elevated parts of the landscape on both sides of the road for endless acres.

'*Awu,*' someone ventured, '*esikaDaliwonga! Ilizwe lembalela.*' (A land of drought). 'That is why he has left it to pick out the richest parts of the land for himself elsewhere; to bulldoze the people out of land that they inherited from their fathers.'

'*Ewe. Nathi uyokusixina ngaphaya.*' (Yes. He also crowds us into the parts that remain ours.)

I was confounded by those words because they came from simple people. Things being taken for granted as they generally are, who could have expected them to nurture any misgivings concerning their share of that wilderness? I say wilderness because that was the most suitable description of what was unfolding before my eyes compared with the white-owned Free State country I had seen the previous day. Proof of its being wasteland lay in the fact that they had surrendered to the inhuman migratory way of life rather than stay and try to eke out a living in their 'homeland'. It showed there was just no way to suck blood out of a stone. The illusion of freehold in a free land had long faded in the imagination of my cheated people. Independence, *uhuru*, had come, avowedly to break the chains of blackness and drive away poverty. Instead it had brought an ominous fog of helplessness that hung over a land marred with eroded ravines which gave one a clear picture of what the earth might look like after an earthquake. From the silvery trickles that traced erratic courses on the sandy beds of some of the shallow dongas, I concluded that they had been rivulets many aeons ago.

The maize refused to grow higher than a foot without water and scientific agricultural methods. It would cost decades in time and billions of rands in the form of irrigation, fertilizer and technology before one would see any advance beyond cross-plantation on the slopes, which was the only scientific land treatment about which I could write home. Where would the billions come from? Obviously from 'white South Africa' with her own sick economy.

If anybody out there had figured that he could temporarily depend on South Africa by sending people there as slaves, hoping that they would earn enough to be self-sufficient after some time, he had dreamt up a nightmare. Slaves don't earn anything; they live from hand to mouth. His country would forever remain both a labour reservoir and a vacuum to suck discarded human labour units out of the South African economy.

We passed a village with a dusty filling station or garage that might have been constructed from the home-made mudbricks of the rondavels. Even if I had a car and happened to have a breakdown near that place, I would never risk taking it there.

Another Railways bus was roaring towards us, then slowing as we slowed. Finally both buses stopped, side by side. Without any explanation the driver left us and went to have a chat with his counterpart. Some of us took the opportunity to go and relieve ourselves at the roadside while the two sets of passengers upbraided one another.

'Why did you come back at all, you fools? Don't you know that *umbona awukho?*' (There is no maize.) 'Didn't your wives write you about it?'

'*Unxilile, sidenge!*' (You're drunk, stupid!) 'Where are you going? *Ngoba uya kubanjwa phaya eRawutini.*' (Because you're going to be arrested on the Reef.)

'It's you that's drunk. Coming all the way from eRawutini to shepherd *umfazi* for a month and then leave her for a whole year or more. Who do you think watches over her while you're gone?'

'*He-e-e! Uhamba wedwa?* Why didn't you take yours along? Don't you know that there are no women for country men where you're going?'

'*Uyaxoka, kwedini!*' (You're lying, sonny boy!) 'There's no place without prostitutes.'

'Your children are going to eat water, then. If that's your aim iRawuti is going to strip you down to your underpants.'

The man-child suddenly blurted out: 'You're going to resort to sodomy in those compounds . . . '

'*Hayi kaloku kwedini.* There are women on this bus,' chided one of us.

The drivers had finished chatting and in another moment we were eating up the tarmac. I had lost interest in the bus talk and was storing mental imprints of the landscape and the few animals and people that I saw.

Many times I fell in love with most beautiful, traditionally dressed maidens and women. An inexplicable nostalgia for the unknown past swept through my whole being. Maybe it was inspired by those examples of African femininity untainted by western standards. I saw them, and I believe they saw themselves, as Africa had seen them centuries ago. I loved them so, and wondered how compatible I would be in matrimony with any of them. Perhaps it was that thought which brought the flood of nostalgia. I was not so sure of my virility in relation to them, and this made me feel that I had lost something invaluable in exchange for my westernization and therefore could not partake of those things which remained purely African in my existence. You can say what you like, but there is nothing more beautiful than a woman, an African woman, for I have been taught to see only her as a woman and not the other shades; there is nothing like an African woman dressed in the tradition of the Continent. The dignity that goes with it! The virility that it stirs in the soul of a son of the Continent who has been robbed of his own evaluation of beauty by the superimposition of foreign criteria of what is beautiful! Africa will survive in spite of her scarred visage!

We were tearing through land that abounded with pine plantations that lent some green to the otherwise desolate countryside. I saw more of my beloved womenfolk, skilfully balancing loads of firewood on their heads, homeward bound: there is an adage among the Xhosa that a woman's merit is judged by the amount of wood that she keeps *egoqweni lakhe* (in her wood store). The skill was apparent from the way they carried their long loads with the point of contact on their heads slightly forward, so that the wood hung behind them at an angle which gave an onward thrust to their movement.

Some kind of avenue with plantations on both sides. Hey! I once saw a box of matches with a Transkei trademark. The sticks must have come from the pines I saw. At least they could produce matches. But where could they export them to? There is only one 'product' that they can export, and that is illicit in most parts of the world. Moreover, say it were a legal product — which country would enter into dealings with a 'state' regarded as non-existent?

Arrival *e*Ngcobo. I had travelled a whole century backward in the South African Railways' time machine. Animal transport appeared to be still the standard. Men bounced proudly on ponies to and from the dusty streets of the nineteenth century town. We turned into one of these, our innards jarred by its uneven surface. People of all the semblances one might expect to find in such a backward town lined both its sides. My beloved turbaned women, men in old misfitting western clothes, girls in school uniform, a few trying to look fashionably modern — like the young woman whose transparent cheesecloth shirt drew damnation from my travelling companions. Behind them, modern houses alternating with old Dutch-styled houses, a large white Mercedes Benz outside one of them.

After a hundred metres we turned left, past a bus terminus with people crowded next to a goods shed into a yard with old battered buses: there we made a U-turn and came out facing the direction from which we had come.

The engine's noise had hardly died before we were inundated by women carrying open cake tins containing oranges, apples, pears and fried fish, screaming their wares at the tops of their voices. Others had cans of warm 'cool drink' and beer. The can of beer, a small one this time, cost eighty cents!

All these vendors were desperate for a sale. Very near to tears, at least that was what I thought, they shoved their cake tins into passengers' faces, both scolded and implored them to buy.

One heard: 'Please *khanithengeni!*' (Buy!)

And: '*Thengani maan, nivela eRawutini!*' (Buy maan, you come from the Reef!) as if each of us was a miner who dug his own gold, sold it and returned home with seam-bursting suitcases of money.

An apple was bought here and there, possibly out of sympathy.

The black conductor wore a home-knitted woollen jersey which had long lost its elasticity, leaving the garment to gravity, so that it looked like a dirty woollen mini-skirt worn over shining, knob-kneed grey flannels and a pair of parched, sharp-pointed once-black shoes, more trodden on than trodden in. This guy had to wrestle each sales lady out of the bus. And each time he pushed one outside with a vehement, '*Niyasilibazisa maan!*' (You're delaying us!) another one opened the door and got inside. In the end he stood just outside the door with his hands on his hips, his face a mirror of surrender and frustration with the head tilted to one side, saying: '*Heyi, heyi bafazi.* Can't you hear when someone is telling you nicely to leave the bus?'

A few men, eager to be on the way again, came to his rescue: 'Either leave the bus or come along for the ride to *eMtata.*

When everything was settled we left, and the people remaining behind seemed to want to break down and cry about it. Maybe they really did have something to be sore about. I felt a tinge of it too, when I thought that I would never see them again. Once was enough and they would virtually die out of my life, out of my memory. And who can face that death with apathy?

A small bank. The cake tin pedlars would never set their bare dusty feet in there. Only the shylock owning the wholesale shop with sugar and mealie meal sacks and tea cartons stacked outside, across the street, had the right to. The teller, there could not possibly be more than one, must have been spending days like eternities of boredom in there.

A modern three-storey school building for the passing stranger's eye. I could not imagine it being built in the middle of that hinterland. I therefore conjured up a suitable, though out of the way, explanation for its presence — it had simply been hoisted with helicopters and placed on the slope of the knoll like a toy house.

Ngcobo disappeared from sight. The bus now seemed to stop every five hundred metres or so to let someone off. Only school children joined us. No adults appeared interested in going to their capital. An indication that there was perhaps nothing for them there; only for the Transkei elite, whom I was so eager to meet after having travelled the whole distance with my third denomination comrades without meeting any sign of affluence except maybe the modern houses and the big Mercedes. I wanted to measure the material gap between the upper and the lower classes of an illusory independent state. Why, you may ask — and straightaway be told: I needed to know just how tight the screws are on us, so as to estimate the exact amount of exertion we need to snap them, if everybody ever becomes aware that we have to in order to survive as human beings and not as sub-human slaves.

I observed that none of the returned migrants had people waiting to welcome them at the bus stops. Their arrival was obviously unknown to or simply ignored by their folks. So many had gone and come back, and so many had gone and never been heard of again, that no one seemed to expect them anymore.

Young men like identical multiplets, all wearing starched new overalls, yellow golf caps, yellow duster bandanas around their collars, new gumboots, all holding bead-decorated sjamboks like sceptres in their hands, off-loaded shining new tin trunks from the bus carriage and made a regal advent into their district. They beckoned to a group of women walking along the road to come and carry the trunks for them. They had been to 'dig gold' in the city and could afford to imitate their employers when they arrived back home. The women tore their ankle-length skirts to get to them first.

The bus was by then half-empty. Only the man-child remained in the last seat with me.

'How far are we from Umtata?' I asked, for something to say.

'It will not take you more than fifteen minutes.'

'You also going there?'

'No. I get off just before.' All the time his attention was divided between me and the surroundings that the bus was invading, which seemed to have taken him by surprise. His were the eyes of one who had come home after a long time to find things not exactly as he had left them.

He expressed his apprehension in a pained voice: *'Kutheni ingathi kubi nje apha?'* (Why does it appear to be bad here?)

'You think so?' I asked, trying to draw an explanation out of him.

'Ewe. The world looks forsaken!'

I still did not comprehend his meaning. To me, the nearer we got to Umtata, the better the face of the earth appeared to become. The maize was higher in the fields, the mountain slopes greener, and larger herds of well-fed cattle speckled the landscape. Even rain clouds hovered in the sky. But then how could I discern degeneration when I had never been there before?

At least a friend was waiting for him at the bus stop. He had not been completely forgotten, like the others, and I hoped that that would cheer him up a bit.

Umtata. The broadening of the road and the number of vehicles on it told me that we were very near. It began to drizzle and faraway, to the left, I saw a wide muddy river which I guessed to be the Umtata River.

My mind was thrust back into the dubious past. Only one thing was I certain of: Nongqause had been a daugher of those parts. It was in the Transkei that her tragedy had occurred. It might not have been on the Umtata River that she had seen the vision. Maybe another river. But the vision came back to my mind in clear detail as we hurtled towards Umtata, for seemingly it is repeating itself during this, my own lifetime. In order to understand my interpretation of past and present events in relation to each other, I think it is necessary to review the tale I heard from my instructional voices.

The age was tender, the soul timid and unfortified. The voice as harsh and as uncompromising as the biting wet switch. The palms of our hands as receptive to the fire of the switch for wrong answers as our minds to doubtful information for the sake of the 'enlightenment' of the South African black man.

The voice could not be wrong. It was the instructor's and what's more he was reading from a book, and never a book was wrong:

Nearly a hundred years ago, a little more than that. You must remember that. In eighteen fifty-six . . .

I thought that my father should be about that age.

. . . a maiden of sixteen years . . .

As old as the girl next door, I thought.

. . . the daughter of a councillor or his niece. It doesn't matter which . . .

My uncle had been home the weekend before from the mines and I had become an object of derision to my friends for his drunken singing, although my mother and my father did not seem to mind.

. . . This father or uncle of hers was councillor to a paramount chief called Sarili . . .

The instructor made us repeat the names of the characters of his story several times.

. . . The daughter or the niece was Nongqause, her uncle or father, Mhlakaza and the paramount chief, Sarili . . .

My father and his friends were always arguing about who the rightful leaders of the African people were, as if they were confused about the historical issue. They had only to ask my instructor if they wanted to make sure.

. . . This girl went to fetch water from the river. When she returned from the river she told her people that she had seen a vision . . .

He went on and on about a tale which I found hard to believe. For that reason I tried to construct my own version of the story: the conquest, the dispossession and the vision.

When the maiden discovered that the water was finished in the house, she decided to go and draw some from the river. Usually they went to the river at daybreak and towards sunset. But it was a long time till sunset and people in the kraal would want to use water. The basic household chores of a maiden were to keep the home supplied with water and wood.

Otherwise why would she have gone to the river alone, and missed a talkative outing with the other girls? The river was about five hundred metres below the village and it would not have bothered her in any way to carry two or three gourds. However she had chosen to take only one, because if she fetched all the water at that time she would miss the late afternoon outing with the other girls.

The sun was hot. It had been hot for days and the unworked land appeared to suffer from it. She suffered from the heat too and, both to protect her skin and to enhance her beauty, her face was smeared with *ingxwala*, the white stone, the rest of her with *imbola*, the red ochre. A piece of tanned skin wrapped her pelvic girdle, otherwise she was naked except for the colourful bead jewellery around her neck and wrists, above her elbows and ankles, below her knees.

She went out with her gourd easily balanced on her head, her arms dangling at her sides. The young men of the clan sang praises to her body that was undergoing a fast transition from girlhood to ripe maidenhood and, but for the state of the land, it would not have been long before one of them came forward to ask for her hand in marriage: that is, before one of them drove her away to his father's kraal, as was the usual practice.

Coming to the river, she removed the big clay gourd from her head and set it down under the tree where they usually sat and talked about the warriors of their hearts' choices. As maidens, nothing captured their imagination more than their marriage prospects.

There was a rustle in the reeds across the brook, which she ignored. It was the age-old *xam*, the water lizard which guarded *isiziba*, the silent pool, part of the river from which she had suckled life since she was a slip of a girl. As long as *xam's* path to the water was not hindered, she would not attack. Trouble started only when *xam* wanted her way to *esizibeni*. Then the lash of her tail was like that of a thong whip.

She went as near as she could to the water and scooped three potholes in the moist sand.

'While I am waiting for the water to filter through,' she thought, 'I will go and scrub my feet. And grind a little *imbola*, *nomemezi*.' (The latter: skin-lightening tree bark.)

The stone and bark were kept in a bead-decorated bag of soft skin that her mother had stopped using for tobacco when she made another one out of goatskin: there had been an unprecedented slaughter of livestock at that time. The corral of their kraal had only a few head of cattle left. The cows did not bring forth milk anymore.

Down the sandy bank she walked, beyond the pool to a place where she could wash off her make-up and scrub her feet without defiling the place where drinking water was drawn. Coming to the flat and smooth riverside rock upon which they ground the ochre and the bark, rubbed their feet and dried their garments, she knelt and leaned forward to distribute her weight evenly between her arms and haunches with the intention of scooping water with one hand and rinsing her face. But her reflection in the still water looked back at her with such clarity that she stopped herself from disturbing it.

She was puzzled by the face that looked back at her because it was incompatible with her age. It was the face of a woman and not a sixteen-year-old girl. There was the stricken look of a child robbed of its childhood about the eyes, and the corners of her lips drooped to reflect an angered soul: '*O mawethu!* Is this the face of a maiden that hopes to win the heart of a warrior? The girlhood is fast vanishing from my features because there is no room in the mind for youthful thoughts. The natural course of life has changed. Girls become women long before they are married. At a time when they should be rejoicing in their beauty they, together with their mothers, are counsellors who fan the flames of resistance in the hearts of their men. Many times have I answered, '*Zemk' iinkomo magwala ndini*' to a young man trying to please my heart with praises. It is true. Young men cannot be singing praises to maidens while the cattle are being driven away to the stolen land by raiders: they must substantiate their praises with *lobola.* And if the corrals are empty, so are the praises.'

She paused and lifted her eyes to the reeds where it was believed that the spirits lived in dark waters, where *amagqira* the fighters of evil vanished: 'To learn the laws of life, to heal, to gain immunity against witchcraft, the power to know the future and to bring the messages of *amathongo* unto the people. O, would I were also a custodian of custom and tradition and knew what is to be done when the land is dying with the people!'

For some time she did not say anything but surrendered herself to her thoughts and the feelings of her soul. The feelings brought tears to her eyes, which overbrimmed and made little streams down the white desert of her face, the cheeks that were caked with *ingxwala*, the white stone. This she did not notice until one of the streams had meandered to one corner of her mouth and she tasted the salt.

In the blur of her tear-soaked eyes she began to envision herself, a mere maiden, standing before the elders of the tribe, imploring them to put into effect the only practical plan that was left to save the tribe. But the vision filled her with fear, for how could she, a mere maiden, face a panel of elders and tell them what to do? The place of the woman was in the home, her duty to rear the tribe and not at all *enkun-*

dleni, at the conference of *amaphakathi,* where the future of the tribe is decided. If she had earned the respect accorded to *amagqira* for their ability to make contact with the ancestors, then she might be able to put her message across.

'But they say Mantatisi was able to gather a formidable horde,' she thought, 'and lead it on a trail of destruction across vast lands. She too was a woman. She sat in council with her generals, who surely were men, and they accepted her leadership. But it is said that she was of a belligerent nature, which is a rare characteristic among us women. Seeing that none of the strength of Mantatisi exists in me, I am left with but one alternative if the solution which I envision is to be given any thought by the elders — to say that I received the message from *amathongo* while I was alone at the river. Alone I am indeed, and it will be hard to prove that I did not see the ancestors. In my soul I feel them, in my mind I envision them and hear their voices.'

The first voice spoke from the depths of her mind: 'It is a long time since *amathongo* directed the people to fight for their natural heritage. Two decades have passed since their voice was heard by the people through Makhanda. And two decades they have waited for Nxele to return from the island of banishment to lead them once more against the usurpers of the land. The two decades shall pass into three; the three into four; the four into five and the five into eternity, and the great warrior prophet will not return for he has taken his place among *amathongo.*'

This much she knew, for he would have returned long ago if he were alive. Those who had escaped with him were already old men. Through her own voice poured out what the message of the first voice meant to her: 'O great seers of our forefathers, to whom shall the people look for direction now? Will all the unwavering faith of the tribe in the return of Makhanda be shattered by your words? The word of Makhanda was unity! The elders tell us that he said *maze sibe yimbumba yamanyama* when he left to give himself up; meaning that we must remain as close together as muscle fibres. What shall be done to keep the scattered clans together when the hope in his return is dying? Your ominous revelation has thrust like a spear into the heart of this maiden's hopeful soul!'

The pain of her realisation sent convulsions through her body. More tears flooded her face, until her cheeks were rinsed of the white stone. She could not allow herself to let the hope die completely, and when the second voice from the depths of her mind spoke, it was as if to ease the pangs in her soul: 'Do not give up all your hope, gifted maiden. There must still be one way in which he can return to guide the people.'

Hearing these words from the depths of her mind the maiden stopped crying, although the tears still gushed out of her eyes. She opened her mouth to speak with all the ardour of her soul: *'Camagu, milond' ekhaya!'* (Hail, the protectors of home!) 'Your words have set my spirit once more aglow with hope. Tell me the way the warrior prophet can be made to return, so that I can go and reinforce the people's beliefs and hopes, for the tribe is drowning in despair.'

She implored, and then she sat quietly as if the two voices of her mind were holding conference to resolve upon a way of getting Makhanda's message back to the people. After they had come to terms it was the first which spoke: 'The only possible way in which Makhanda can return is through a medium who will be his voice and representative among the people.'

At these words the sixteen-year-old lass felt the limitations of her kind and expressed them to herself: 'I am but a girl, O great ancestors. How can I speak to the people, for they would not listen to me. Such is a task befitting a warrior, a man. Or shall I quickly go and seek a warrior to come and listen to the word of the ancestors and carry it to the people?'

The second voice of her mind spoke in disagreement: 'Where are the warriors? For there are no longer any among you, young maiden. Their blood drenches the soil of the lost fatherland.'

In spite of that, the maiden clung to her belief that by virtue of her sex she did not qualify to take the message to the people except through a man's voice: 'O great ancestors, there must be at least one warrior left among the people. Speak and I shall go and find him, wherever he may be.'

But the first voice of her apparition would not accept her word: 'The vision has appeared in your mind only this once. And already it is too late. It is your obligation to take the message to the people, for your young heart bleeds most for the fatherland.'

The maiden's body was convulsed again like one of the reeds of the stream: 'But my maiden's heart is struck with fear. My status in life permits it not that I address the tribe.'

It was with assurance that the second voice spoke this time: 'Your maiden heart shall be fortified by the voice of your father *u*Mhlakaza, a man of some standing among the people and councillor to the paramount chief *u*Kreli. Your father will listen to you, the chief will listen to your father and the tribe will listen to the chief of chiefs of the clans that make up the tribe. Your word, through him, could gain the power to unite the tribe.'

The same heart that had gushed out the gall of despair was now filled with hope and courage: 'Speak, O great ancestors, and I will convey the message to my father, he to the chief and the elders, and they to the people.'

While she listened the first voice declared the message: 'Go then, and bid your father relate to you the affairs of the present world. And bid him help you find the solution to these affairs by giving an explanation to the following riddle: *The people have placed greater faith in witchcraft than in uMvelinqangi, amathongo and themselves to reverse the conquest. The first is a futile and evil practice; the second and the third constitute the cult of the tribes of the fatherland and are therefore the pillars of the tribes' faith in life, beliefs that have sustained them spiritually throughout time. But these beliefs cannot be manifest in real life by any means except through those people who adhere to them. When the rites prescribed by cult are performed accordingly, the spirit of the people becomes like a powerful whirlwind that sweeps every adversary that intrudes on the fatherland into the seas, which in turn swallow them.'*

Although the maiden could not comprehend the meaning of the words she sowed every one of them in her fertile memory for exact recital later to her father. But she desired a little more enlightenment: 'Is that all, O ancestors? No allusion to the solution?'

There was no answer forthcoming from the depths of her soul except this: 'Only the people can save the land from conquest, or else be turned into slaves of the invaders.'

'Slaves' was a word which shook the very roots of the maiden's feelings: 'But the people have never known such a state. It is beyond the extremes of my imagination to picture the tribe in subjugation.'

There was no pity in either of the voices that contested her imagination: 'They shall know it for centuries if they fail in the defence of the heritage now. Many who accepted defeat and remained in the old land to the west have begun to be slaves.'

Of the two voices the second was the one that was inclined to say the more soothing words: 'To avert the disaster, there must first be a great sacrifice. The people must sacrifice their very existence. For as long as the people believe that they can survive from the little that is left, they will not remember the lost heritage. When the livestock pens are empty and the land is parched they will long for all that was lost and they shall be forced to go over the mountains to reclaim it.'

The vision began to fade away before her mind, which reached out in one last question before the voices of *amathongo* vanished: 'When shall these events occur and what will they lead to?'

It was a faint voice and apparition, drifting away out of the scope of her mind, which answered: 'The sacrifice is taking place even as your ancestors speak to you. Let every drop of blood that flows from a warrior dying in defence of his people, as well as that which flows from the vessels of an animal from the cattle pens, be seen as a sacrifice. And when all is over the people shall rise like a whirlwind and sweep evil and the enemy into the sea.'

When the voices of her mental images of *amathongo* finally vanished, the maiden was suddenly thrown back on the reality of the gleaming stream and the glaring sun. It was as if her mind had transcended space and time. She felt a vigorous upheaval in her soul and a powerful voice emanated from her very being: 'A maiden has found a solution to the plight of the tribe. Because her heart has bled for her people the voices of *amathongo* have crept into her mind and told her what is to be done. I will go to discuss the voices with my father, the wise councillor, and implore him to convey their messages to other men of wisdom who sit in council with him.'

For the first time in ages there was excitement in her soul. Her father had been sitting for long hours near the cattle pen, lost in his thoughts and speculations, for the councillors were burdened with the heavy task of producing a solution to the problems of the tribe that was beginning to die in great numbers because of famine, caused by the concentration of many people on an undeveloped piece of land. She could not wait to see again the smile that had graced the now taut face when there was still a little hope left in the tribe. When the people were beginning to believe that the invaders had stolen enough land and stock, and that the commando raids and the burnings would abate. When it had not dawned on the tribe that there might be more invaders from the sea, who would come to squeeze the people out of their lands, burn the villages and drive away their cattle.

With these thoughts she rose and retraced her steps to where she had left the gourd, and using a small calabash ladle she filled the gourd from the small pools she had dug. The village already seemed too far for her to carry the heavy message to her father and the tribe. Were it not for the water she carried on her head she might have run home faster than an antelope.

When she arrived in the kraal she sent a small girl to take the water to the women's hut, the message of her mind searing through her soul.

The corral made of stones was above the group of huts at the base of a hillock. The maiden knew that her father would be behind it, sitting on a small stone with his head on or between his knees, his long pipe smoking incessantly, his eyes almost shut, the leathery face that had been carved into a godlike gauntness by meditation over the affairs of the tribe dead to his dying surroundings. She found him there, much as she expected. One hand held the pipe and the other formed a cushion, palm down, between his grey-bearded chin and his knee. His cowhide blanket covered only one shoulder, the arm which held the pipe exposed and reflecting the slanting rays of the sun like polished ebony. He was not aware of the intrusion on his thoughts until the maiden's shadow fell over him.

His had been a warrior's body when he fought the frontier wars in the prime of his life. It was these wars which had won him promotion to *iphakathi* to the paramount chief. It was the experience gained in the defence of the land, and in the resolution of the internal strife of a tribe in the throes of being uprooted, that had placed on him the heavy mantle of councillor. When the tribe was in distress men of his standing were expected to come up with solutions. Now the last valleys that remained to the tribe were sick, and the corrals that had been the pride of men's eyes were like rocks surrounding the sepulchres of a dead heritage. His own cattle pen confined the last five lean and perishing cows. They could not be left to wander far in search of nutritious grasses for fear they would be driven off into the usurped land or slaughtered by the thousands of starving people scattered across the hungry valleys.

The maiden thought that perhaps her father was trying to hold on to his crumbling pride, his corral, by spending whole days where she had found him.

She knelt a few feet away from the old man, whose pondering face did not show even the slightest sign of acknowledgement of her presence. He wondered silently what had brought his daughter to speak directly to him. It was seldom that a maiden approached the family head about her personal problems. The mother had always been the go-between. He thought with pain in his heart that perhaps his status and the tradition of the tribe were going with the cattle and the land. He looked as gaunt, as defeated and as impotent against the factors which determined the further existence of the tribe as the animals in the pen behind him.

His sixteen-year-old daughter was the most fiery of the women of the kraal. With all the manners befitting a maiden and the restraint in the presence of men expected of her, she somehow managed to slip out of those traditional chains and state her mind. Many things that she said provided food for the thoughts of old men. She cherished the history of the tribe and believed in Nxele's (Makhanda's) words that '*maze nibe yimbumba yamanyama,*' that the clans should unite — and actually helped to seek this togetherness by the infinite stretching of her imagination.

The old man prepared himself for searching questions but did not flinch from his position. His eyes remained fixed where they had been when the girl first appeared. Only his taut cheeks hollowed as he drew the smoke, the only thing which satisfied him these days.

He listened with a gradually softening face as the girl captivated his attention with the recital of his praises. When she had finished and was waiting for response the old man turned his face slowly to look at her and spoke: 'It is a solace to my despairing soul to know that there are a few people remaining, even if they are only my womenfolk, who still sing my praises in earnestness. Therefore be at ease *ntomb'am,* and speak what has brought you before me.'

The maiden considered awhile how to introduce her tidings before she said: 'I have come to seek enlightenment on matters concerning the tribe, my beloved father. For, when I was at the river, it was as if the voices of the great ancestors spoke to me, telling me what is wrong with the tribe: that there is so much suffering, and that the land is being stolen from the people.'

Her father cleared his throat and spoke with a confidence that contrasted with his beaten look: '*Camagu,* daughter of my fathers! I will soon acquaint you with the affairs of the tribe, even though you may be only a maiden and such matters belong to the thoughts of men. What is it you would like to know about?'

Nongqause had the look of a woman who had long stood by the men of her tribe in times of strife: 'I would like to know about the state of the land these days, father.'

Mhlakaza smiled, removed tobacco from a bag that hung over one shoulder, and began to fill his pipe: 'Let me first stuff my pipe, dear maiden, then I will give you the light that you seek. You see, my daughter, as I believe your quick mind has observed, people have come from beyond the south-western mountains destitute and full of fear of the strange men as pale as *amathongo* . . . '

Nongqause's eagerness to know and her desire to express her views could not be suppressed: 'Why, father? Why will they not stand up and resist like their forefathers?'

Mhlakaza raised the palm of his free hand: 'Let patience rule your mind, young woman. Listen well for the knowledge you seek, lest it sink shallow in your mind.'

She saw the wisdom of the old man's words and apologized: '*Camagu, bawo.* It is the excitement of a young heart. I am listening.'

The old man counted silently on his hands and then proceeded to instruct his daughter: 'Many years ago, two decades ago and four years before you were born, a conflict broke out among the white clans and the clan that is known as *ama*Bhulu, who shared the western country which is the stolen land with other white clans under British rule, broke their allegiance to their queen and moved north, to the land beyond the great river, *i*Gqili, that is vomited by the mountainous land of *abe*Suthu who are ruled by a wise king *u*Moshoeshoe. The land to which they moved had been laid open by *imfecane.* Only scattered clans remained here and there to be harnessed into the service of the invaders. Thus it is the white rebels who hold the land north of *i*Gqili. To the south and the west of where we stand, the British rule; to the north east it is Moshoeshoe. To the east rules Mpande, he too but a defeated king, installed in place of his brother, Dingane, after the latter's defeat *ngama*Bhulu at Ncome river. Such is the standing of the fatherland today, my maiden. So that we can neither move the tribe north, nor west, nor east, nor into the sea in the south. Hemmed in from all directions, with very little left of our pastoral life, the tribe is suffocating.'

The maiden felt cold fingers of despair clutching at her heart and just managed to hold back her tears. 'The heritage of the Nguni tribes is all but dead and the slow suffocation of our own tribe will continue unless something is done to turn the tide against the invaders.'

Mhlakaza felt like his daughter: 'Yes, maiden. Something must be done. The need arose long ago. That is why the great prophet warriors of yore, *o*Makhanda the left hand, *no*Mlanjeni *no*Maqoma would not give up the task of fighting that they had been bequeathed by the ancestors. But then, at that time there were still many warriors and the tribe had not despaired.'

It was the desire to overcome this despair in the peers of the tribe which had inspired her vision of 'The Great Day of the Lord' where-upon the tribe, devoid of even its last subsistence, would rise like a whirlwind to claim what had belonged to it long before the invasion. Nongqause proceeded to describe the vision to her father.

The old man sent a jet of nicotine-coloured spit to one side and fixed his eyes on the same spot which had held his attention when the maiden arrived from the river. The battle was nearly over and yet the people still looked towards them, as councillors, for salvation. Although they did not scream it out, he knew that they expected the councillors to do something to alleviate their despair. The councillors, not the paramount himself, 'because the latter never thinks up anything but sits and waxes fat on the thinning remains of the tribe's subsistence.' The councillors had to prod the tribe to act in the face of a crisis. But how? What could they promise the people at that stage of the conquest?

His daughter's voice reached his ears as from a great distance, for he was only half-listening while his own thought continued to digest the vision. He stopped himself from thinking in the manner he had about the chief: 'When men are faced with extreme difficulty, the tendency is to heap the blame on others, even though these others may be innocent. The paramount has followed his father's road and has done much to keep the clans together even after Mlanjeni's war.'

Again pity and despair clasped at the young maiden's heart as she witnessed the dejection in her father's soul: '*Camagu, bawo*. It was not your daughter's aim to bleed your heart.'

She knew when his calm was disturbed and she sat silently waiting for it to be restored before she went on to present the solution her mind had envisioned. However it was he who continued with the rage of a man used to dignity breaking down in the face of deliberate humiliation: '*U*Grey, their chief, wants to destroy the people's self-sufficiency and turn them into slaves of the white men who have stolen our lands and driven away our cattle. *U*Harry Smith, his general, it was who drove the people out of their grazing lands and laid them waste. *U*Grey it was who stated that we 'must be totally deprived of arms; kept under subjection by military force for years to come; ruled at the outset through chiefs, whose power must gradually diminish; they must be held in subjection and taught their insignificance . . . Peace is not the word,' he said, my daughter. 'They must surrender and implore for mercy.'

At that the maiden stared at her father with the wide-open eyes of horror. She stammered: 'Are . . . is . . . are the chiefs going to let him repeat what he did and effect his ambitions?'

Mhlakaza raised his brows in perplexity at his daughter's retort. 'What do you expect, my little one? What can the chiefs do with starving warriors? The land into which we have been pushed is too small to keep the whole tribe. Many of the chiefs have worked miracles to keep the tribe together. Maqoma the old fighter and Sandile have deviated from their father Ngqika's treacherous ways and brought their people together with *ama*Gcaleka *ka*Sarili the paramount chief. *Aba*Thembu *nama*Mpondo have also thrown in their lot with the other clans. This dispossession of a heritage will unite the people, *ntomb'am*, it will unite the people. Your hope must not die. All the wise kings will rally themselves and their people together. Moshoeshoe has sent word of unity. Dingane was rallying the clans of the east but was defeated by the treachery of his brother.'

This feeling of hope brought back some of the old man's calm and he signalled his daughter now to relate what her fertile imagination had conjured up. He always listened to whatever she said, for mixed with her dreams was amazing wisdom. Moreover he sometimes felt that he cherished her above her mothers, 'since she is the only woman in the kraal who takes pains to help me in my search for an alternative to the slavery to which the dispossessed tribe is surrendering.'

The maiden remained silent for a while although she had been given permission to go on, like one collecting wandering faculties. Her eyes withdrew from her immediate world and what she said took both her own and her father's minds back to the river.

Mhlakaza saw reason and wisdom in his daughter's vision.

His eyes began to shine like those of a blind man who has suddenly found himself able to see. The voice that left his lips conveyed the excitement that might accompany such a fortune: 'My pride in you exceeds everything in my life, my daughter. Many days have I spent here behind the kraal, searching and praying to the ancestors that there might dawn in my mind a plan to curb the disintegration of the tribe under the onslaught of the people from the sea. Infinite distances has my mind wandered in pursuit of this goal without arriving anywhere. And each day that gave way to night I rose from my sitting place, afraid to cast my eyes upon my dying kraal, the belief that *amathongo* have left the tribe to die sinking deeper into my mind. In the end I was addressing myself to *u*Mvelinqangi Himself, without any hope whatever that The Great Day of the Lord would arrive. Go on my daughter, feed my hungry soul with wisdom and I will be your voice *enkundleni*,' (at the court).

Her father's words had fired her spirit with confidence and her words came out like a new spring in a dry wilderness: 'Let the people abandon their faith in witchcraft and place it in themselves, father. Let them eat what is left in the corrals and the granaries of the tribe; and let those who still have a little share it with the destitute, because even when they hold onto it the raiders still come and still will come, to wrest it with guns and carry it to the stolen land.'

Mhlakaza nodded repeatedly as his daughter explained the vision of her mind. At intervals he said, *'Camagu,'* under his breath to express appreciation that *amathongo* were shedding light upon his mind through the voice of one who was only a maiden.

She continued without pause: 'Such an act will be like a great sacrifice to *u*Mvelinqangi, for to share at times of dire need is His great law; the law that will hold the tribe together.'

The father interrupted with a sign of his hand. That voice which had analysed the thoughts of wise men had returned: 'In what manner can such an act of sacrifice help save the tribe when what little is left must be preserved and defended? It cannot be sacrificed, my daughter. The cattle are the race. You ought to know as much.'

There was a pause as the girl's mind searched for the right words with which to elucidate the meaning she attached to sacrifice. 'Your words are full of truth, father. But who will stand in defence of what remains when the warriors are perishing of famine, burying their spears and returning to the stolen land to offer themselves as slaves to the conquerors? Did the great Makhanda not tell them to sacrifice and attack even though the bullets would pour down on them like rain torrents, and did they not obey? And did they not almost raze Fort Grahamstown to the ground although armed only with spears, thwarted only by the army that, mistaking them for Tshaka's warriors, attacked them from behind?'

Mhlakaza kept nodding and pulling at his pipe, as he would do when in complete agreement with the speaker.

Nongqause was now gripped by rapid, intense thoughts. 'Courage, father. Courage to make a sacrifice is what the tribe needs to survive. Not resignation to conquest. A quick death at the enemy's feet is better than a slow death away from him in hiding.'

Mhlakaza found himself surrounded by the dawning of his daughter's vision, the daybreak fast approaching, and he coaxed her to hasten the advent of light with these words: 'Your vision of life and of things to come is much deeper than I measured it, my daughter. Go on and tell me in exact words what you feel should be done, for I believe it should be seen as advice from the ancestors.'

The encouraging words fortified her confidence and she continued: 'If those who still have stock and grain and land will not share with those who have been completely deprived by the dispossession, this disintegration of the tribe will proceed faster, my dear father. But if they share what remains, many who have already resolved to opt for slavery may stay with the tribe and, perhaps, with a little in their stomachs they may gain some strength to till the uncultivated soil while the warriors stand a better chance to resist the plunderers and . . . '

It was Mhlakaza, the warrior, Mhlakaza the scatterer who concluded the girl's hope and belief: ' . . . the sprouting of new crops from formerly untilled soil will give the tribe back the hope, belief and strength that it used to derive from great leaders and warriors of the past, oMakhanda, noHintsa, noMlanjeni whose word was courage and sacrifice. It will be as if they had risen from the dead and the spirit that will be infused in the tribes will be like a great hurricane that will sweep the usurpers out of the stolen heritage into the sea. Truly you will grow to be a great seeress, *ntomba'm.* Your mind's vision of the affairs of the tribe is a treasure of wisdom.'

The face that had been a portrait of despair became once more a face of determined leadership. Mhlakaza stood up from his stone, not with the tottering slowness that had lately become his mark, but with the vigour of the Mhlakaza — the scatterer, the analyst — of old. He was already striding away when he said: 'Call any of the boys that you can get hold of and bid them report to my hut. I will be sending them to different places this evening, some of them faraway. And start preparing lasting provision for them.'

Inspired by the awakening of the old warrior in her father, the maiden rose from her kneeling position and sang silent praises to him, for she could not call her father's name in the open.

He stooped and vanished into his hut, there to confer with his soul. The girl went to join the others in the women's hut. She received a barrage of questions relating to the content of her meeting with the kraalhead. When she would not divulge anything to them, they all froze their dispositions towards her.

She took a grass bowl and went to the fast-diminishing maize pit for some dry grain to grind. Striking a rhythm in her grinding strokes she brought a song out of her soul. It was a long time since a sweet maiden's voice had risen from the confines of the kraal.

The bus was already half-occupied as it hummed over the last hill before Umtata. A lonely radio mast probed at the cloudy sky and some construction work was taking place a few kilometres ahead. Someone pointed to our right, at buildings that reminded me of the migrant labour camps, respectfully known as 'hostels', back home and said: 'The barracks for KD's troops.'

The slope faced Umtata. I was not intrigued by the sight, but by the way the man had described it — 'KD's troops.' Not his, nor anybody else's, but KD's. He might not have attached the same meaning to his words as that which I drew from them but, to me, that did not matter. I had heard what I had suspected all along: for the power-hungry to achieve their goals, the prior condition is the setting up of an armed bodyguard, the function of which is to intimidate the ordinary man into suppressing whatever reservations he might harbour about the way his life is to be run. The subject would come up at a later stage when I came across a man who did have misgivings about the 'bantustan' arrangement.

My first impression was that there was little, if any, architectural enterprise in the few buildings that dominated the 'capital'. They were just blocks of concrete, brick, glass and corrugated iron lumped together at the lowest possible cost. Only a residential area consisting of a hundred or so houses to the right of the road could lay claim to any style in its buildings. I guessed that it was a legacy of the pre-independence days. To make sure I asked, 'Who lives there?'

'*Abelungu* who remained after *umaziphathe,* and a few affluent black people who have since moved in there,' was the answer from a man two or three seats in front of me. I had no further questions.

The town was relatively bristling with people, predominantly colourfully-dressed young women. I gave my own explanation of the sex and age ratios — there were few men in the Transkei who could ever hope to strike gold at Umtata, few able-bodied women who could ever hope to leave the 'bantustan' as migrants to 'White South Africa'. The aged men and women clung to the ruins of that past that had attended our journey from Queenstown.

A house with a rusty plate that said it was a Roman Catholic cathedral, cars parked diagonally on the other side of the street, stretches of dusty sidewalks under ancient verandas in the shades of which sat ragged-looking women selling shrivelled fruit. I remembered how it had been back at *e*Ngcobo. We turned into a mucky bus terminus with one long railing in the middle hoisting a narrow corrugated-iron roof.

Everybody alighted but a woman, her young son and me. A queue stretched from one end of the terminus to the other, again dominated by young women carrying small parcels after a Thursday afternoon's shopping.

The bus roared away towards its final stop, the railway station. I started wondering whether my friends would be waiting.

The station looked deserted except for a few people who might have been waiting for a train at one time. The carriages that I saw seemed not to have budged on their rails for years.

My friends burst out of an old-model white car and raced each other to the bus before it had stopped, with Pumzile, the woman, oddly out-pacing my other friend, a man. They nearly stampeded over me when they came to where I stood grinning. Pumzile had put on some weight which had rounded her figure very well. The man had grown a beard since I had last seen him. I was the only one who had not changed, and they had not had trouble in making me out.

We got into the car and drove off in the direction from which the bus had come. I sat tight-lipped, almost on tenterhooks. I was in the presence of friends who were now citizens of a bantustan. How they felt about it was all that occupied my mind. I so longed to know what they thought about their position in the world that I nearly blurted it all out in a direct question. My special interest was aroused by the fact that Pumzile had been born and bred in Port Elizabeth and I knew how hard it had been for her to leave it for the Transkei, her only alternative after months of enforced idleness despite a B.A. certificate and all but one of the library science qualifications. What stopped me from asking how she had come to accept the alternative was the embarrassment that I thought such a question might have caused her and her companion.

The sight of two young men in military uniform reminded me of the barracks. Their gait reflected a belief (theirs) that they had been assigned the all-important role of being on hand for the maintenance of 'Law and Order' and the defence of a fatherland.

Before I could proceed along that line of thought we crossed the Umtata river into a suburb, called Norwood I was told, in which every house had some backyard rooms to let: the beginnings of a squatter situation.

Pumzile lived in one of these backrooms behind a spacious house belonging to her landlord. There were four rooms in all, built like . . . I cannot easily bring myself to repeat what thoughts entered my mind when I saw them for the first time. They were built together, three of them opening into a common passage in the middle of the block and the door of the fourth facing the landlord's house. Each room was occupied by a different tenant or tenants. What completed the public toilet impression was a wall that stood three feet away from and opposite the passage.

We went inside, made ourselves at home and started talking.

'How was the journey down here?' they wanted to know.

'Fine. I came third class.'

That brought chuckles from them.

'No passport problems?'

'I came Queenstown way. Can hardly tell when I crossed the "border".'

We went on to talk about our old times together while Pumzile prepared food on a gas stove. A light-complexioned, tall and thin man with a golden earring joined us. He was introduced and we shook hands before continuing with our conversation.

I could no longer suppress my thoughts about the barracks and the two soldiers I had seen in town. So I said, as if joking: 'I see you people are making headway with your "independence".'

'Why?' asked the newcomer with surprise in his eyes.

'A whole barracks as I came into town and two soldiers as we were coming here.'

'You must be out of your mind. Actually things are worse than they have ever been before. Only a few — KD and his lot, relatives mostly, have ever reaped anything from the whole show.'

Seeing that we, the newcomer and I, were on the same side of the fence I started a discussion.

'The barracks and the soldiers that I saw are there to remind you that complaint and opposition will not be tolerated — neh?'

'KD would not survive a single day without them. He would crumble without his props.'

I got straight to the point: 'This is what puzzles me about you people. Those soldiers are drawn from among the ordinary people, aren't they?'

'They are. Why?'

'Why do you ordinary people not refuse to serve in a military bodyguard that's intended to threaten your very selves?'

'With what?'

'Why, violence of course! Why do you think they are armed and trained to kill?' I asked, trying to sound vehement.

He looked thoughtful and then said: 'One reason strikes my mind, namely the distortion of the concept of patriotism. We, the poor, are drawn by well-phrased but fallacious arguments into the illusion that we hold some stake that is worth defending in the land of our birth. Whereas we have nothing like that. We are landless and have not even the smallest share in any other means of production. If we have any land rights, we cannot exercise them because we haven't got the capital to make our land productive. That is why we have been relegated to the ranks of migratory labour.'

'Will you explain?'

'Because we have no money or other implements we can use to live off our land, we are forced to abandon it in the hope of bringing back enough to get started.'

'Has anybody succeeded so far?' I asked. 'Have you ever heard of anybody?'

'Naw, I don't want to lie. Not any that I know of . . . You see, ours is a drone's life; ours is just to work and work to make South Africa rich while the rewards go into KD's pocket. He lives in a forty-roomed mansion with glorious chandeliers and twenty servants, and we stay in grass huts lit with wick lamps at night. Now, is that fair?'

'Naw.'

'That's it, bro. But there's also a second reason why we allow ourselves to be drawn into KD's army.'

'I'd like to know it too, brother.'

'When we serve in state-established institutions we automatically feel that we are part and parcel of the power-structure and therefore obliged to defend it.'

'Against whom?'

'Against the poor, the have-nots.'

'But who are the poor? Are they not your very kinsmen?'

'Then, perhaps, we also feel that we are defending a "nation", the reasoning behind it being that this particular "nation" is composed of our kinsmen and we are for that reason defending our own kinsfolk.'

'Is that not another distortion, my bro?'

'Of what?' he asked.

'Of the concept of nationalism, its being equated with tribalism?'

'How?'

'By turning tribes into nations. Tribes combine to form one nation.

So tribes are the components of a nation. A tribe cannot be a nation by itself in a country that it shares with other tribes. Can it?'

'Naw, *mfo*. You're right.'

'Unless it's in South Africa. Here black tribes are taught that they are different, and as soon as they begin to see themselves as different, they naturally develop differences which evolve into antagonisms which in turn will lead to physical conflict between the tribes. One tribe wants to outdo all the others in all spheres, even that of mere existence. That is the law of divide and rule.'

'And one man is responsible for making us victims.'

'You need not mention him. We all know him, and others who have done the same to their tribes. Here's food: eat, you must be hungry. Especially the traveller.'

Women and their nurturing instinct!

After the meal Pumzile asked: 'Would you like to go out somewhere with us?'

'Where?'

Now, that was not the kind of question one would normally ask from one's hosts in a place that one was visiting for the first time. I found it strange that I was not keen to discover more of Umtata.

'Seeing friends . . . ' She studied my reaction to her suggestion. 'Or would you rather rest after the long trip? I know it cannot have been pleasant.'

I agreed that that was the case: 'Better tomorrow, during the day when I can also get to look at this place.'

They hung around for a while and then left me.

Lying on my back on the bed I let my mind go over what I had seen or heard of the dying illusion so far. The scenery from the 'border' near Queenstown right up to Umtata, excluding the picturesque traditional remnants — the huts and the women — had evinced to my searching mind the treachery of Apartheid and its Bantustan policy in no uncertain terms. I tried to piece together all the scraps of truth about the history of our fatherland that had sifted through the mesh of lies to which my mind had been subjected in the name of 'education' since I started learning. This was so that I could reconstruct the making of the wilderness in the middle of which I found myself that night.

At the end of my musing the whole artifice through which our humanity had been subverted stood in stark clarity before the eye of my mind. Briefly outlined it bore the following historical visage.

Sixteen fifty-two anno domini — the seed of colonialism was planted at the toe of Africa. I could imagine the Khoikhoi people playing the rôle of puzzled welcome party on the sands of Table Bay. And then in the following years, their gradual displacement by the initial waves of burgher expansion into the interior. Sixteen eighty-six anno domini — meeting of the new white race and the old black race, the Xhosa people, on the banks of the Buffalo River, followed soon by the Seven Xhosa Wars of Resistance, recorded in our history books as the 'Kaffir Wars', the last of which was that of the warrior prophet *u*Mlanjeni in 1853, the same year in which Britain granted Representative Government to her Cape colony. Four years later came the tragic act of self-preservation inspired by the merciless land-gobbling onslaught of colonialism on a people who had for centuries unknown practised an African communal culture, where everything was shared in times of need — as reflected in my version of the sixteen-year-old maiden's bid for unity. The act she inspired was, unfortunately, to be the last nail in the coffin of the old way of life for the Xhosa people.

In terms of Representative Government the dispossessed could vote, provided they were twenty-one years of age, could read and write, earned a minimum of fifty pounds a year or owned landed property worth no less than twenty-five pounds. Few could read and write, many had been dispossessed of their land, a handful, if any, earned fifty pounds. In other words the vote of the dispossessed was insignificant. Even if it had not been, all that it could have achieved was the 'election' of a white representative to parliament.

However by the time that the Ciskei and Transkei, the last retreats of the Xhosa people, were annexed the vote of the dispossessed was beginning to count, and with the annexation and the subsequent increase of the Cape population it spiralled from fourteen percent in 1882 to forty-seven percent in 1887 — which necessitated the finding of means to disenfranchise the conquered.

The first move towards this goal was the decision by the Cape Parliament in 1887 to disqualify all voters by virtue of occupation of tribal land, thus reducing African voting power by a considerable percentage. The franchise qualifications were also made more stringent, and in 1892 the Native Franchise Act increased the property qualification.

Then came the Union of South Africa in 1910 to mark the beginning of a systematic removal of the Cape African from the common roll. Dr. Jameson found the African franchise to be the obstacle in the way of White unification. When the Union Convention met it was decided that no African would enter Parliament as a representative of his people. This agreement was then made binding by the South Africa Act which was passed by Britain and enshrined racialism to this very day in South Africa. African protest to Britain against the passing of the Act fell on deaf ears.

From then on followed an avalanche of laws, culminating in Hertzog's 'Unholy Trinity' of 1936 — The Native Land and Trust Act, the Native Laws Amendment Act and the Native Representation Act. By these three Acts the Black people of this country were effectively excluded from participation in the government of their fatherland.

The Native Land and Trust Act released thirteen percent of South Africa's land surface, scheduled for black South African occupation under the Native Land Act of 1913, and kept the rest of the country as a white area, thus bringing into effect the balkanization of our land.

After 1948 the scheme for the ultimate burial of the black man's right to the viable part of South Africa was put into practice. The Bantu Authorities Act which designated chiefs to head Bantu Tribal Authorities was passed. I found myself laughing alone when I remembered that these chiefs could be deposed by the Governor General on whose proclamation the new Authorities were established. He aso fixed the minimum and maximum number of councillors to serve on each Authority and could oppose any appointment by power of veto. The Governor General's role brought back to my mind old Sir George Grey's idea of governing blacks through their 'chiefs whose power must gradually diminish.'

As to what happened after that, dear reader, you may reflect on the recent history of the now 'independent' bantustan. In 1955 the Bantu Authorities descended on the Cape, and particularly on the Transkei. You will remember that the Act established councils along tribal lines through which Apartheid and Bantustanism were forced down the people's throats through the manipulation of the appointed chiefs, doubtlessly chosen, as has been proved, according to their pliability.

I went to sleep thinking just how pliable some people — those with a vested interest in the exploitation of their own kind — had been. The goal of those who believed in racial discrimination and oppression was almost achieved: but for its economic impracticability, of which I had personal witness, to be confirmed over the next two days.

It was late in the morning when a knock on the door woke me up. I washed and joined my friends outside. And, guess what, they were driving in a snow-white Mercedes Benz! This ultra-modern machine with maroon seats took us to a house on the other side of town. All the time that we were driving out there I felt like a fly in the milk container.

At the house, which was indescribably furnished with tables that stood on carved ivory legs, a stereo that looked like a spaceship, Oriental carpets and walls that seemed to have been decorated by Michaelangelo himself, we watched television tapes of the Muhammad Ali-Spinks fights while sipping beer and fruit juices out of tinted glasses. I'll admit that I was impressed, though in my own negative way. In order not to appear a peasant, I tried all that I could to pretend that I had been in better houses than that one before.

After some hours in the house I could not suppress the desire to go out among the ordinary people of my third denomination, and I asked: 'Have you people got any "spots" around here where I may chance upon some of our old colleagues from Alice?'

I sensed that they would have burst out laughing if they had not known that I was a stranger to Umtata. One did not meet people that way in the capital of the Transkei. One kept to one's own rank. Classes were too well defined, as I would learn with the passage of time. However, make no mistake about this, it would not be through my friends' aloofness or "class consciousness" that I came to know of it, for they took me where I wanted to go, what is more they went with me.

Discretion, brought about by insecurity I reckoned, was the outstanding characteristic of the people of the capital whom I met. A lightweight world title fight in Cape Town dominated conversation and next came football, with guys describing matches taking place at Orlando Stadium hundreds of kilometres away as if they had been there. They went to this particular 'spot' which was run by a cute sister in their brand-new Cressidas, and bought with ten-rand notes: perhaps to make an impression of affluence on her. Apparently they wanted that cocoon of new-found comfort to follow them everywhere, and they shunned other things that disturbed it.

All in all, the company only became enjoyable when I abandoned my curiosity, explaining to myself that consciousness differed from one place to another. But then I had not figured on so vast a diversity of awareness between the people where I came from and those of Umtata. Wherever one goes in Soweto or, for that matter, in the whole Rand complex, among the people one cannot miss the sense of bitterness in the black man's soul. The black man knows that he has been divested of his natural heritage of human dignity. He feels it on his way to and from work in the crowded trains, buses and taxis; in his crowded and sub-economic habitat, be it a hostel room or a township dog-kennel; when he is asked for a pass or given the shakedown; and at his place of employment where he works under Napoleon Bonaparte's glare; just about everywhere and at every hour of his life. I had actually expected people from Umtata, at least those with reasonable mental training and financial security, the rural petty bourgeoisie who could afford cars, suits and beer at extortive prices, to be even more outspokenly critical of the forces that determined their lives: more critical than the migrants on the bus and myself, who could not lay claim to any 'independence'.

I could not understand them at all, and that is why I dismissed them as being discreet about their views because of insecurity. They had to cling to the little they had and remain silent. What had happened to Vuyani Mrwetyana and others before and after him must have had a telling impact on their attitudes. We left the place late in the evening for supper and some more television, and then went to bed.

The following day, a Saturday, revealed nothing more than a newly-built prison on a hilltop and the dominating Volkskas building in town. I excused myself and went out on my own. The Umtata River was muddy, the bus terminal was busy with buses coming and going, and a man peddled fish out of a cardboard carton at the top of his voice. A 'traditional' woman sat on the dusty pavement not far from the terminal, sharing a loaf of brown bread with her parched brood of four, three little boys and a girl wearing a woollen blazer. Another young and loudly made-up woman drove past in an arrogantly roaring blue Alfasud. The fruit vendors sat forlornly where I had seen them on my arrival. The Transkei Hotel with its beer lounge attracted me.

It was full of men huddled around small, low tables full of beer bottles. Not a single face looked familiar. I let my eyes roam across the room in search of the friendliest mob, waited for a chair to be vacated and carried it over to the group I had chosen. I ordered two beers, although I did not feel that thirsty, added them to theirs and introduced myself. They were all migrants from Port Elizabeth, East London and other nearby places, home for the Easter weekend.

On Sunday we went visiting, one place to another, mostly in vain. People were out for a breather in 'white' South Africa. I, too, felt I wanted out, and the following morning I was back on the Queenstown-bound bus with my migrants. I vowed all the way that I would never again place my foot in the Transkei of my own accord. My friends there would have to come to me if they cared about me.

Behind the Veil of Complacency

Behind the veil of complacency
Are two human loyalties.
One, when it is uppermost, is destructively real
And the other only abstract and intangible.
They are War and Peace.

You tear a Rembrandt or a Da Vinci original from its gallery wall, break the frame over your knee, cut the canvas to shreds and set fire to the fragments.

Or, nearer home, you take a graphic that has been painstakingly completed by Mzwakhe and put it into the fire.

Tell me, how would we who care about art feel towards you? Or the masters themselves if they were watching?

If you can't answer this one, you'd better stop reading right here, because you won't understand the real outrageousness of what I am going to tell you about. You're apathetic, a robot that continues to function as long as its computer is in good order.

Sunny Friday afternoon, the eighteenth of May this year, 'seventy-nine. Sunshine in their united souls too. And, around them, comfortable expressions on the motley Johannesburgers' faces. Why not? The capitalists had already gone beyond the point of no return in their weekly obligation to part with some of their wealth for services rendered, and so, for them, there was no use in crying over spilt milk: perhaps a look at the unspilt milk cheered them up a bit. The workers, to reserve the honourable and precise word 'slaves', ignorantly or resignedly found reason to smile too; maybe because that night they could take their girls out for drinks without the fear of running short of money while the 'spots' were still hot.

Their reason for smiling I've already stated: two united souls walking side by side, oblivious of the many people, of the buzzing traffic, or even their route to their destination. Part of all this and yet infinitely removed from it all.

And after all, it had been a wonderful day. The fixedness of the concrete walls had been unable to hem in their souls, the height of the buildings unable to bear down on them. It had been so from cool sunrise. In the train he could swing and sway on the holder, never normally the case at rush hours. People had given to the blind, rattling their tins down the aisles, seeing their way through the eyes of little ones holding their hands. The girls who had been standing opposite him and Pro had talked animatedly, each one striving to be more beautiful than she was or could ever hope to be. The ways of our sisters! Yet on this day beauty seemed well within the reach of the plainest girl among them.

At the university: twelve thousand white youths minding their books and ignoring, to the point of forgetting, his presence and that of a few other black people of African, Coloured and Indian strains — these, incidentally, disregarding one another too. It is a disunited world in which they all live. Sincere apologies for labelling people.

If being left to go about his affairs like any other human being was not courtesy to him, then he did not know what he wanted. That was the least he prayed for under the trying conditions of his life.

The papers. They go a long way towards the make-up of a bright day. Very little good news in this rat race city of his, he had been thinking. Behind the veil the whole country, the whole sub-continent, is strife-torn. We know this but it is 'too ghastly to contemplate': as long as it is still just outside, on the doorstep, and has not poked its head inside, though the doorknob is already turning. Nearer his consciousness: people thrown into the winter night with babies because they do not have rent, do not work and cannot employ themselves. Mh . . . no money for black education. Mh . . . parliament: the destiny of the father land tossed to and fro across the floor like a ping-pong ball, while true patriots hold their breaths in prison; vile insinuations concerning the black man's future. Mh!

That had almost spoiled the morning but, it being a part of his life, an unwanted part, he viewed it as such, with an unwavering belief that some day they would all of them up and do something about it. 'You never can tell when a person who is a fool or pretends to be a fool will suddenly see the light.'

The latter hope had balanced the dejection brought by the morning dailies. On the whole, the day was wonderful. Porridge and potato chips for lunch, shared with Mapula at the labourers' canteen, was one of the best meals he had ever had in his life. Before they left the eating place, they bought oranges.

Apartheid, prejudice, was far, far away from their minds and, if it had been meant to separate, it could never succeed with them: for they were united in their blackness, appreciating each other wholeheartedly. They talked about almost everything, excluding hate and violence. If there is indeed a benevolent God somewhere or all over, as we were made to believe from childhood, He must have smiled upon them that day, pleased with Himself that He had done the least he could for black humanity by blessing them with each other. The least that they sought of Him.

A few of the white people they regarded as friends nodded to them in passing or stopped to chat encouragingly, pushing apartheid further out towards or beyond the margin of life.

With warm souls they set out for the location, the darkness, the smog and the claustrophobia. Their spirits their torchlight. The motorists, few black, most white, gave them extra seconds to cross the path of the gathering traffic, hand in hand. They smiled at the motorists in sincere gratitude and the motorists smiled back in acknowledgement of their thanks.

Don't make any mistake about it. They both of them, and maybe even the benign motorists, knew that the prevailing mood was nothing but a complacency which they might liken to a layer of ice, upon which all of them were stepping gingerly, with doubtful hopes that the ice was thick enough not to break while they were still in the middle of the deep frigid lake called Johannesburg. 'If only we could reach land, our different locations, still wearing the affable mood,' everybody must have been wishing. This is a virtue that some of us true South Africans aspire to every day of our lives — that where the 'races' encounter, it should be in harmony until they depart in repulsive accordance with what is decreed by the powers that be.

The sad thing is that it is an illusory state that we aspire to. Harmony also has its pre-conditions.

'Darling, I need a packet of cigarettes.'

Those most beautiful eyes regarded him accusingly.

'You know what the habit does to your lungs, but you continue.'

'I know, I know. You need not tell me because you've never even tried it. I'm the one who smokes. Moreover I've switched to golden milds. They don't do the same amount of damage. I've cut down on nicotine, on the way to killing the habit.'

'*Mcf!*'

'Why *mcf*? Why? What do you want?'

'*Mcf!*'

'You make me sick. Not the cigarettes.'

She smiled at the lie.

'But what do you enjoy in that bitter and nauseating smoke?'

'The bitterness.'

'Go ahead and kill yourself, darling. I'll cry like a rainstorm to show just how much I loved you. Here's a shop.'

'*Voetsek.*'

They had no milds at that shop.

'There's another shop further down towards the station.'

She was what he called a creative conversationalist. She also had a constructively critical outlook on life. Most of all she was awake to and detested their state of subjugation. A sister who knew to which side she belonged; concerned with and thus giving courage to a young man the driving force of whose life was the conviction that he hated oppression and its resultant exploitation of man by man.

The man himself explained to her how he saw this world and their position in it. She understood and contributed ideas that reinforced his philosophy. This, he believed, he constructed through a personal observation of their common environment rather than through accepting other people's comments on it without question.

'*Eyi* maan!'

'What is it?

'I wish I were already through with this schooling so that I might apply my mind to concrete things.'

'Like what?'

'Matters of life in general. Matters that are more relevant to our own lives. For instance, get a chance to study black South African literature, rather than spend hours trying to imbibe *Silas Marner*. Or, learn something new at a higher level rather than repeat in English for matric purposes what I did in *si*Sotho for primary school purposes and in Afrikaans for Junior Certificate purposes. The way we learn really bores me.'

'I bet one has to take it, if only for the certificate.'

'Time wasted, darling! The certificate can't make up for that.'

She was beautiful, but fumed when she was reminded about it. That was no priority in her life, and this was reflected in her manner of dress, denims and other types of trousers most of the time, occasionally a frock or skirt which 'makes me feel uncomfortable'.

'How?'

'Like an ordinary *skebereshe* (tart).

'Whereas you're what?'

'A person! What do you think?'

'A woman.'

'*Mcf!* I'm not like any other woman. Many useless things that occupy most of their minds most of the time hardly ever enter mine. For instance, have you ever seen me smudged over in make-up, resembling a spectrum?'

'Naw. You don't need any of that stuff. You're right as you are.'

'But you wouldn't be surprised if you saw me like that, would you?'

'Naw. You're a woman, *mos.*'

'You see? You expect it from me simply because many other vain women do it. So you conclude that all women are vain. I'm not impressed by that attitude from you. One would expect you to have sound criteria for evaluating other people, not just their sex.'

He wondered what she was driving at. He supposed that if she were sophisticated enough she would have labelled him a male chauvinist pig.

'It's nobody's fault that you're a woman.'

'I wish I were a boy, y'know. Then I'd just be ignored, permitted to do what I liked and not what is expected of me.'

'Tomboy. Go kick a ball.'

' 'Strue. I want to be a motor mechanic.'

They had found that very funny, perhaps picturing her greasy face in greasy overalls.

Only semi-conscious of the world, they had passed the shop to which they were going.

'Hey, the cigarettes!' he suddenly remembered.

'We've gone past the shop, maan. Why don't we forget them? You won't die.'

He caught her petal-delicate arm and pulled her back towards the shop. She tried to resist but only playfully.

It was gloomy inside, almost ominous. By normal city restaurant standards the young man reckoned that it would not be long before the owner received a sequestration order, or decided to sell up his shop and give those who had been meant for capitalism a chance. All the shelves were only half-full. His wife was apparently his servant both in the shop and at home.

He was selling an assortment of sweets to a white man, doubtlessly disappointed that that was all the man wanted. Of stature he was short, with a back that reminded the young man of a camel; pale and dry of complexion, with a long nose that must have been bent or shifted to the left by a blow from a hard object. He did not strike the united black souls in his shop as being anywhere near pleasant.

Mapula remembered the oranges which were in the bag that was slung over her boyfriend's shoulder. '*Hoo wena, di-orenji.* I nearly forgot,' she said and dipped her hand into the bag to remove one, which she immediately began to peel.

'*Wat* can I do for you?' asked a throaty voice without any of the mollifying tones of an aspirant capitalist getting on with his job.

'Oh!' The customer did not know what had surprised him but he guessed that it was the lack of merchandizing skill in the shopkeeper's approach. 'Give me a packet of Rothmans Golden Milds,' he said, placing a fifty cent coin on the counter. Mashonisa promptly snatched it.

From here onwards the shopkeeper shall be known as Mashonisa.

He put a packet of Peter Stuyvesant in front of the young man.

'I said Rothmans Golden Milds.'

'You said Peter Stuyvesant, maan!'

'I said Rothmans.'

Mashonisa brought the right order but held it in his hand. 'What else?'

The young man had looked at Mapula, who was beginning to part the orange segments with her fingers. 'What else can a guy get out of fifty cents after buying a pack of fags?'

'Matches,' she suggested.

'Ya. And a box of matches.'

Shylock brought it.

'Is that all?'

'Ya.' He was wasting their time. The trains for the townships were leaving. They would be caught in the rush.

The little hawk-like eyes moved from the young man's face to Mapula's. For a split second the two thought they had seen a flicker which could only have been seen once before, in Shylock's eye as Shakespeare first imagined him.

'I want five cents for that orange.'

There could be no mistake: he was indicating the one that Mapula was eating.

Perhaps it was an attempt at capitalist humour. Mapula's friend smiled at her. 'Tell him where we bought it.'

She answered, smiling: 'You saw me taking it out of the bag, didn't you? We bought it at Wits.'

'*Wat?* Wits!' The eyes were by then like a snake's. 'You took it there!' He pointed at a box of oranges displayed on a fruit stand ten feet away from Mapula.

Mapula's friend wanted to cut Mashonisa's tongue out for insinuating that his love was an orange thief. 'You want to say that she would just walk into your shop, take an orange, peel it and eat it without paying for it?'

'Don't talk to me like that, *jong*. Pay the five cents or you're not getting the cigarettes!'

'Okay then. Give back my fifty. I'll buy the cigarettes elsewhere!'

Mashonisa drew his hand with the fifty cents, the cigarettes and the matches close to his chest, to his heart, as if to say that was where the fifty cents belonged.

'Hey, man. She's telling you we bought the fucken orange at Wits!' Mapula's friend screamed. 'We can't pay for what is ours.'

'Mutluhele, lovey. Give him the five cents.'

'What! Leave him alone, you say? Give him the five cents for our orange?' the young man shouted at her.

'But . . . but . . . what is five cents?' she stammered.

Her friend nearly blasted off through, imagine, the floors above, right through the roof two reinforced concrete strata up, and out to the furthest outskirts of the universe. Not even a Soyuz or Gemini spacecraft could have outdone the force of his anger. '*Heer-r!*' He hated, hated! What was five cents to him, to Mapula, to Mashonisa, to the blind man playing a guitar out in Hoek street, to the shortlived existence of a child dying of malnutrition down Transkei way! What was five cents, to whom, in this capitalist world?

'That was a relative question, my darling, a very relative question,' he thought. He forgave her for the look of fear in her shiny beautiful eyes. Even to her five cents was a lot of money, not to be picked up on the dusty streets of where she came from. He knew her. He knows her now, as he reports to the world the presence of an abominable soul — address, Mashonisa's shop — in the midst of a humanity starved of peace.

He forgave her, and miraculously resisted an irresistible urge to vault over the counter and kill.

'Give him the five cents, *mfowethu*. That's what they want, *mos*,' said another voice, nearer the true explanation of the petty capitalist's behaviour. 'They' want to rip off the last few cents from natural, love-engrossed young people.

'But if I give it to him, he will be five cents the richer and I five cents the poorer.'

'Give him, nevertheless,' said the brotherly voice of a man who knew where Mapula's friend would end up if he allowed what was imminent to happen.

Mapula looked with silent fright, mixed with disgust, at inherent male violence pent up and ready to erupt. She did not know what to do with the orange.

The servant-wife did not approve of the threatening violence, either. She tried to intervene on behalf of the two young people. The orange was theirs . . . but she was gagged by a tirade of venomous language from Mashonisa.

'Okay, then. Here.' The young man searched himself.

Mapula took out two two-cent pieces and a cent from her breast pocket and gave the coins to her friend. The latter dropped them on the counter with a trembling hand.

He had won. The capitalist had won. He had won, over a bad loser who would tell him what he was and tell humanity about it, too.

Mashonisa handed over the cigarettes. Looking back at the event later, the young man regretted that he had not demanded his fifty back.

It was not over. That had only been the opening scene of the show.

'You know what you are?'

You only see the smirk that was on Mashonisa's face on a baby's, when it is suckling at its mother's breast.

'You're a THIEF!'

That went home like a red-hot poker into a pile of dry paper. The baby's smirk now belonged to the young man as he turned away.

A burst of violent commotion behind him told him that the paper had burst into flame. Mapula took off. The young man turned to look at Mashonisa rifling among his merchandise like a dog trying to dig a rabbit out of a hole.

'He is going to shoot me. If he does, let it be outside his gloomy shop.' He retreated outside.

Mashonisa went after him like an enraged, wounded rhino. He had a two-foot-long club in his right hand. He was growling, and punctuating his venom with '*Kaffer!*'

The young man said: '*Kaffer* is your mother!'

Mashonisa moved much faster than his age, which might have been in the vicinity of seventy years.

The young man wanted to draw him further out and then kick his feet from underneath him. That way his case would stand a chance, though a slight one, in court. He was like a magnet to Mashonisa's hate and aggression.

Thirty feet away from the door the young man put the bag down and taunted Mashonisa to approach him. He had lived through the 'seventy-six hostel-location 'factions'. What was a camel-backed old man dying of seven decades of hate?

Mashonisa stopped and the young man inched closer to him.

Then Mapula shouted: 'No. Don't! Watch out!'

The young man looked behind him and there was a police van crawling towards them up the short street of the block. His body went limp. The old abominable soul gained courage. He charged at the young man with his club and the young man went to the van, which had stopped, with an explanation.

Not one of the four eyelids blinked. Four green onions stared through the windscreen of the van. It crossed the plaintiff's mind that the four ears were blocked. The faces were as inanimate as the brass-shouldered blue jacket and the caps. The nearer was wrinkled, as if moulded out of baked red clay. The driver's was smooth, with almost girlish blushes. But they were equally indifferent, with the slightest trace of exasperation on the nearer, and of indecision on the younger.

'Dammit, I made a foolish mistake!' But, though he thought this, he repeated the cause of the disturbance in near fluent Afrikaans.

Jong! It was a real disturbance.

The bitter soul of Mashonisa was vomiting all the blasphemy it contained, with the scream of a bird of hell. 'You *kaffer!* Go to Soweto, you *kaffer . . . kaffer . . .*!'

Nineteen seventy-nine.

'You hear what he's saying? What should I do?' the young man asked, feeling sick. He was begging the very representatives of justice to realise that this was the kind of racial confrontation they were supposed to prevent. It made him feel silly, impotent and bitter all at the same time. He knew what he was. The gale of profanity that blew at him from Mashonisa was what he was before the brass-shouldered blue-coats. Mashonisa's *'Kaffers!* Go to Soweto!', his own vain wait for action from the only people empowered to defuse the tension, their inanimate response, the beautiful and frightened Mapula, all captured the attention of many a passing motorist, who viewed the scene with marked detachment while waiting for the robots to wave him on his way.

'What should I do?' the young man screamed, in order to be heard above the abuse from the star of the show. Something crossed his mind. The word *'kaffer'* had been declared an offence in law some time ago, 'public disturbance' was an offence in law, an attempted assault with a dangerous weapon was certainly worth a reprimand from justice. All legal myths.

Mashonisa was now barking like a watchdog trying to impress its masters.

'I want to lay a charge against him.'

Baked-clay shifted on his seat. Life sprang into the young face at the wheel as he looked towards his senior for an answer. The senior might have yawned before he said: 'Go to Hillbrow police station.'

Three to four kilometres away! No pass on him! Never!

'Let's go, darling.' He hitched the light bag over his shoulder and put an arm around his soul sister. 'I should have slaughtered the old goat for the ancestors.'

'You're blaspheming,' she said. 'One with a soul so full of evil would bring bad instead of good luck.'

'And those two just sat there like corpses. *Nxa!* The day shall come, I'm telling you my love. No man can stand being humiliated before the most important people in his life forever.'

She had fallen into a sudden pensive mood, chewing the nail of her forefinger.

'I hope you do not consider me the coward of the moment, lover-girl.'

'They could have shot you through the head. *Molimo!* What could I have done? I would have implored them to shoot me too.'

'It's always they that start the violence, that create the hostile atmosphere and racial antagonism, but in the end it is we who are declared terrorists and hanged.'

'There is no such thing as a terrorist. They are told to shoot and they shoot. They are told you are an enemy and they don't ask why.'

The young man pondered this. The behaviour of such people as the three they had met tended to have a centripetal effect that swallowed everybody, pulled them into the fight. It tarnished any goodwill that might have been sprouting in his heart towards 'the other side', excluding his few genuine friends.

'Surprising how one is mostly torn between two loyalties: to war and to peace; the former, when it is uppermost, destructively real and the latter only abstract and intangible.'

In their instance, his and Mapula's, there was, however, a third loyalty towards each other, and they were thankful for it, because it made them feel human. One thing that they could not be denied.

They passed the shop not more than four days in a week and they laughed, holding hands. They had still a long time to live if they took care of themselves. Mashonisa had but a few years, even months of hatred to live; and then he would die, a slave to a base prejudice.

You know what Tyler, a friend from Mdantsane near East London, would have done to even up the score?

He would have visited the shop a few days later, sure that Mashonisa would have forgotten him. He would be conspicuously holding a ten rand note or two for Mashonisa to see, even as he entered the shop. He would then start ordering goods from any shelf upon which his roaming eyes rested. Maybe Mashonisa would even be compelled to fetch a step ladder to reach some of the orders. Tyler would wait until everything was packaged and the price added.

Then he would have smiled in his own mischievous way and said: 'Remember that day you swore at me right in front of the blue-coats and they just sat there like they were made of clay?' And then Tyler would have pocketed the greenbacks and walked out.